DIFFERENT

WALKS

BY

TAYLOR HARTSHORN

Acknowledgments

There are so many people I could thank for encouraging me, but no one measures up to Mom & Dad.
This one's for you.

PART I

BEFORE

September 1, 2016

SAGE

It had been far too long since I sorted through the box labeled in purple crayon: 'Sage Riley's belongings'. As I pulled it out from under my side of the bed—the left—with ease, anxiety crept in; the anticipation for what I'd find there almost unbearable. The word fragile was misspelled on the opposite side of the box, this time in orange rather than purple. A carefully planned route was finally depicted on a map in my right hand. Setting it aside, I intended to find the letters. The map was pointless to me without the letters that went along with it.

It had been just over fifteen years since I had seen Max, but his letters were pieces of him that I couldn't wait to delve into, wondering why I had waited so long to begin with. Opening the box, I dug through some old treasures, my eyes diverting to and fro to find one thing and one thing only, before Tom got home.

I had one hour, give or take a few minutes.

The letters were at the bottom of the box, as luck would have it. The only one out of one hundred some odd letters I had read before laid casually on top of the stack, as if it were waiting for me.

Sage,

> *Enclosed is a stack of letters, one for*
> *each day of my journey. Don't open*
> *them until you're recovered and ready;*

ready to take your journey. Hopefully, that journey will then lead you to me.

Until then, I'm going to stay here, in Virginia. My mother needs me now more than ever, and I need her now too. If ever you are at a crossroad in life, you know where you can find me.

I'll always be here for you, even if we can't be together. This journey has been refreshing, and after all I've been through the past few years, I've been given solace, and maybe just a sliver of clarity.

Even though you think I'm crazy, Sage, don't overcomplicate things in your life. I hope that one day we can be together again.

When times get tough, I challenge you to just get out and walk. Don't read the stack of letters until you're ready for your journey. Read one letter each day when you do. I'll be here...waiting.

All the best, be strong and don't worry about us. Here's hoping this isn't goodbye for good.

In a way I'll always love you, Sage.

Max

I was desensitized to it now, but remembering the devastation I felt while I read that exact note at sixteen years old, made me want to tear up for everything that was my past. I had come so far…

Running my fingers over the return address I had memorized so many years prior, I verified that it matched accordingly to the final destination on the map in my other hand. Smirking at my correctness, I slid the box back under the bed, the stack of letters secured under my arm.

A filled backpack already sat nearby. I added the letters to it, just enough room for them but not much else. Everything was falling into place fabulously and it made me giddy with excitement.

Dash, Tom's bulldog, lifted his head out of slumber from the corner of the room. I had all but forgotten he was even there, but his gesture indicated to me that Tom was home. Dash waddled to the door to greet his owner and I followed suit. Erasing evidence of my journey to come, I wandered to the couch in my slippers, a half glass of wine in hand. I tuned into a reality show. Looking as if I could have been there since I got home from work, I nervously expected Tom to know I had been up to something.

My heartbeat quickened steadily as the lock turned and Tom walked through the door.

"Hey, honey," I said, almost too nonchalant.

***

The coffee was cold again this morning, matching my attitude at the very least. Nevertheless, I sipped on it sporadically as the afternoon encroached. The phone on my desk rang, scaring the life out of me. I hadn't had a call all day. My mug of decaf in hand splotched on my dress unintentionally as I jumped back in response to the ringer. At least then I was glad the coffee was chilled.

"Fredrick Publishing Company, this is Sage speaking," I clenched my teeth in attempt to sound friendly. For the next eight minutes and forty-two seconds I played with a hangnail as the person on the other end rattled on.

I hung up the phone to blot the coffee stain from my dress, which luckily wasn't my favorite to wear, anyways. I got ready again with the lights out in my own damn bedroom because Tom was asleep, being courteous as I tiptoed around our dark bedroom. By default, I picked out a dress that screamed mediocrity, having not been able to see my other clean options.

I finally let myself admit that I was miserable and perhaps had been so for quite some time. All round, nothing was going right. I'd always lived convincing myself that there are no bad days, but rather, there are good days, and then there are days that make you want to give the world an extreme eye roll and a choice finger.

There is definitive beauty in recognizing your own insanity.

Being a book editor, I've read about adventure all too often, but experienced little adventure in my own life. A lot of that was fiction, but sometimes it was nice to escape into an idea that arose when I read through the transcripts of novels submitted to me by hopeful authors.

I looked into my rearview mirror on my way to work to make sure my makeup and hair weren't as in shambles as it felt. For the first time, I saw my mother looking back at me. I am at the point in my life where I am cordial to my mother, but nothing more; not after all we've been through.

I'm a head in the stars, lofty, free spirit type, but I'll be damned if I end up anything like my mother.

A glance in the mirror that turned into me gazing to get a closer look because, *Dear God, is that a wrinkle!* is just a reminder that I am not getting any younger these days.

At only age thirty-two, I had to convince myself repeatedly of my youth and that just didn't sit well with me. I needed something that made me feel alive in my life instead of sitting at a desk, the typical nine-to-five. I barely knew my cohorts, with our heads buried in manuscripts all day, anxious to meet short deadlines. The commute from one end of New York City to the other bustling side was equally as miserable as the next person's.

There were times I felt the need to barge in the door of my boss Seth's office to check for a heartbeat. Too frequently his head appeared to be super glued to the blotter on his desk, dozing off. A hand printed message on a torn off sheet of notebook paper hung on his door reading, "Left for lunch. Be back in 30." It had not left its location for twelve days, yet he'd be the first to appear at my cubicle if I was just ten minutes late on a deadline. That's why he's not fired yet, because when it came down to it, his employees would do all the dirty work for him. On his accord, the office evidently lacked any type of personal flare.

At four in the afternoon, I snuck out of the office earlier than usual. I had no particular reason for leaving other than that I felt like it.

I was skimming through the nonsense of my most recent cookbook, deciding what to whip up for dinner. I tied my long, dark hair into a loose braid down my back, how I was most comfortable. Tom would be home from work in an hour, and although not expectant, I should have a dinner prepared. If anything, I was starved.

The cookbook was more of a prop, because I actually knew what the hell I was doing when it came to cooking. I settled on an Alfredo pasta dish. After setting up the water to boil, I checked back in with the mirror. I had never looked—or felt—so aged as I had, for the second time in one day. Shaking the thought, I washed off, changed into the comfiest sweatpants I could find, freed a wine cork from a bottle of the most expensive red we had in the cabinet—$14.95!—and let Tom's nuisance and poor excuse for a dog back indoors.

Living with Tom sounded all fine and dandy until Dash entered the picture. Now I was stuck taking care of a massive bulldog with a very misleading name. I don't think I've seen Dash take off after anything a day in my life.

Lost in thought, I recognized I was stirring around a pot of water without noodles. I added them equally as effortlessly as I had done everything else that evening because every night blended together; I barely referred to my agenda.

As time passed, I tidied up here and there, because if I didn't do it, it'd never get done. Tom would give the excuse that he was too tired, which he might be, from all the time spent away from me. I know when he leaves and gets home, but what he does in between, remained a mystery.

Downstairs, I heard the faint sound of our cheap doorbell. It was Tom. Even though he had a key, he preferred not to scramble with it but instead introduced his presence via ring. I buzzed him in routinely, right on time, per usual. The monotony of that man's timing had grown sickeningly familiar. I had mastered it down to the minute.

I set the table for two, stirred the pasta some more, and wished it were anyone but Tom walking through the door to join me.

***

"Smells good," Tom came prancing through the foyer and tossed his briefcase on the couch—something I'd have to move later.

We sat down and discussed how our days went. He, being a pediatric doctor (which attracted him to me initially) had to deal with hypochondriac parents, a few common colds, and today, his clothes fell victim of projectile vomit, which seemed to happen more often than one would expect.

I told him of all the amateur fiction pieces I read. We sat at opposite ends of the table, almost so we had to shout at each other. *PASS THE SALT!* Our tiny, yet overpriced, apartment only had so much square footage, yet there we were, feeling miles apart.

For some reason that night, I was bothered by the redundancy of our conversation more than most, accrediting that to my visit with Max's letters. Plus, talking about what I experienced in the office made me dread my time there that much more the following day.

"Everyone submits these pieces with weak protagonists. Anyone who knows anything about writing knows the protagonist carries the attitude, even sass of the novel. Leave the weak characters for the supporting roles. Yet here I am, falling asleep at the pages before me. I bet that's Seth's exact diagnosis. He's bored by weak protagonists that he just falls asleep at his desk day in and day out," I flailed my arms for emphasis and even slight exaggeration. Although not exciting at all, it was sadly the most riveting part of my day.

I felt myself redden in the face, hoping it wasn't too obvious to Tom that he was one of my life's weaker characters. I don't know what it is that drives a person mad, but I'd have to guess predictability has a little something to do with it. I wasn't usually that pessimistic toward Tom, but recently, I just didn't have the patience to tolerate him.

13

I wished Tom would cheat on me or do something to legitimize my growing hatred toward him, but he was just the plain old Tom I had always known. How horrible of a girlfriend am I, for wanting a mother of a sick child to walk in and seduce my boyfriend just so it justifies my reason for leaving?

In a place of children's wellness, for crying out loud!

But he would make some woman happy someday and it just wouldn't be me, and I had to settle with that being reason enough to leave him.

As I laid my head down next to Tom's after a few episodes of network television, I said my goodnights. My thoughts drifted off as they always did. Always to Max. In a way, I've felt guilty because although I had never physically cheated on Tom, I've never felt about Tom what I've felt for Max.

Tom reached over to pull me into him.

"Not tonight, Tom..." I said, rolling over.

I was too preoccupied to put up with him any longer, my patience wearing thin. I was overcome with fear at what my life with Tom was becoming. I wasn't happy, and I knew I didn't love him as he did me. I was too restless for my own good. I turned to face him; it would be the last time I saw him, potentially. I absentmindedly played with a curl on Tom's head while he drifted into sleep almost too easily. There was a time when he meant something to me, everything actually. Obviously, I moved in with him after not much convincing and only seven months of dating. He was a doctor, and I, a struggling author. He worked while I stayed home and pieced together my debut novel.

However, when my novel flopped and my storyline ran amuck, I knew I had to begin my job search. It was all too comfortable for so long that it led me to this current state of madness when things *had* to change.

I got a job at the publishing company to appease whatever feelings I could not suppress from my failed attempt at a novel all my own. Somehow it was a happy medium.

Another year went by, which led us to where we were currently. I remember placing his framed picture on my desk at work, face down. I was on a conference call and it was distracting me. Even in the picture I felt he was judging me with zoned in eyes. Now suddenly, I felt guilty for that action.

He was sleeping so peacefully, yet little did he know that when his alarm went off at 5:30 the next morning, I'd already be long gone.

"Goodbye, Tom," I whispered breathlessly.

***

It was one in the morning when I finally obtained the courage to leave. I scribbled Tom an extensive apology, because despite his little shortcomings, I felt bad for the guy, and I didn't need a missing person's report hanging over my head when he found me gone.

In fact, I was leaving for the opposite reason—to be found.

I planned on calling my boss Seth once the office opened. I'd have to apologize for leaving so abruptly, and I dreaded that conversation, but it was nothing

Mandy and Mindy, or whatever the names of the interns, couldn't handle. I did wonder what would happen to the man in the novel I was working on but I was rooting for it to get published, so hopefully I'd see it on shelves soon; my leaving took precedence.

I already knew people wouldn't grasp it. They wouldn't understand why I was doing this. But as people continually do, they'd jump to conclusions too quickly, anyways. I think that's the problem with most people, actually. If you knew more about people's stories, you'd empathize with them. Their insanity is almost justified if their history leads them to it.

I decided when people questioned my journey— soul search, if you will—that they won't need an explanation. I was sick of owing people things. I owed Tom dinner when he got home, I owed Seth my articles by a short deadline, I owed my friends an explanation of why I was still with Tom, I owed it to the neighbors to clean up after Dash, I owed money for bills...

The list went on and on. I was still young, I craved adventure. I was too in over my head with responsib-ilities.

I owed it to myself to leave without explanation and with reckless abandon. And that's exactly what I'd do.

PHOEBE

I looked at the clock posted above the tacky educational posters in the back of the classroom what felt like fifteen minutes prior, yet in actuality, was only three. I rolled my eyes, perhaps subconsciously but probably intentionally, and inhaled the largest deep breath my little lungs could manage.

I dated my science quiz September 1, 2016. The date reminded me that my birthday was in just a few days, which baffled me, although it shouldn't, it came this time every year, I suppose.

Mr. Bailey passed out the quizzes and I racked my brain for all that I didn't study the night before. I had intentions of reviewing my scarce notes like they would have helped, but something better had come along. Colin invited me over and I couldn't say no. I looked over at him sitting just two rows and some odd seats ahead of me in class, running a hand through his hair all calm, cool and collected. Just like him, not even phased.

Our teacher liked to add mock answers to his quizzes, which he thought were comical, but in reality sold the class on all reasons they should not take him, his polka dotted ties or his class seriously. If the teacher considered the class a joke, so would I.

I hiked up my skirt to find where I jotted down just what I assumed was *D, all of the above*, but I had to verify my lack of knowledge. I did a solid job of summarizing the second chapter of our science book in entirety on my thigh. Although I had to skip my third period art class to do it, I needed a good grade in Mr. Bailey's class, and in a way, it was an art form all its own.

I was about to have to start looking at colleges and needed all the help I could get. Holly, my nearest and dearest (this week, anyway), took the test second period, so she helped me narrow down what I needed to know. I had the ingenious idea of writing it all down on my right thigh because what was Mr. Bailey going to do, ask me to lift my skirt in front of the class? Not this day in our oversensitive age, I don't think so.

Colin caught my eye, turning his quiz in when I hadn't made a dent in mine. He too must have cheated in some way because there was no chance he would have finished before me. He might be—is—the best looking and most popular guy in the room, but what he had in looks, he definitely lacked in brain cells.

He eyed me coyly, bit the side of his lip ever so slightly and placed a tiny note on my desk, taking the long way around so he bypassed my desk on the way out.

The answers to the last five questions are: C, C, A, D, D, B. Now hurry up and finish the quiz, and meet me out by my truck.

Because I saw every other girl death glaring me from all corners of the room, I couldn't help but blush. I didn't ask for Colin and I to click the way we had, it just happened…and all so quick. His jocular demeanor, tall, dark and handsome vibe matched with his athletic build just didn't align with my unruly head of curls, rounder figure and flushed completion, but I wasn't one to complain about the particulars.

Recognizing that he provided me with six answers when he claimed five, I reviewed the quiz in front of me as steadily as possible. Adjusting my skirt to hide the evidence as I glided effortlessly out of my seat, I turned

18

my quiz in with an undeniable giddiness overcoming me. Mr. Bailey nodded jovially as I turned in my answers.

"Have a great Thursday, Phoebe," he said, his positive energy making me as uneasy as it always had.

I don't know where we were headed or what we were doing, but I walked out of the room with conviction and a dull pencil, a smile plastered foolishly on my freckled face.

SAGE

It was 2:12a.m. when I left the apartment for good. I had a backpack full of granola bars, peppermints, and clean underwear—the essentials. There was a little less than five thousand dollars saved up between my credit and debit cards. After rent, basic bills and maintaining an energetic lifestyle, I was not left with much wiggle room when it came to saving money. Asking Seth for a raise was out of the question, as I discovered through trial and error. It should be plenty to last a while, though. I've never been good at saving, only ever spending, so this would be a crash course in learning on the spot.

I decided I was going to Virginia. Where Max was and hopefully still is.

Max and I practically grew up together, at times our relationship stronger than others. It was nothing short of love for a few sweet, yet short and childish years of our lives. He was the freest soul I had ever met, but entirely put together all the same. He cared about his appearance, maintained a healthy lifestyle and always was very gentle and thoughtful. He and I had a great life, or the potential for one together, but his family had deep-rooted issues of their own. His mother struggled to make ends meet after his father died abruptly. Going a little crazy as a new widower and a now single mother, she did her best, but undeniably needed Max's help.

A year into our relationship, Max decided he needed to move back to her in a small, yet overly rundown town near Virginia Beach, in order to get her back on her feet; more out of guilt than anything else. He received a call from his mother one day demanding he come be with her, what a sad excuse a last blood relative he was to her, and that she was ill. Whether this was true or a mere exaggeration, I may never know. All I knew was that Max was rattled. This was the call that everything changed for us.

Without a car, Max took off on foot to be with his mother as immediately as he could. Perhaps to prove a point, perhaps he too had just given up. He was always too kind for his own good and I admired that most about him.

Thinking of the problems I was running from now, I could easily see how they paled in comparison to Max's struggles and what I watched him go through those last few months of our relationship.

I used to classify problems by a sort of hierarchy, some being more severe than others, and although to some extent I still find that true, I have loosened the reigns. A problem is a problem, no matter how you spin it.

Never hearing from Max after he left saddened me more than anything I thought ever would. He was just gone, and for so long. For what I thought would be ever. My sixteen-year-old self couldn't fathom life without him until I had no other choice to.

Until one day, I received a package of notes, and a ton of them. There must have been one hundred, at least. I was already in college at the time. I'd write Max just to reach out sporadically and let him know I was thinking of him, all going without a response.

I'd never forget the numbness I felt walking back up to my apartment after seeing his handwriting on the package. I snuck it under my arm to avoid confrontation with my overbearingly nosy roommate at the time. She would have made me read them all aloud to her, had she got her hands on the box.

He wrote me about his nomadic ways on the journey to be reunited with his mother, who I did find out was never even ill at all, just heartsick, as a woman who lost her husband of twenty something years often is, and admittedly deserved to be.

There was an individual letter for each day he was out walking. Even though I knew the relationship with him was over, I was ecstatic to have a pile of letters with his name in the return address. We had been through more together than some people would experience in a lifetime, so for that reason I felt forever bonded.

I intended to read them all right away. He knew I desired a sense of normalcy in our relationship that he just couldn't give me. I hadn't moved on from Max at that point because I didn't know how to love after him. No one compared.

Although I always found her kind, his mother's shortcomings were a constant embarrassment in his life, but he wasn't an ex-boyfriend like the ones my friends talked about. They were always bitter, and out for revenge, on a mission to prove how much happier they were without him. How could someone I hadn't talked to in so long, at least a year and a half at the point when I received the letters, still hold such a tight grasp around my heart?

The note on top was dated with the end of Max's travel time—the day he finally was reunited with his mother after a journey of hundreds of miles on foot. I did what math I could and calculated his traveling to four months and fifteen days. His shaky handwriting wrote me the note I read in preparation for my trip. It was motivation in a way.

Enclosed was an address where he'd be waiting.

As simplistic as his first note was, I've replayed the last lines of it in my head constantly over the past, what, fifteen, maybe sixteen, years since I saw him last? I unceasingly wondered what the others revealed. Every time I looked at Tom these past few days, my curiosity in Max would sneak up on me stronger than ever before.

Maybe I'd gone a bit mad, but maybe that was the beauty in it all. I'd had this longing to be as refreshed as Max had become, to be with him again and I felt newly inspired by his quest.

Then there was that twisted reasoning at the back of my mind signaling to me that now more than ever, Max needed me to fix my mistakes, taking ownership once and for all.

It was time for me to go, and I'd walk as far as it took to get there.

PHOEBE

I was never into all that mushy, romantic crap most girls my age were. Holly's new boyfriend asked her out "officially" last week with a promise ring. All the girls at my lunch table gushed, but a stale taste of vomit crept into my mouth, perhaps from the sappiness of it all, or perhaps from the terrible cafeteria food. Probably both.

It wasn't that I didn't like romance, I just felt awkward around it. Almost that I didn't deserve it and unknowing how to react to even the slightest romantic gesture. *"Ohh, ahh, so sweet!"* they squealed like they'd never seen jewelry from a vending machine before.

Last year, a boy—bless his heart—too far out of my league (and I am confident in admitting it), told me he loved me after we made out at a small party in Bradley Duckett's basement. So small, I'd call it a gathering over a party, really. It meant nothing to me. It just so happened to be the first time I drank beer.

After a long, well thought out speech and confession of love, all I could muster was, "Thank you…you are kind." We sat in what felt like a staring contest for thirty seconds too long afterwards. Who even says the word "kind" anymore? It was a word my grandmother would use repeatedly. *"The new neighbors made us pie! How kind!"*

I avoided him ever since.

Do I think I handled the situation well? No. Not at all. He probably cried his eyes out. He was that type, overall just very immature and overly emotional, as all high school underclassmen were whether they wanted to admit it or not.

Colin was different though. He didn't make me want to be any more romantic than I had been in the past, but he certainly made me feel some kind of way. And I liked it. I liked it a lot.

Typically, as any love story goes, there was an immediate flaw. He was a bad boy. Now, I was by no means a good girl, it wasn't *that* cliché. But see, I didn't want to end up with a bad boy. Two negatives do not make a positive in this type of scenario. I found that I made any excuse plausible as to why it was okay to be around him, and I hated to think his popularity had a little something to do with that. I liked the attention I received when I hung with him and his crew.

What would my mother have thought of Colin? She wouldn't be pleased. And I definitely wouldn't let him meet my father. Your typical "don't bring home to mom and dad for burgers on the grill and a get-to-know-you session" was out of the question on that one. I went into the relationship knowing well and good that it was going to end in a heartbreak. How horrible!—I know. When you're a little girl dreaming of love, you never envision the bad. I envisioned the good just like the rest of them, so knowing Colin wasn't good from the beginning put me at some sort of advantage.

Plus, this was high school, where I was supposed to have fun, be rebellious and free. Boys like Colin didn't always go for girls like me so once I scoped out to make sure he had no hidden agenda (which didn't take long), I figured I'd give him a chance.

His life couldn't have been further on the spectrum from mine, but that's what made it interesting. At my home, I'd have to sneak a boy up to my room, careful to avoid the creaky steps accordingly, but at his place— where not only the kitchen counters were made of marble but also the multiple columns serving as base supports to the mansion of a home—I'd walk right in and if I didn't get lost, found my way to his bedroom shortly thereafter. His mother was too consumed with her own vanity to be concerned and his father was always out of the country on business. I reveled in the novelty of it all. They were untouchable and I often would have to pinch myself in disbelief that I was in their presence, feeling inclined to wear my best pearls as if to impress.

They were after all, just humans, and conceited humans at that; and yet, they fascinated me.

After making my way to Colin's room, I'd sit bored on his bed as he played video games, myself feeling idiotic.

We always did what he wanted to do, but somehow I never minded. At fifteen, I was too naïve to know any different. Whereas at fifteen for him, he seemed so adult to me, if not in his actions, certainly his lifestyle.

I made my way to the bathroom to scrub off the answers peeking through my skirt with every move I made. Colin didn't even notice my absence, he was so glued to the game.

Looking in the mirror, I reminded myself that one day I'd find someone who would treat me as I deserved.

SAGE

Max's journey was driven by obligation. Mine, I felt had a more romantic twist. I didn't know what I would do for food, shelter or basic necessities, but somehow I wasn't scared at all. I had what I would compare to a runner's high. I used to run in college, so I know first-hand how that felt.

Did I feel invincible? Yes. Did I feel obligated? No. Deep down did I feel a bit of both? Maybe.

A girl I used to work with, Gracie, hiked the Appalachian Trail once. This is comparable I would assume. She lived to share about it. God, it's all anyone ever talked about with her post hike. Poor thing. I'd get bored just overhearing the conversation—again—from just a few cubicles over. However, it did seem like a worthwhile experience, so maybe I wasn't as insane as I seemed.

Far easier than expected, I jumped up and walked out the front door. I had devilish dreams of sneaking out the window with my pack, bouncing from balcony to balcony until I reached ground level. Secure and on my feet, I'd start my journey. But like most things in life, it was anticlimactic. I stood up out of bed as if I was just using the bathroom and I'd be back in just a minute. Instead, I beelined to the front door; Tom not batting a lash or quivering the slightest.

I had a backpack busting at the seams with random things. I always had a tendency to over-pack and this trip would be no different, however this time, I came to terms with the fact that I may need to shed some belongings as I went. Alongside it I had my map, one that was so clean when I bought it at the convenience store but now had markings all over the east coast. Baffled by how little I knew about maps, I brought it to work and did some research, using the brightest yellow highlighter I could find to mark a safe and strategic course. I had been planning this trip for weeks, just waiting on the right moment to pick up and go.

When I finally did, Dash looked up in my general direction. I put a finger to my lip making the s*sshhh* motion, as if in some strange turn of events he'd understand the gesture. The only one who slept heavier than Tom was Dash, slapping his head against the floor of the kitchen and falling back asleep, after verifying I posed zero threat.

Convenient.

I wondered if Max felt this way at this point in his journey. Adrenaline pumping, knowing he was about to embark on the most silent, yet loudest thing he'd ever do.

In my head, I complained immediately, but I begrudgingly walked what must have been ten miles at the least before stopping. Actually, I knew it'd been a solid ten miles, because I spotted my favorite café in the distance. It was nearing 6a.m.

I was never athletic by any means, but at least in shape, and I knew I wasn't making great time, but I was making good time, and both would get me by. Additionally, I wanted to get to the outskirts of town and out of sight of Tom's work route so he wouldn't catch me on the way. Imagining him urging me to get into his car so he could talk some sense into me would be worst case scenario.

I stopped and downed a large coffee from Maggie's Cafe, my favorite place to sit on a Saturday afternoon and forget it all. I was usually found there later than the crack of dawn, but regardless, I was grateful they were open.

"Sage! The regular?"

"Yes, please."

"You off somewhere? What's with the backpack?"

"Just felt like being a little adventurous."

"Oh yeah? Where ya headed?"

"Virginia."

"On foot? Oh honey, you're gonna need more than a coffee."

I couldn't help but chuckle. It was nice to know that soon people wouldn't recognize me. I wouldn't have a "regular" at the café in town. It'd just be the world and I out there together, one out to get the other, and vice versa.

"Crazier things have happened," was all I could think to say.

"Well, you keep safe out there. The world is a brutal place."

"Hmm. The coffee is perfect. Thank you," I said, casually changing the subject. I paid, but didn't tip as I usually would. I realized I was going to need to budget accordingly for the venture. I loaded my coffee down with sugar and low-fat milk, so much so that it could hardly be considered coffee at that point, but rather a warm swirl of sugary goodness. But I believe that your morning coffee sets the tone for the day, so I had no choice but to make mine strong.

I could see the disapproval, reluctance, confusion and a pile of other mixed emotions in Maggie's eyes as I turned to leave, not because of my absentee tip, but because of my future absence in general. She'd been a motherly figure to me out here. When Tom and I had our first fight, she was the easiest to talk to. I would go there to edit papers every Saturday, my computer plugged up to the wall like it was on life support to keep charge for the numerous hours I knew I'd be perched there.

She knew more about me than I'd like to let on. Now, something was different in her tone. Her eyes screamed, *"Do you want to talk?"* but the other piece of her knew me well enough to know I was too far gone and the decision was made. I should have been flattered she was worried, but I caught glimpse of the girl on the wall and got distracted.

The girl in the photo. It was me, but it was not. It was the old me. *Customer of the Month, March 2015* is scribbled under the photo. I kissed the palm of my hand and hit my plain self on the wall, kissing who I used to be goodbye on my way out.

***

I walked for twenty-four straight hours, my heavy pack an adjustment; the knot in my neck reminding me so. A sense of purpose had already washed over me, though. I finally admitted to myself that this journey certainly wouldn't be easy, nor would there be many twenty-four hour commitments once the adrenaline ran its course.

It was fear that kept me from sleeping that first night. Afraid of where to stop, afraid that if I gave my legs a break, they'd give up forever; a journey incomplete.

Now, while still in New York, I hopped on the subway, fearing I was still in close proximity to my home, where I could potentially see someone I knew. I'd take it as far south as I could before getting off. Having not set definitive rules for myself yet, I wasn't sure if this was cheating mileage or not and I was too exhausted to care.

Letting my muscles take a break, I didn't want to lose sight of what I was doing too easily. I took the stack of letters out of my backpack. My head rested upon the nearby window, scuffed up with children's fingerprints. Not paying mind, I took the first letter off the stack and opened it, hoping it would provide me some hope, enough to keep me going. After all, I felt more than deserving of some guidance.

It was appropriately titled *Day 1*.

I recognized what the letters were immediately when I received them so many years ago, I just never

30

thought I'd do as they actually intended. I got the hope I longed for and the reassurance I needed in his comic relief, and then some.

Sage,

The first day has to be the worst of all the days on this journey. It may be too soon to declare, seeing as I have yet to experience the other days to come, but it can't get much worse than this. It's raining and I'm finding shelter under the awning in Bennett Park.

Yeah, I know, you're laughing. I only made it here in one day.

I have the images of you in my head from the time we came here last summer. Falling asleep tonight will be easier, envisioning you before me on the swing. The memories of you and I will keep me going.

Until tomorrow,

Max

I did laugh at the vision of Bennett Park. It still remained not too far from my apartment with Tom, but it was different in every way I remembered Max and I sharing it. Currently, small children infested its slides and swings, joggers congregated there to put in some mileage and dog barks could be heard from all corners, whereas it used to be desolate. We'd go there to be alone and it was there he first told me he loved me.

I remembered it like yesterday. It was memories and the short notes from Max I was certain would get me through. With them, this was all less scary.

***

As I stumbled across my first state line into New Jersey, a feeling unreal washed over me. Stopping to smile up at the state sign turned into an eruption of laughter. It was definitely becoming the simple things in life I took pleasure and pride in.

I walked some more before setting up camp for my first sleep outside. I found a space off the beaten path. Surprisingly, the ground was dry and I slept rather soundly. I was fresh off walking twenty-six straight hours, so dozing off was a breeze. I went undisturbed for a solid ten hours, which my body thanked me for. Likewise, It took me no time at all to wake up once I realized where I was. It was daylight when I heard birds chirping and cars soaring down nearby streets. Packing up my sleeping bag and gathering my pack from the brush, I knew I must continue on, despite how much my body was in opposition. I ate to refuel and with not much to commit to in the beauty department, I was back on the road.

I didn't get too far into my day's travels when I stumbled upon a suburban neighborhood where an older gentleman had set up a yard sale in the corner lot. Who would have thought I of all people would be enthralled by a yard sale? High society, perhaps materialistic Sage...I wouldn't have been caught dead at a yard sale, let alone purchasing something of used value. Yet, there I was, hoping to score a good deal on something that would be of assistance while I was out venturing.

It was the bicycle I caught glimpse of first. A rusted hue with a hint of mint speckles covered its frame, as if the paint had run its course. No doubt it had seen better days, but I needed it to be mine. I crossed my fingers, hoping it wasn't too expensive.

"How much for the bike over there?" I inquired.

An overweight man, who looked like walking himself would do some good, eyed it coyly.

"For you? Twenty bucks."

"Sold."

It could have flat tires for all I knew, but it was a risk I was willing to take because not only could I move faster on a bike, but it acted as some sort of protection. I had yet to feel threatened, but after only two nights, I knew the darkness could become an unsafe and even scary place for a young woman like me. I was prepared for worse, inevitable nights ahead.

I could feel my eyes start to droop just thinking about the darkness. I had pulled several all-nighters in college, but nothing compared to this.

The night that followed I wanted to sleep, and I wanted to sleep good. Tempted by the thought of walking home played on repeat in the back of my mind. I was still close enough...

I thought about the letters in the backpack that was quickly starting to weigh me down. There was no way I

33

could stop then and I knew it. Max had this journey set out for me long before I knew the journey existed for myself. It's enough for you to believe in yourself, but when someone you've fallen in love with believes in you like that, it's something special all its own.

I hopped on the bike. In better condition than I anticipated, I went twice as far as I expected in one morning; happy to have my home state of New York— the Big Apple—behind me...the city that never sleeps…

***

My only saving grace was the McDonald's cheeseburger I ate for dinner. If I was being completely honest, I ordered two of them. The following day, I stopped and got some dry-sealed groceries. I was too preoccupied reveling in the moment to care about anything else. The burgers may in fact have been the best things I'd ever tasted. Anything tasted gourmet when you were famished, I suppose.

My next order of business was scouting a good area for a place to sleep. I spotted an abandoned shopping cart in the distance. Like the bike, it seemed a bit rusted.

Walking to it, the haunting realization and shame at the very idea of resting my head down for the night in a rusted, old shopping cart and being okay with it, set in. Then again, what other options were there? I rested it securely against the corner backing of a bridge, lining it with my sleeping materials. It was sure to be tight, but better than nothing. This is what my life had come

34

to…but the fleeting reluctance was nothing compared to the adventure in my heart.

Sleep came and went, as typical when sleeping in a rusty, beaten up shopping cart at the corner of town, I assumed. My mind drifted to Max yet again. Wondering if tonight he sat down to a table packed with roasted turkey, salted mashed potatoes and fresh-cut green beans—not the flimsy store bought kind—that his new girlfriend or wife cooked fresh for him as he got home from work.

"Honey, I'm home!" I imagined him saying as he entered their chic and almost too modern two-story split-level. The dog running to greet his faithful owner, just like my life with Tom.

The thought disgusted me, mostly because it reiterated my second-guessing and the purpose of my travel. He may have moved on and that frightened me more than the journey itself. Also, returning to something so similar from what I was running from, was definitely something I wanted to avoid. I didn't sign up for the same life with a different man. I, however, believe people change, and that life with Max would be different, no matter what.

After all, in a world of redundancy, isn't it the different things in life we have to fight for?

PHOEBE

I could never grasp the concept of fighting in any regard, not even in a boxing ring or wrestling match, where it was considered acceptable, and God forbid, entertaining. Colin watched wrestling all the time when he wasn't buried behind a gaming console, and I couldn't grasp why. Thinking he was a tough guy himself, he'd stare down any guy that attempted to talk to me, threatening them with his eyes, even if at the end of the day he'd do nothing about it. All bark and no bite.

Once in the lunch line, in a genuinely absent-minded mistake, I forgot my wallet. My lab partner at the time was in the line in front of me. He was a good-looking guy who happened to be a perfect gentleman. He was the perfect combination to spew jealousy. I saw Colin eyeing me from our unassigned, yet unspoken assigned lunchroom seats in the far back corner. If looks could kill...

I was lost in conversation with my 7-out-of-10 lab partner until I hit the end of the line and I was forced to pay for my meal. I fished around my purse in search of a wallet I couldn't quite find. I already had a chicken Caesar wrap on my tray and was growing increasingly frustrated when I couldn't find what I was looking for in the first ten seconds of my search. The crumbs at the bottom of my purse annoyed me. Why were they even there, as if I were snacking over my bag? I grew ever more frustrated at the crumbs, who were third party in the matter, as I continually struggled to find my wallet, which was misplaced in the seemingly bottomless pit of a fashion statement. I immediately racked my brain for where it could be without trying to look too unsettled, which would in turn make my company uncomfortable and potentially subject them to secondhand embarrassment. Instead, I settled on the simple statement, "Dammit, I must have left my wallet in my locker. Will you hold my place in line?"

"Oh, I got your lunch today. You've already come this far," My lab partner said in a *don't be silly!* tone. I acted surprised by the offer, an Academy Award winning performance, "Oh, are you sure? You don't need to do that! I definitely owe you."

It was those little games I played with Colin that kept it interesting, knowing he witnessed everything that had just happened, but making far worse assumptions as to what really went on.

I thanked my lab partner twice over and made it known I'd return the favor.

"What was that about?" Colin could hardly contain himself, hanging halfway off the seat when I reached mine.

"What was what about?" Innocence is key, because after all, I wasn't guilty...

"Did he just buy your lunch?"

"Oh, that," ...duh, it finally hit me... "Yeah, he did. I can't seem to find my wallet. Have you seen it?"

Playing it off as no biggie, I took a bite of my wrap, all tortilla and no substance. My hunger was making me irritable, so I suffered through the waste of calories.

"It wasn't my turn to watch it," he said as if he was the authority on anything and everything. He got defensive too easily, but I saw true anger in his eyes, almost defeat. Colin was very aggressive and naturally argumentative. I knew he was envisioning knocking my lab partner to the ground in one steady hit. He loved to

37

fight as much as I hated it but if he really wanted me, he'd fight for me—if not physically, emotionally and mentally. Because after all, didn't every girl want someone to fight for and in turn be fought for? It was just inconvenient that I had to play games for him to fight back.

SAGE

As I walked, I thought back to when I was eleven years old living near the coast in a small rundown town in the heart of New York. Not much had changed now, except I traded in living in the dirty outskirts to a well put together studio apartment.

It was just my mother and I back then. She tried to do what she could to make a happy childhood for me, but one day she just gave up. My father left us when I was just five weeks old, the stress of a newborn taking a toll on him.

Not like they were married when I was born, he "just wasn't ready," from what my mother relayed to me later in life. He was always there though, which was reassuring, just at a distance. He lived near Times Square so visiting him once a month always turned out an adventure all its own.

She could tell I was upset whenever she talked negatively about him, despite her not picking up on many social cues. My mother didn't have many friends, but the ones she did have were just like her. She was a strong-willed and opinionated woman, I will give her that. Albeit, with little education, her statements were often nothing more than an ignorant jumble of words and phrases.

I appreciated her raising me, but she was entirely too sluggish for her own good. Sometimes, I wondered if the reason my father left was because he wasn't ready for a life with her; it having nothing to do with me whatsoever.

"He's guilty!" I could hear my mother's raspy voice yelling at no one in particular from the couch where she would watch endless episodes of courtroom television. She'd always input her lack of criminal justice knowledge as if it'd make a difference. A sad excuse for reality TV, and a sad excuse for a life.

"Aww...that's wrong...he aughta be locked up!" She'd shout when it didn't go her way, flailing her cigarette into the air. I hated when she smoked in the house.

"What's the square root of 112?" I would ask from the kitchen table in an attempt to do my homework in my late elementary days.

"Look it up!" She'd typically answer when she herself didn't feel like thinking. Now a question like that was mindless to me, which revealed a lot about her intellectually. However, even at that age, I knew the answer damn well. I was smart, but had to vie for her attention in any way possible.

"Is Roger coming over tonight?" Roger was my mother's boyfriend who would come over only after I went to sleep. He wasn't creepy or anything, but I always found it bizarre he only ever showed up after 10p.m. But, he stuck around for more than a week, so he must have been something special. Apparently he came over late because of his job, another novelty in the line-up of mom's boyfriends.

I never had a solid male figure in my life (although Roger hung around for a couple years, I can't say he was a *good* example, among other things), with my father in and out constantly, but I knew enough to know what not to look for in a relationship. I still gravitated to bad boys during my early teenage years, as all girls do, I suppose.

I'd never forget the fateful night the week after my thirteenth birthday, just some years later. I slid on my best leather jacket, skinny jeans, and threw in my biggest hoop earrings. I parted my hair all to one side to cover up the burn on my right ear as a result of my hair crimper; a new birthday gift. Rookie mistake. My mother splurged on what was the best brand in her opinion, but I knew it cost no more than a whopping $12.99. Like I said, sometimes she'd have her shining moments where I knew she tried to at least give me what I wanted.

I wasn't one to complain though. It got the job done, I looked good. When I heard my mother quit crunching potato chips on the couch, I'd sneak out and meet Ethan McBride outside where he'd be waiting in his brand new sports car.

Some of us got hair crimpers for our birthday, others got sports cars. It is what it is.

Feeling accomplished for skipping the creaky stair on my way down, I opened a window that led to the front porch (a task much more tedious than I anticipated). Much to my surprise a voice startled me, "Well don't you look nice!"

Dammit. My mother was sitting on the porch in a rocking chair, cigarette clasped between two fingers. Just rocking.

"Oh, I…um…thought you'd be asleep by now. I'm sorry, I'll just head….um, back upstairs now."

"Sneaking out are ya?"

"Something like that…I'm sorry, I'll…"

"Why don't you sit down with your momma for a minute? You in a rush?"

"Not really, no. What're you doing up so late? It's almost midnight."

"Couldn't sleep."

"Oh. The house was very quiet."

After a minute of silent to moderate rocking, she took a long drag from her cigarette, "It's okay if you want to go out. You don't need to sneak."

She said it in a caring way, no condescension.

"I mean, I get it," she continued, "It's fun to sneak. But you're a good kid. I don't know how you turned out so good. Coming from me and your father…" This was the part I almost interrupted her, to deny her statement with "*No, mother, you're wonderful, you did a great job raising me,*" however, I didn't feel so inclined because at the end of the day, she was stuck in her ways, refusing the help of anyone who sought a tiny ounce of kindness. If a rebuttal was what she was hoping for, I couldn't serve one up.

"But I trust you. Who's the boy?" she was always so forward.

41

"Why do you assume there's a boy?" Perhaps a fault of mine was reacting too defensive too quickly.

"Well look atcha! You're not my little baby anymore, are ya?"

Caught.

"His name's Ethan McBride." I didn't mention the fact that he was three years my senior, although I'm sure it wouldn't have made a difference to her. She may have even commended me for it.

She chuckled a bit. "So there *is* a boy…"

I chuckled too, I couldn't help it.

"Listen to your momma, now, don't be like me and fall for a little boy's sweet talk."

So I had her blessing, if nothing else. It was the best I'd get. I hurried off the front porch steps after spotting Ethan's car in the distance, perhaps too giddily for the late hour.

It was going to be one amazing night at a greasy twenty-four hour waffle establishment. I could almost feel my happiness gushing through every little stud on my faux leather jacket.

***

Amazing is one of those words I've always hated. A word with a double meaning. Good and bad things alike can be amazing. Coincidences are amazing overall. Whether a situation is good or bad depends on the point of view. What happened to my mother that night ended up being amazing, little did she know it then. It would be one of those, *we'll look back on this and laugh* moments, but instead of laughing, we'd be grateful.

Ethan was dropping me back off at home when I saw the blue lights of a cop car flashing from the driveway through the trees on the other side of our neighborhood. Something either happened to my mother or she did the something. In that scenario, I would put money on the latter every time.

"You can drop me here." I interrupted Ethan's story about some timeshare his father invested in.

"Your house is a good half mile up the road, I can drive you." He was oblivious to the situation, but I knew something had happened with my mother. I had no option but to cut him short.

"It's been a really great night, Ethan, but *please* let me out. My house is closer than you think," I was nearly begging, never able to hide panic very well.

"Oh…oh…okay." He screeched to a halt right there, flat in the middle of the road.

"I'll see you at school," I muttered through my embarrassment. I was so praying for a kiss. My friends would have just died at the thought of me kissing Ethan McBride, star basketball player. Mr. Popular himself.

I sprinted home as Ethan swerved his car in the opposite direction. Poor boy was probably so confused.

Cutting through the thick brush, I made it out with a solo scratch. That was a good record, considering I'd used the shortcut numerous times, never once escaping scar free. This time the pain was irrelevant because I was so focused on the police car's lights raging on in the driveway of our house. *What could be going on at this hour?* I saw my mother crying from the kitchen window as I made it to the mailbox at the end of our drive. I stared at her for a minute, not going inside yet, catching my breath. So frail, so damaged, so hurt.

"What happened?" I walked toward an officer who was briskly moving down the front porch stairs, replicating what I had just done to my mother two hours prior to meeting Ethan.

"You live here?" he asked.

"I do. That's my mother in there."

He motioned me inside. I caught a glimpse of Roger in the back of the cop car. *What was happening?* was all my thirteen-year-old mind could process.

"You know your daughter was out and about this evening, ma'am?" he asked my mother, who was being looked after by a second police officer, this one much taller and thinner than the one who escorted me in.

"I did, yes. She was out on a date."

I cringed. For some reason I didn't want her to call it a date, and I didn't want the officers to know about it.

"Little late for a date. You've been drinking?" he asked me.

"No sir."

The officers eyed each other in a "were done here" manner, like they had an understood pact.

"Okay, well ma'am it seems we've done what we can here. Please take the information we provided you with utmost seriousness. We don't want you in any further trouble."

I noticed a handprint on the side of mother's face, but I could tell she was trying hard to hide it. There were also some bruises on her shoulders. I started to piece it together as the officers made their way out, signaling to me on their way the tall one said, "Help your mother." Little did he know I had, without fault regularly. I just nodded because I did appreciate his guidance. They left and we were alone, just my broken mother and I.

"What did he do to you?" I asked my mother harshly, my voice perhaps too accusatory in reference to Roger.

For the rest of the night, I held my mother in my arms as she cried. When she finally drifted off to sleep, I compiled crumbs of chips and snotty tissues off the floor near her spot on the couch. There was a brochure on domestic violence and another for a drug rehab facility laying on the table. I knew this was the "information" the officer was talking about taking seriously. She slid them nonchalantly under an outdated magazine when she thought I wasn't looking, but I took them and hung them front and center on the refrigerator where they belonged. Somewhere she'd see them, and hopefully take the hint. I knew as horrible as it was with my father leaving, and how heartbroken she was, she and I both knew that he would never do this to her.

Once I saw that she was in her bed sans Roger, sleeping more soundly than I expected her to, I stroked the side of head, kissed her cheek, and made my way to my room. It was a cluttered mess, but I'd deal with it in the morning. I climbed into my own bed after brushing my teeth and sending up a special intention to God.

I never spoke to Ethan McBride again.

**

I noticed the brochures were still on the refrigerator a week later, but that they had been rearranged and possibly leafed through. Roger was convicted of domestic violence, something that had been going on for longer than I knew about. Maybe I was a bit oblivious to their relationship.

Finding no substances in the house, they didn't arrest right then and there, but the cops knew my mother needed help. Anyone who looked at her knew she needed help. If it took someone in a position of authority to get through to her, I was glad at least someone could.

And help is what she got. Since that night, she had been sober. Clean off everything, and although she struggled with being supportive still, I knew things turned out for the best.

Since then, she married a man named Bill, moved to Tampa, and worked part-time at a retail store. My mother met Tom once when I first met Bill. It was a reunion of sorts. My mother didn't like the guy I was dating, and I finally liked someone she was. Ironic how that worked.

I thought of my mother and what she might be doing at that very moment, wondering how she'd feel if she knew what I was doing in that very moment. I suddenly missed her. This happened sometimes, more sporadically that consistent, but I did miss her. I always intended to make the trip out to Tampa, but never seemed to bring myself to do it. Maybe if I felt ambitious enough to walk…

As if.

PHOEBE

It wasn't hard for me to fall into the popular crowd when I made that awkward transition from middle school to high school but it was certainly unexpected. I was pretty enough but never would admit it aloud in fears of jinxing myself. Naturally outgoing, I never minded talking to someone new. So in due time, I too was invited to sit with the popular lunch crowd in the cafeteria full of cliques. I was initially approached by Summer, Colin's ex-girlfriend, and she wouldn't let you forget it. *When I dated Colin...* was how every other one of her stories began, as all wonderful and juicy stories often do. She was anatomically perfect in every way and it was intimidating...until she spoke, releasing air-headed thoughts one sentence after the next. Summer's name used to be Autumn, but the season's change, and so did she!

Sickening.

Everyone made a huge deal of Autumn/Summer's name change like it was something monumental. We all just waited in patient anticipation to find out if Autumn/Summer would show up as Winter the following semester.

I saw the jealousy spring up in all the Kinsey's and Cameron's from across the room with the announcement of her name change, of which she had made a public spectacle in every way possible. To Summer's defense, at least she didn't have a cookie cutter name like theirs. Maybe I was the jealous one because I was "blessed" with a grandmother name for the rest of my life, rather than a youthful, time appropriate name. My grandmother did name me, after all.

Yet, I got my father's mannerisms, and my mother's rebellion. It was a mix made of gold.

As I felt the other girls' eyes on me as I accepted Summer's lunch table invite that first day, a piece of me had won. I had conquered another girl's high school bucket list. Someone roll out the red carpet as I make my way to my new cafeteria seat!

"My parents are out of town this weekend, Pheobs, and we're having a party, you should totally come."

It was the first thing Colin had ever said to me. I didn't even know he knew my name, and then suddenly a nickname. *Oh, Phoebs, that's me, he's actually talking to me!*

"I'll have to check. I might be busy actually, but if I find I'm free, I'll totally stop by."

I played it so cool it was crazy. I was getting good at the game. That's all being popular ever was.

Mr. Jameson asked us all to write one word to describe us later that day in English class. Would cool be too conceited? I considered it for a while and with nothing else coming to mind, I jotted down those fiery four letters because at the end of the day, you can't help being who you really were. My shift in the lunch table that day solidified everything. Now what outfit should I wear this weekend? That was the real question. I had my first high school party to attend…

SAGE

Things hadn't gotten any easier on day three. Quite the contrary, actually. My indestructible watch read 7:12p.m. Because I could not move my legs any longer, I retired to a barstool. The older the pub, the better the drinks, in my opinion. There was a soccer game on and not a soul to be found in the place. Pennants lined the wood paneled back wall, alternative music established the atmosphere. I did a double take to ensure that they were actually open.

The bartender, an attractive man of about twenty-seven years old or so (if I had to guess), served me something he was sure I'd like, as if he knew anything about me and my drink preferences.

"You'll like this, it's strong too."

I drank quietly, suddenly aware of the aroma radiating off my body, self-conscious, because he was becoming cuter with each and every sip.

He was right, it was strong.

After sitting there for about fifteen minutes alone pretending to watch the soccer game with valued interest, he made his way to me and leaned over the bar, his muscles erupting from his plain white V-neck.

"So what brings you out here on a Monday evening? Where you from?"

"Is it a Monday?"

"It is…"

"Oh well, time sure does fly when you're having fun."

49

When I started saying cliché phrases that made me sound like I was aging myself, I knew I was in trouble. The bartender was engaging, the type of guy I'd pursue. If not end up with, he'd make for a fun night.

I thought of Max and how heroic I felt on a quest for a lover, as if he was my very own prince charming in this modern day fairytale and I, the damsel in distress.

It all sounded so romantic but I knew it was all in my head. The heat, weariness and booze must have been getting to me, yet there I was, stupidly leading the bartender on. He made it almost too easy. Besides, it wasn't like Max and I were together, nor Tom and I, so I convinced myself I deserved a bit of fun.

I did look forward to reading Max's letter later, though. It was the last thing I did before trying to get some sleep each night.

I realized my mind was wandering, and it must have showed in my expression, because cutie bartender said, "Everything okay?"

"I'm fine, just taking it all in. It's been a wild day," at that he topped off my drink. "I'm from New York, actually," circling back to one of his original questions as he poured.

"Oh yeah? I've lived so close to the state my entire life but have never been. I've lived in this house for as long as I can remember. When I say house, I mean the bar. I live upstairs." He pointed a finger north and my eyes instinctively followed the direction as if I were familiar with the place. "Family owned and opera-ted…one of those."

"You gonna drink with me?" I asked randomly. I could tell he wanted to chat, so if that was the case, I figured why not formally invite him to.

"On the clock? Nah…wouldn't be professional."

"Oh that's right, all these customers might judge you or something…" I signaled around, placing emphasis on the emptiness that was the bar. The air growing evermore stale, making it harder and harder to breathe, I tapped my empty glass on the bar as if to say "pour me another!" Although done jokingly, he obeyed with no questions asked.

"Well after all, not many people are looking to party on a Monday night, I suppose." A subtle, yet well-deserved jab. He slid the full glass in my direction, impressively spilling not even a drop.

"If you knew the week I've been through, you'd be here drinking too."

"Let me guess, break-up?"

"Well, that's part of it, I guess, but that was my doing, so I wasn't too caught off guard on that one."

"Well still, I'm sorry to hear that."

"It was for the best."

"I'd say I'd get you a drink but I guess I have been all night in a sense," he winked at me and my heart skipped a beat. "What's in the pack? You carry that with you everywhere you go?"

"Oh, no," I laughed, feeling my face flush with self-consciousness, "I'm on a mission. Like a little journey." I had assumed he made the connection that I had walked but apparently he hadn't.

"Oh are you? To where, might I ask?"

"Virginia."

He raised his eyebrows as if impressed.

"I'm walking," I hesitated to add. I sucked out the juice of a lemon he threw in a water and winced just the slightest at its tang.

"Excuse me? You're walking? To Virginia?" His voice heightened with each new question.

By then he just thought I was crazy.

"Mmhmm." I must maintain my confidence.

At my nonchalance, he just burst out laughing. His hysterics should have offended me, but I was feeling giggly too so I laughed alongside him. Besides, it really was utterly ridiculous.

"Well, you stopped at a great place. We'll take care of ya!" I think he threw in the "we'll" part of the sentence to make it seem like it wasn't just the two of us in the room even though I had yet to spot another employee and didn't intend to.

"Is it always this dead on a Monday night?" I attempted to change the subject.

"I closed down the place awhile back but missed it too much. I decided to reopen it, so I'm just now getting back on my feet, if you will."

"Hmm, must be nice to have found your calling."

"You haven't? Wandering isn't your life calling?"

"It's a mission, remember. I have a purpose for all this. Don't call it wandering. Wandering seems… aimless."

I felt comfortable around him, like I had known him for longer than the forty-two minutes I had. It made the casual banter easy.

We talked for another four hours. Time was flying. I lost count of how many drinks I consumed. I knew if I kept this up, I was in for a miserable tomorrow. Walking was a pain as it was, the last thing I needed to do was add a hangover to it.

Mr. Bartender started to get handsy with me and I knew this might not end well if I wasn't careful, but I also knew he resided upstairs, where he had a bed… a nice, warm, comfortable bed. Probably equipped with multiple pillows and a down blanket…

A girl can dream.

"What time do you close this place?" I eyed my watch, secretly hoping it was not too close to last call, although I felt like he'd make an exception for the sake of some company. We seemed to be hitting it off quite well.

"You think I'm going to send you back out into the night knowing your nomadic ways?"

"Umm, yes. I'm almost getting used to it now…"

"Not in this drunken state, you aren't. A girl can get hurt out there if she's not careful."

"So what am I to do? Hangout on this barstool until my drinks wear off? I have too many miles to trek to waste time. Plus, I'm an adult," I rolled my eyes. I may as well be on my knees begging for an invite upstairs…

"Stay with me tonight. Don't you want to shower?" Ask and you shall receive.

"A shower would be nice…too nice."

He extended a hand to help me up, topping off his glass and downing it with the other. Bartender perks, I supposed.

I stumbled out of my chair much more tipsy than anticipated and followed him up a flight of stairs. We made small talk all the way up because now the

53

atmosphere was nearing awkward. He cut the music off, turned the open sign around and dimmed the lights.

Everything was smooth until the idea of me agreeing to go upstairs and take my clothes off, even if it was just for a clean shower.

He put the key in the door, but didn't twist the knob. Instead, he looked back at me, put my face in his hands, and kissed me hard. It took my breath away for a split second, but I found myself kissing back, just playing along.

After I showered, we kissed some more. We did more than kiss, actually. Besides being at my final destination, lying in that bed was the greatest sensation I could have asked for in that moment.

His place was quaint, definitely a bachelor pad. Wall decor was simplistic but not scarce. There was a hint of cotton air freshener filling the room.

Overall, I just felt clean there; the rejuvenation much needed. It was refreshing to watch the layer of grime crawl off my skin as the hot water dripped casually down my body. Lying under his white sheets, I felt rescued. From what, I still hadn't decided.

We laid there in silence, both of us overtired, me from walking, and him from pouring drinks.

"My name's Liam, by the way."

"Nice to meet you Liam. Sage Riley."

I knew this would just be a one night thing, yet, it was nice to lay there and do much of nothing but waste each other's time and breathe each other's air.

PHOEBE

I typically despised parties, but I felt an obligation to live in my prime. I didn't want to get to my older years and regret not living while I was young.

I mostly went out because Colin invited me, but he was already sloshed out on the dance floor that he wouldn't have realized if I was there one way or another. Yet, I found myself being the bigger person—what else was new?—and made my way over to say my hellos.

"Phoebs," he shouted when he saw me. We embraced in an awkward hug.

I had a beer nursed in my hand that I sipped on casually until it was flat, more just so others wouldn't offer me a drink. There was a discomforting pit in my stomach that was brought about by peer pressure, but I smiled through the uncomfortable element for the sake of my growing popularity.

Colin caught me off guard in an unexpected twirl out on the dance floor. His eyes were glassed over. He'd have a pounding headache in the morning at the very least.

"Come dance," he said, twirling around borderline violently. With that, a sticky Jack and Coke spilled down the front of my blouse.

"I'm ser sorry, babe," he stuttered, his hands like little feathers trying to dab away the damage.

"You know what, it's fine. I'll be right back. Going to clean up," I managed to shout over the loud music,

55

with no plans of actually returning to the obscure dance scene.

I had my eye on a pile of napkins over by the punch bowl. After giving up on excusing myself from the crowd of people surrounding the DJ, I nudged my way through as swiftly as possible.

"You okay?" A voice near the punch bowl startled me, but I smiled when I saw the face it belonged to. It was a boy I'd never seen before. He had a sketchbook tucked under one arm and a pencil protruding from his left ear, barely visible through his wild mass of dark hair. He was seemingly out of place.

"Just a little accident. I think I'll survive," I said nonchalantly. Thankful it was dark in there, as the flush in my cheeks certainly revealed embarrassment.

We laughed a small laugh together before he said, "I'm C..." He said a name like Chris but I had a hard time hearing him over the commotion and I felt rude asking him to repeat it.

"Phoebe."

We shook hands.

"Want to leave this place and go walk on the beach? Is that too forward?" He asked so very innocently, putting his hands up as if in defense.

We were at Colin's gorgeous house right along Virginia Beach. It was a regular party spot for this group because not only was the house huge, but also the water right there. Slowly people would slip out one by one to escape to the shoreline.

Normally, I was more cautious, but for some reason I trusted this guy, so I nodded my head in agreement.

He pulled my hand, nearly out of the socket, so by default I followed where he led to a nearby chair where he handed me a sweatshirt.

"Put this on," he says, "It'll be much warmer than what you've got."

"It's yours?" He nodded, smiling too widely, perhaps at my dumb question, as if he'd provide me some random person's sweatshirt.

I maneuvered it on and my wet blouse off in one fluid motion and in a very ladylike manner. Feeling much better, we made our way outside.

The water crashed to the shore like it would in a sick romantic movie, as the sand chilled my bare feet. Seeing I had my shoes in my hand, Chris, Cole, Cooper, whatever he said his name was, slipped his off too.

"What're you drawing?" I asked out of curiosity although it was really none of my business.

"Just some sketches of things here and there," he responded. "Nothing special."

"I'm sure they're great," I said as if I knew anything about his artistic background. "Seems like there wouldn't be enough lighting in that party to sketch anything."

"It was an experiment, I guess. Something to do to pass the time," he said smirking. "I'm not too into the party scene. Not really my thing…"

Although I wanted to skim through the pages, I quit the inquisition when I noticed his slight attempt to change the subject.

"Mine either to be honest," I said because at this point there wasn't reason to pretend any longer.

I listened to him talk and ramble on and I'd nod time and again like I was interested, but when I did pay interest, I found that I genuinely was captivated by the things he was saying. It struck me as bizarre that I had spoken more to this human, who I considered a stranger just forty-five minutes prior, than I had spoken with Colin in the last two months.

We talked and walked for a bit longer before we realized how late and how cold it actually was. Like a perfect gentleman, he walked me back, holding my hand in a special kind of way before leaving a simple kiss on my cheek. I had never seen the boy before and didn't know whom at the party he knew, but I didn't care much where he came from, I was just glad that he was there.

Then he was off into the night. A strange feeling lingered though, as if that wasn't the last I'd be seeing of him.

Suddenly I wanted more, and so much of it.

SAGE

Usually, I regretted staying with a man I just met the morning to follow, not that it happened too often, barely ever actually, but his bed was too comfortable to regret anything whatsoever except that I had spoiled myself. Not that I didn't deserve it, because I did, but God only knew when the next time my body would lay as gracefully in a bed as it had that night.

I'd already experienced a journey most people, let alone a small young woman, wouldn't imagine embarking on alone. I also knew I needed to make some serious time on the road. Those miles weren't going to trek themselves as much as I wished they would.

It was already 11a.m.

Shit.

Luckily, Liam was nowhere to be found, and I hoped I could make a quick escape, thinking he'd already be mopping some floors or cleaning up what he didn't get to with the night's turn of events. I snagged a banana from a basket on the kitchen counter after bouncing up out of bed, and was on my way.

Speaking of things we didn't get to last night, I decided to open Max's next letter.

Sage,

I was crazy to ever encourage you on this journey. It can't be safe for someone like you. So naïve, so fragile, so beautiful. It's dangerous and I don't want you doing it. I take back everything I said. It's difficult and I'm struggling.

Forever thinking of you.

Until we meet again...

Max

I knew Max was still stuck in his old ways because, to my knowledge, he still didn't have a cell phone. I looked him up on the Internet one day and nothing popped up. No sign of him anywhere. How nice it must be to be nonexistent this day in age.

Max was always wary of the long term effects of the Apple Era. He hated the idea that cell phones were gaining popularity at the turn of the millennium, and that companies and schools were becoming more and more reliant on technology.

"No long term studies have been tested on these things! How can you trust them?" I'd recall him saying at age sixteen. In a way there were so many little things that I admired, that ultimately made me fall in love in Max's personality. He was so simplistic, in the most beautiful way. Too often, I worried about things Max wouldn't dream of wasting his time with. When he told me he made a mistake by recommending I walk this walk, I knew it was him being overly cautious. The rarity of his worry didn't make me hesitant though. He knew I was crazy enough to do what he told me, and that was why there was a continuing stack of letters. He would have stopped writing letters if he really wanted me to give up. If I start something, I'm going to finish it and he knew that about me.

It was too late for me to turn back now anyways, but definitely too early to be feeling this lethargic.

I stepped outside and was immediately furious to find that my bike was missing from where I had tied it up. I will admit, I didn't have a legitimate bike lock, so I rigged one together out of rope I had in a totally makeshift manner. The rest of the process relied on trust. Max would have cringed at my attempt and showed me twenty more effective ways before settling on what I had, but Max wasn't there. Not yet, anyway. If he was, the bike would have probably remained there too.

My natural instinct was to panic. I felt behind me to make sure that at least my pack was still there, and thankfully it was intact. As intact as it could be.

I cursed out loud and didn't care who heard. I was angry, and rightfully so. It shouldn't have been that godforsaken difficult that early on, but then I wondered what inside me ever believed any of this would be *easy*. That word just didn't exist out here.

Once you've been robbed of something important, you're on automatic defense. I walked with conviction and let my frustration lead the way.

How careless of me! I instinctively patted myself down, as if I expected to unlock yet another surprise. The bike was an impulse buy unlike any other so I settled on it being gone. I shouldn't have cared so much. Plus, it was becoming a pain dragging it around everywhere I went. It wasn't necessarily compact. So at the end of the day, I decided it was a blessing disguised as thievery.

My mind wandered aimlessly while I walked to the randomness of anything and everything. It took time for me to admit that was normal when there was no one else to talk to, convincing myself I wasn't crazy, just delirious. After all, I was walking so many miles for a *guy*.

I'd walked about twenty miles from what I could gather from street signs and my map, which so far had

61

been very trustworthy. Long hours at the office sometimes allowed me to veer away from the novel in front of me and focus on my own kind of creativity. Who knew I'd be a decent cartographer?

Whoo, whoo!

I heard briefly what sounded like a police car, and it was. It was behind me with lights on so I stopped walking, not sure of the protocol for this. In a car I'd pull off to the side of the road, but walking, I was already there. The officer stepped out of his car.

"Ma'am, can I ask why you're walking out here? You do realize this is an interstate highway?"

"Oh…um, yes sir." I was suddenly more nervous than I expected.

"Where are you off to?"

"Just up the road, I'm meeting a friend for dinner."

"And you chose to walk…?"

I lied. So naturally I had to keep lying. Elementary school morals 1-0-1.

"Yes sir, for exercise."

Now I just sounded crazy. He was probably calling for backup, or racking his brain to rank me among the other crazies he dealt with on a regular basis out in these parts.

"Well, I got a call from someone driving along the road about you. They seemed concerned. You could get hurt out here. Also, I feel it's my job to add that it is in fact illegal to walk along the interstate…even if it is only to meet a friend for dinner." Was it just my delirium, or did he seem skeptical?

"Illegal? Oh, I never meant to do anything illegal."

Great. Now I'd have to change the course of my map to pick-up back roads here and there. How stupid of me not to look up something like that before I left.

My world felt like it was going to crumble around me in that moment. The directness of my journey was too good to be true.

"I'm going to let it slide but can I give you a ride to wherever you're off to so I can ensure this won't happen again?"

"Oh yes, that'd be nice. Thank you…very much." He didn't know the weight of his gesture. My legs throbbed in muscles I didn't even know I had. I was too dehydrated to speak to the kind officer properly, and I thought I still might be a bit hungover from the night before.

He drove me all the way to the edge of the city. I wanted him to keep driving…and driving…and driving…until we covered a million miles. Or at least until I was at my Virginia destination.

"This will be good," I found the courage to say. There was a quaint café called Raymond's on the corner with an outdoor patio I would be content with trying. I pulled a ten dollar bill from my pocket, allowing myself to spend no more, only less in order to maintain my finances. I moved it to the forefront of my wallet for spending control purposes.

"Raymond's?"

"Yes."

"You be safe now. Next time I might not be as nice. Have your friend give you a ride back."

"Will do, thank you." Little did he know…

63

I got out of the car and walked to the side where they had outdoor seating. I was just about to sit down when I heard, "Sadie?"

I turned to find a young man with a wiry smile and wide framed glasses, too eager to hand me a bouquet of flowers.

"Excuse me?" I asked as I felt him leaning in for a hug.

"You must be Sadie! I won't fault you for being late. It's so great to meet you." He hugged me aggressively.

Putting two and two together, I began to assume that the poor boy had just gotten stood up on a blind date by such Sadie, which might end up a free meal for me.

Sage…Sadie…same thing.

"I am so sorry to keep you waiting," I said, going along with it. Little did he know I just hopped out of a cop car, and before yesterday, hadn't showered all week. I was just thankful I was somewhat cleaned up and half presentable, seeing as I just walked roughly twenty-one miles prior…

"Sit down! I have some calamari and red wine on its way."

Rich taste. I picked a good night to do something illegal and then swipe a rude girl's identity, all the while hoping she was for sure a no-show.

"The flowers are beautiful, thank you." It was a shame they'd have to die so soon, as there was absolutely no way I could maintain them as I moved on.

We talked on and on about his interest in becoming an engineer, and the ever-dreaded relationships of his

64

past. My own mind interrupted him mid-sentence and suddenly I was no longer paying attention to whatever Cindy, an ex-girlfriend he met at church camp did to him that was so traumatizing. Instead, I was transferred to my own thoughts. Although I didn't want to sleep with the guy, a place to sleep would be nice. I was getting good at the wandering thing. This could potentially be night two I got to cuddle with a cute (and obviously harmless) guy all the while taking advantage of the crinkles in his sheets and his overabundance of pillows. It was all too easy to picture.

"More?" He raised an eyebrow inquisitively in reference to the wine. I shouldn't have but I did because I had a new outlook: never deny something you can consume for free. I had my map and a budget, and when I could use other's transportation to cover that map and the sustenance someone offered me free of charge toward that budget, I didn't deny.

We chatted on and on for another hour more. I learned his name was Dustin by creeping over his shoulder and eyeing his credit card after he went to the restroom. Dustin and Sadie must have met online. Talking to him, I could envision his online dating profile, and it made me smile at how accurate I probably had it.

"I'll meet you outside." He told me as it was my turn to excuse myself to the restroom to check out what I really looked like.

Dustin was friendly, maybe too friendly, but I thought he found me equally as personable. In a completely innocent sense, I was almost giddy myself. Not because Dustin gave me butterflies or anything like that. He was definitely not any guy I'd go for. Not my type. I was giddy with the fact that my journey was thus far so successful. Maybe I was getting too confident, but I'd stay that way until I was given a reason not to.

"Sadie! Sadie!" I heard the voice getting closer.

Oh right, that's me, I was Sadie.

Dustin had pulled up, curbside service like a perfect gentleman.

I suppose it was assumed I was going back to his place. I hopped in the car, only to find out he lived in an apartment with some roommates who all attended the local community college. I was dealing with a boy several years my junior here, and perhaps far smarter...but if it'd get me a little bit farther, then I was ready, set, go.

In the moment I was loving the small talk, taking in the bright lights. I was headed back to college with each tap of the gas pedal and it was wildly refreshing.

We came to a halt at the red light. I couldn't help but notice a cop car parked catty-cornered to Randall's. It was the one that stopped me earlier. The officer made eye contact with me and smiled, happy to see I had a ride home.

I smiled back, because I had never felt so safe in such a strange situation.

PHOEBE

I had made some life choices as of recent that were somewhat uncharacteristic of the way I'd usually gone about things. I had a new cloud of arrogance that followed me consistently. I sensed a maturity shift the past summer and with that brought a new attitude.

"Are you Colin's new girlfriend?" a girl named Britt asked me in history class one day. She sat beside me, and we were cordial. We didn't talk outside of class, but we had a solid grasp on understanding each other.

I didn't know where I stood with Colin right then, so I gave her the most ambiguous answer I could think of, "It's complicated, but I guess so, yeah."

She smiled smugly. Somehow, me confessing that yes, I did in fact date Colin, made me a hotter commodity than it should have. Britt and I had exchanged small talk daily but I didn't think she liked me *that* much. Now suddenly, it would have appeared we were best friends by the way she was giggling and going on about boys...

"Colin's a cool guy," she said, as if confirming the general consensus. "We should hangout sometime, too."

"We should," she seemed normal enough, I had no reason not to want to hang out with her. I was always open to new things.

The bell sounded, releasing us from the musty, cinder block classroom. We had one class left and we'd be done for the day, but somehow, Britt couldn't fathom having to wait.

"Let's go hangout now. Let's skip class and go do something fun."

I didn't really want to, but Britt and I skipped class and went for a drive. She was having some educational troubles and I didn't feel like learning about the branches of government.

"You hungry?" Britt asked as we turned into a pharmacy. She needed tampons, mints, and some magazine.

"I'm fine to do whatever you want to." I was struggling, but I wanted to go with the flow.

"Good, I have an idea."

I waited in the car while she went inside. I twiddled my thumbs for a second, and subconsciously started snooping through Britt's car out of boredom. I didn't mean to, but my phone died, and even if it didn't, I didn't feel like checking in with everyone with where I was at.

Not that Colin would have cared too much where I was at. Skipping class had become more common for me that he probably just assumed. Plus, his shorthand text messages were difficult to decipher, and, God, his imperfect grammar killed me.

Britt popped in the car out of nowhere.

"Ready to go?" she asked.

"Depends where we're going."

"My cousin Larry owns a tattoo parlor. Just opened down the road. I've been wanting this one tattoo for so long now. Typically, you must have parental consent if you're under eighteen, but Larry's really chill and will hook us up if you want something."

"Oh, yeah, I mean I don't really have…anything in mind, but I'd be fine to go and watch or something."

You could tell they just opened the place. It was practically being built as we sat there. I watched Britt get some dragon looking tattoo on her shoulder blade. She was "edgy" like that.

I skimmed through the books at all the compiled tattoos in disbelief that some people committed to having them inked on their bodies forever.

"Pick what you want and I'll give you one on the house," Larry said, the toothpick in his mouth waving up and down as he focused on Britt's dragon design.

"Oh, no that's okay."

"C'mon, I need the practice."

He wasn't exactly selling me on the idea, but at the same time, when did I ever require much convincing?

"Well, there is one thing I've had in mind…"

"Okay great! Britt is almost done here, she'll have to come back later for some touch-ups, but I can have you in the hot seat in just a bit."

In a weird way, he was very charming and had a way of making me feel comfortable. Plus, Britt's didn't look half bad, considering. Not my style, but I was open-minded, or trying to be anyway.

"Did you find a picture of what you want?" Britt asked, acting braver than she was revealing through clenched teeth and teary eyes.

"I think Larry will be able to freehand mine," I responded.

"Woah. Let's not rely on good ole Larry here to freehand, I just opened the place, remember," Larry stated. I didn't understand the correlation between his artistic ability and how long he'd been employed, but I shook it off.

I'm getting my first tattoo! I smiled to myself, suddenly feeling like a little kid in a candy store. A much less cleanly candy store. Much darker, too.

Larry cleaned what he needed to, grabbed some new utensils, and told me to *come on down*! like I just won a car on a game show…

I took one, solid deep breathe. Taking a second one, I may have reconsidered. The scent of incense filled my lungs and I deemed myself ready as I ever would be.

"Whatcha want, darlin'?" he asked, throwing a fresh toothpick between his teeth.

I pulled up the sleeve of my sweatshirt to reveal my wrist.

"Two straight lines up and down, side by side."

"How tall?"

I motioned with my fingers about half an inch.

"Like the number eleven?"

"Just like the number eleven."

I sat there calmly, and it surprisingly didn't hurt me at all. Instead, I liked the rush that overtook my body in the small moment.

The tattoo appeared seamlessly on my wrist as if it had belonged there all along. Britt just shrugged her shoulders at my odd choice, but didn't comment further. She was too enamored with her new creation to question.

I just smiled at Larry, "See, I knew you could freehand it."

SAGE

I spent the night playing video games with Nick and Harold, the roommates, until I passed out on the couch, all the while being Sadie.

I had never been on a blind date before, and this night affirmed why. While Dustin was washing up before bed I saw Sadie's dating profile pulled up on his laptop. I couldn't help but sneak a look at her photo to see what I was working with.

Granted, it is a tiny photo, but the slight resemblance in hair color and length were there, the deep brown eyes. She was wearing lipstick, something I wouldn't be caught dead in, especially while out walking layers of miles.

She was pretty enough and looked older than her age, which was why I was sure he thought she was me. I definitely am youthful looking for my thirty-two, but I couldn't pass for a college sophomore even if I tried. I was flattered regardless because catching glimpses of myself in mirrors here and there haven't been doing me justice lately. I attempted to fix the out of place strands of hair or blot my eyes to somehow make them less swollen, but I was still just the raggedy nomad who should probably invest in some suntan lotion sooner than later. I looked burnt to a crisp.

I drifted into sleep too effortlessly, but when I woke up, Harold was cooking breakfast. Rather, he woke me up in the process of making his breakfast.

He whipped up a fruit smoothie with probably thirty times too much protein powder. While it mixed, he dropped and did push-ups.

"Training for something?" I had to ask.

"Oh, Sadie, I'm sorry, I forgot you were here."

"No, no, it's fine, do your thing."

"Want some?"

I watched as he cracked a raw egg and threw it into a glass that already housed two others.

"I'm good. I should get going myself."

"Not going to say bye to Dustin? He's out at an early class. Must have snuck out."

"I'll leave him a note."

"Cool. Well you have a good day."

"Yeah, thanks for having me…" I watched his surfer boy self grab the cup of raw eggs and leave the room, which I was thankful for because I didn't think I could have watched him down it and not have gagged myself.

He was probably lunging down the hall to his bedroom.

I did take note that he had cleaned nothing up in the kitchen, instead only adding to the pile of stacked dishes already in the sink. I was immediately grossed out at the thought of the couch I just slept on. Who knew who plopped down on that thing before me, or what the cushions hid underneath. Cleanliness was not key there.

It was 8:17a.m. I assumed Dustin's class began at 8a.m, so hopefully I'd have time to hop in the shower and still escape in time to avoid an awkward goodbye.

Two showers in the past two day—quality. I was anxious to see where the next night led.

I cleaned off quicker than anticipated because I was ready to be on the move. It now become somewhat of a high. I had noticed how toned my body had become. My legs were much more solid and my stomach much flatter, pleased with myself because I wanted to look good…no, great…when I saw Max again.

A giant box of several band T-shirts sat in the corner of Dustin's room. He never mentioned a band. It looked like his face on the front of the shirt though. I held one up, hoping he wouldn't notice if a size small went missing.

I scribbled a note *(Thanks for a fun night. Keep in touch. –Sadie)* and left it on his desk.

I was getting bolder in my decisions, but I also needed more clean clothes. I snagged a small, throwing it on under my pack, and grabbed a medium for the road, considering it a souvenir.

The last thing I took from them was a Pop Tart for the road. It was the strawberry frosted kind so I couldn't resist.

I felt like I was back in college all over again with an overloaded backpack weighing me down, a mediocre band T-shirt on, munching on a Pop Tart with tired eyes from playing video games all night. Minus the stack of love letters bursting at the seams with my name etched on them.

I found a park bench about a mile and half from campus and read the next letter from Max:

Sage,

73

*I wonder if you think about me as much
as I you. You know they say "not all those
who wander are lost," but I must be in the
small percentage that is in fact lost. I pray
every day that my mother is okay, and that
she'll welcome me with open arms when
she sees her long lost son.*

*I hope you're feeling well yourself.
I'm only a few days into my journey
and missing you more and more as
each day goes on.*

Am I crazy?

Don't answer that.

Max

PHOEBE

I watched the school soccer team run past as I walked to my car. I used to be one of those girls just last year. Maybe sometime in the future, I'd refocus on something productive. It's funny how it all comes full circle, or in my case a square, because life was often rough around the edges for me.

74

Lost in thought and even a little guilt, I climbed into my car, something my father had invested in for me when I got my permit last year. I was still getting accustomed to sitting effortlessly behind the wheel.

I'd heard a lot about the dangers of distracted driving, so I tossed the sweatshirt lying on my passenger seat to the back. The sweatshirt that belonged to the boy at the party was still in my car, and although a week had passed without seeing him, I couldn't stop thinking about my hour with him.

I don't believe in love at first sight. I think it's basing a very important emotion on physical appearance and immediate attraction, and to truly love someone involves so much more. Love at first sight is a classy excuse for lust.

But I had this sweatshirt in my possession. It was the sweatshirt of someone I thought I fell a little bit in love with the first night I met him.

There were exceptions to every rule.

I didn't mean to fall in love. I mean, does anyone ever? It just happened. As he was talking, and kept talking, I liked what he had to say.

I liked that he could talk to me about things I never thought I was interested in, yet somehow I wanted to know everything about that particular topic.

Surely he knew someone at the party or he wouldn't have been there. That gave me hope in getting some name clarity, or even where I could find him again. I'd hate for his sweatshirt to be a mere souvenir of our one hour together.

I wanted to get to know that boy more so I could really fall in love with him. There was potential there, dangling before me, yet so far away in the unknown. It was entirely too frustrating.

The kiss on my cheek had been burning a hole through my face ever since, similar to the memories in my mind and the desire in my heart.

It was my week with my father. I alternated every week between his house and my grandmother's house. We lived with her until I was ten but once we moved out, I missed her and the house. I would put up a tantrum in the beginning of our move, so much so that my father let me stay with her a week at a time and the routine stuck. To this day, I alternated.

My father calls me his wildcard. I guess he and my mother didn't expect to have me, and then when they did, I was just always full of surprises. As far as family nicknames go, it could be worse. He told me each day I live truer to it, which I took as a compliment; at least I wasn't boring.

He brought this up again when I showed him my tattoo. Instead of being one of those girls that tried to hide it for months and explain when stumbled upon, I thought it'd be better to be upfront.

I knew my father well enough to know he spiked his Mason jar of freshly brewed sweet tea with some cheap vodka. While he wasn't looking, I snuck a shot into mine as well. I stirred it with my finger just slightly as I made my way to the front porch, where we ate on nights the weather permitted.

It was my turn to make he and I a great meal to compliment the unexpected mix drink. It was one of those nights where adventure was in the air.

"How are your grades these days?" We were about to go through the daddy-daughter motions. I looked just like the man, curly light hair, darker eyes, and average height. His glasses made him look more professional than I'd ever look, but our personalities couldn't have been more different. It was why we got along so well. He was the perfect calm to my storm.

"Above average, but the school year just started so it's almost too hard to tell," I said, shoveling a mouthful of garlic mashed potatoes into my mouth. An onlooker would think I hadn't eaten in days, the way I eat.

"Ah. Well keep it up." He took a hearty bite into a rib mimicking my motion. Barbecue begged for dear life as it dripped down his chin, but he appeared unfazed.

"And soccer…you mentioned the other day you'd be joining the team on Monday, and well, it's Tuesday. Any word?"

"I'd rather eat ribs for the rest of my life instead," I didn't really have an excuse and I didn't want to admit how belittling it was to pass the field earlier. He seemed to know I didn't already join the team, but asked more out of obligation.

"And because I'm your father and have to ask…how's your love life?"

Reading about others' love lives in a trashy romance novel sounds enthralling and intense, but hearing your father bring up your love life while

77

chowing down on barbeque ribs is the least enjoyable thing to discuss.

"Daaaad…really." Again, I did not want to get into it.

"Just had to ask! More sweet tea?"

"Sure."

He reached for my glass from across the table. He nonchalantly sniffed it.

"You toss some vodka in here?" he questioned in the most non-accusatory way possible, his right eyebrow raising just a hair.

"Well, didn't you?" Two could play that game.

He smiled and shrugged as he made his way inside, expecting nothing otherwise, because after all, I was his wildcard.

SAGE

I strolled as casually as possible, although I'd bet money on it I was a mess of all sorts, as I walked through the streets of Belmar, New Jersey. I was nearing the coast. My father took me here on many beach trips as a child, but nothing compared to the views before me. Being an adult with real world experience put it all in perspective in an odd sort of way.

I wished I had more time to be touristy, but I felt guilty taking time and spending money on myself. In fact, I had the urge to make money. Not that I really needed it, but it felt continually unnatural not to have some type of check deposited to my account at the end of the month.

I saw a man older than I by about twenty-five years, sitting with his back leaned up against a building and playing a harmonica for tips. The waves could be heard slapping against the sand in the distance with the boardwalk nearby, children excitedly playing amongst them. The man sat before it all, not a care in the world as to the happenings around him.

He wore a plain, and somewhat grungy T-shirt with jeans. His hair was greased back methodically, most of it peeked through the backwards baseball cap on his head.

I racked my brain for a talent I had of any sort with no such success. Instead I approached this man. In awe of his raw talent, I had to stop and revel in it, hoping some would rub off. How pathetic it was to be talent-less. Instead, I just clapped vigorously at the end of his song.

"You enjoying my music?" he asked between tunes.

I was his only audience.

"I am. You're very captivating."

He nodded his head in appreciation.

"Mind if I sit?" I asked not even phased that I was infringing upon his private space. He slid over regardless. He was someone I would have strolled by as I texted or sent emails to clients, my head buried in my cell just two weeks prior, but instead, I felt a need to befriend him.

"I don't see why not," he smiled up at me with the teeth he had remaining.

He was dirty and obviously homeless but for some reason I wasn't turned off at all.

"What makes a pretty girl like yourself want to spend time with the likes of a guy like me? I'm so washed up, yet I'm not at all. Haven't washed up in weeks if I'm being honest," he admitted.

"You're interesting. What's your story?" It was my way of indirectly asking him what brought him to homelessness because in a way I felt I could relate. I had slept outdoors more than half the nights I'd been out walking, the others considered rare and lucky. More nights outdoors were in my near future so I needed all the advice I could get.

He laughed, "Most people lead with 'how are you?' when they talk to me, but I hate that ya know why? It warrants a one word answer and doesn't tell you much aboutcha. Not enough people ask for the whole story. You're doing an experiment or something? What's with all the gear? And the questions?" For a moment I felt he was intimidated and maybe even fearful of me. Had I offended him?

"Well see, I'm on a bit of a journey. It's a long story actually, but I'm walking from state to state to be reunited with...well, like I said, it's a long story," I shook my head and he didn't insist I continue, rather I cut to the chase. "I won't get into, but basically I'm homeless right now..."

"Huh," he paused, and I was afraid I offended him further, "well you came to the right guy." He winked at me, putting me at ease.

"Oh yeah?"

"I've been homeless for years now. At first it wasn't an option. I was forced to foreclose on a house, and couldn't hold a job. I had some deep-rooted problems too, ya know, couldn't get my head on straight," I nodded occasionally, "but now I'm established. People know me. I sit here on this corner every. damn. day. and greet the regulars on their way to work…play for them my music. Some bring me lunch, if anything, their leftovers. I sleep where my head falls. It's simple, really. I've become one with the ground below me. I own nothing, but I feel so very rich. There are people everywhere in this city who know my location and pay me visits. People who appreciate my music. If something happened to me, they'd care. I know they would. I didn't even have that type of support at home. Here I have a very large, unofficial family."

I started to get tears in my eyes.

"You make enough to survive?"

"I don't make much, but I get what I need. God provides, ya know. Some days are harder than others, but you'd be surprised by how very little you can get by with."

I took in everything he said and suddenly knew I was going to be okay.

"I had a daughter like you, ya know?"

"Did you?" I thought of my own father and the wonderful times we spent together in this very town…

"I did. Both she and her mother left me when I started to go through some things. Better yet, though. I didn't need her seeing her daddy in such a state."

81

"I used to be close with my father, but I never saw him that often. One weekend a month was all I got, but still, he was my hero. He was everyone's hero, really. A hard worker, level headed, but also really friendly. But things turn out the way they do…" I wondered why I was elaborating. Something about this place screamed nostalgia.

"It's a damn shame. I regret it. I think of her every day and I'm sure your daddy does too, think of you."

With as many people crowded in the busy streets of that tourist town, I felt like it was just he and I there propped up against the corner store in the unofficial plot of land that belonged to him. I didn't want to mention that my father since had passed to ruin a completely genuine moment; we're not given enough of those in life as it is.

"Ya know," I picked up on the fact that this was somewhat of a catch phrase of his as I listened more intently with each breath he took, "My daughter was seven years young when they left. A beautiful little girl. Her momma took good care of her, but I didn't recognize it then. I remember she'd yawn from a long day of play and I'd tell her yawning was contagious and she'd just laugh at me as I let out a deep bellied yawn myself," He was growing increasingly lost in a memory but I felt privileged to be the one he was sharing it with.

"I think of her every time I yawn as juvenile as that sounds. Just this time, it reminds me of my loneliness when no one is there to catch the contagiousness. I know it's simple and stupid, and I should have better memories of my daughter—Lucy was her name...is her name—but that's all I got. And I know more than

82

anyone that you need to hold onto whatever you've got."

I felt a mix of emotions streamlining throughout me. Sadness for him and the absence of his daughter, anger at not being able to reach out to my own father in a time like this, wondering if he had any special story that bonded he and I together; and ultimate happiness to have heard such a personal tale.

Also, hunger. I felt a strong sense of hunger, but then again, I was sure he did too.

"Want to know what I think?" I offered my two cents, "I think that's a beautiful thing to remember and I think that maybe you've been too hard on yourself. What you do out here, it's tough. Not everyone can survive like you do, and you make it seem like you're thriving."

"That's always been what I said. People can be rich in lots of ways. Rich in love, rich in the obvious sense of money, rich in time, ya know what I mean. There is a certain richness each of us possess, and that's what gives people their strengths."

"What do you consider yourself rich in?" I asked, surprised at how wise he was. I had definitely judged him based on outer appearance and now had bitten off more than I might have been able to chew.

"Hmm…rich in experience overall."

"I think that's the best type of rich you can be. Does it ever get boring, just sitting here day after day?"

"Does it ever get boring out there? Out doing what you do?"

"I suppose it does. A lot actually."

"Exactly. Boredom comes and goes now and again, but so does sadness, and happiness, and hatred, and love."

I sat there and talked with the man, who I found out was born the name Julian, but acquired the nickname Stoop, as one who sits for years on the same stoop in a small town would, I suppose. I chose to call him by his given name, partly because it almost felt condescending to call him anything different, and partly because too much in his life was unofficial already.

I realized yet again as the sun set that I was ravenous. I had not eaten a single thing almost all day, which was not smart for the amount of miles I'd trekked. If my insanity didn't become the death of me, my poor life choices certainly would.

"Julian, I'm going to run down to the sub shop on the corner there, you want something?"

He pulled some change from the tip jar he had propped up beside him and told me to grab him a number six with fries. I laughed because I should have known he was a regular. Baffled at the thought of him even offering me money, I declined because I'd like to think I could be a decent human being at times…

On my way, I stopped at a nearby antique shop and picked up a relatively cheap, yet quality camera, wishing I had more time to browse. It was a modern looking Polaroid style where the picture shot out immediately. As against technology as I was trying to be while walking, the people I kept meeting were too interesting to not keep tabs on. I decided I'd start photo journaling my experience. Max writing to me was his form of documentation, but I wanted to do something more official so that one day I could look back and see how rich I was in the experience.

***

I walked back with a bag in my hand containing dinner for two. As I approached Julian, I saw him in the distance looking to the sky. He let out a yawn and just as we made eye contact, I yawned on instinct. He smiled up at me, letting me know he was grateful he wasn't the only crazy person in this world.

PHOEBE

I woke up to it being my birthday. Hard to believe I was already sixteen, although I acted much more mature for my age. My grandmother told me since the day I could remember, that I was literate in the ways of the world, and that was one of my biggest strengths.

Birthdays for me were never wild and crazy times though. I never got into them. I knew sixteen was supposedly a big one to celebrate, but just like in years past, I couldn't care less.

I'd be totally content with staying sixteen forever. I believed everyone says that around my age, when you start to realize that the glory years are the ones you're living, and if you projected your life to ten years in the future, you'd either be depressed by how little you've accomplished, maybe just content, or God forbid, settled down. It's a scary time for an adolescent in general, let alone the constant reminder of your childhood innocence diminishing with each darkening day.

I subconsciously grasped my necklace, the favorite among past birthday gifts I'd received. How sad was it that no gift had ever topped the elegance and meaning behind the necklace gifted to me the day I was born?

My mother clasped it on, a gorgeous opal bead surrounded by two silver beads. My father, as diligent as he has always been, kept the necklace in a jewelry box for me until I was old enough to appreciate it.

The timeless beads have dangled from my neck for years now. My grandfather gifted my mother the necklace when she was young. Although, I couldn't wear it legitimately until I was a bit older, I hadn't taken it off since I put it on.

I was alone in the kitchen, my father already having left for work. The note on the table let me know he wanted me to sleep in, to take the fifty dollars he left on the counter to buy myself something nice and advised me to *have a great day!*

With that, I blew out the candle on a single cupcake and made a wish.

SAGE

I was saddened my time with Julian had to come to an end. I spent the night on the park bench beside him, not sleeping much, but rather taking everything in, thirsting to become richer from his experiences. It was a concept I couldn't get over.

I gave him a friendly embrace when we said our goodbyes the next morning, like any old friends would.

"Thank you for everything. I'm thankful I stumbled upon you."

"Likewise. Stop by anytime. You know where I'll be." He gave me a small smile before picking up his harmonica for the day.

In awe, I must admit, if only to myself, I had just learned more about life from a homeless stranger in twelve hours than perhaps I had in a lifetime with my own mother. It was nice to talk about my father some too. It had been a long time since I spoke aloud about him after he passed. As busy as he was, and as little of his time was dedicated to me, I knew the time we shared was special and that he loved me for being me, for being Sage. A deep down passionate, yet altogether mess, Sage.

I felt a unique bond with the other people who were up and functioning before six in the morning. It was a whole other world entirely. It was like a whole society of productive people that were awake, even if barely, to tackle the day with productivity. I was not among these people enough, but I was after leaving Julian, so there was no other option but to breathe in the chilly, sewage smelling New Jersey air, and feel honored to be alive.

Inhale, exhale. Inhale, exhale.

I referred to my map only twice that day. I was becoming more familiar with what to expect. It didn't make the miles any easier, just bearable. Making unprecedented time, I had trekked a total of twenty-three miles. Blisters the size of blueberries were forming on every part of both feet. I was feeling inspired though, and an inspired person is oftentimes unstoppable.

It was not until that twenty-third mile when I was completely transfixed in thought that I was brought back brutally to reality. Suddenly, I was surrounded by the first set of strange men I felt genuinely threatened by. Perhaps my overconfidence had become conceitedness. I had wandered into allies and dark places, knowing they may pose a threat, but doing them anyway.

I was invincible. I was free.

Except I was not.

I was still just a girl.

And at the bare base of it all, a very misguided girl.

I vowed to myself not to stay with strangers anymore, no matter how friendly they appeared. I had survived some nights I maybe shouldn't have out here, and I needed to be more cautious. Things could have gone worse. Way worse.

It was a truck full of men that drove up beside me nearly halting to a stop. I felt a gust of wind from their van as they slid by, almost brushing my outer leg with their vehicle with how close they got. Call it whatever you will, but intuition set in, the bad news palpable in the air.

"Need a ride, little lady?" one of them shouted, his body nearly hanging out the window.

"No thanks." I could only hope my voice didn't give away how frightened I felt. I adjusted my backpack, buying time with my thoughts.

"Not at all?"

"I said no thank you." I couldn't stomach trying to be polite.

There was just something about night falling and a truckload of men pulling up initiating conversation that I found a bit unsettling. Which girl wouldn't?

"Whatchu out here walking for anyways?"

If I had heard the question once, I'd heard it a million times already, yet I panicked and I was done with them. I didn't like where their inquiries were leading nor did I want to encourage progressive conversation. Instead, I took off running. Correction: sprinting. I was sprinting through buildings and night air. I turned back and they stopped following, but had instead erupted into laughter; the entire van bellowing at my insecurities.

I didn't care if they laughed, I probably did look pathetic. I'd be surprised if I didn't have some sort of wind burned rash resulting from the episode. Their van revving what tiny engine it had scared me whenever I felt it near. Getting right up beside me, they'd laugh and holler, then retreat as if giving me some sort of head start, then repeat. My tired legs couldn't take me as fast as the game was moving until I was no longer sprinting, but definitely running. I wasn't even losing them at the red lights. As much as I hated to get off track, I knew the only way to lose them was to start weaving in and out of buildings. Literally the last thing I wanted to do.

For as dented, scratched and beat up that vehicle looked, it sure proved how slow I was on foot.

I needed to find a place to rest for the night after all this running. I spied a rather fancy hotel at the corner of a downtown area. It was massive and seemed almost out of place in the historic town. I didn't want to buy a room for the night, but I wanted to sleep indoors. I felt tainted and well deserving of comfort.

Also, if I went quickly enough the van's occupants hopefully wouldn't see me.

I made a mad dash for the hotel with the shiny chandelier and rotating sign. I slowed my pace when I got near. Without the van in sight, I felt I didn't need to worry about them following me. Despite wanting to blend, I was wholly aware I was going to stand out as soon as I stepped foot into the establishment, but felt no other option would do.

Men dressed in business suits and women in fur vests bounced through the lobby. Some people appeared to be walking on a continuous cloud. As anticipated, I definitely appeared out of place, but they didn't acknowledge me regardless. Instinctively, I avoided them too as I made my way to the front desk.

"Can…I help you with something?" The boy with the thick-framed glasses behind the desk looked at me puzzled, his hair gelled to perfection.

"I…um, was just looking for a place to stay the night." I gathered my thoughts but my breathing was still awry.

"We unfortunately don't have any vacancies, but you can try the motel down the way, although one could never be sure the last time they had their carpets done. I wouldn't crawl under the covers there either, but that's me, you know. I'm wearing a bow tie, and you're wearing, well...that," he did a once over my body. I was still wearing the band tee and Nike jogging shorts to complete the look. He adjusted his bow tie in a disapproving manner, rightfully so. It was then he put the pieces together, "Are you...*walking*?" he asked, giving novelty to the word.

"If you mean traveling by foot, yes, yes I am."
"Oh dear!" He flaunted a flamboyant wrist to his mouth while simultaneously reaching across the desk to rearrange a piece of hair deranged from my head, one of many I assumed. Uncomfortable with being touched, I took a step back without seeming too obvious. I was unsure where all this was going.

"I know I shouldn't have come in here, I'm so sorry. There was just a van full of men that were borderline harassing me, and I finally ran far enough to lose them, and you're building is so shiny...I don't know...I was attracted to it." My hand gestures might have made the story more elaborate than it actually was. "But, it is a Friday, so I get it, lots of tourists have already booked their stay...thank you."

Just as I turned to leave, he called to me, "Wait! I can't let you leave looking like that, looking like you've just seen a ghost."

I must have still looked shaken up from my run. Cross my heart I didn't intend to make him pity me, it sort of just happened. I had been getting better at making fast friends as of recent. I guessed that's what happened when you spent your days alone with nothing but your map to keep you company. You'll talk to whatever will say words back, and sometimes you'll settle for something less.

"Please, sit. Let me see if I can work something out."

"Well, I don't have much money…I couldn't possibly afford a room here after all, I don't know what I was thinking…"

"Here's what we're going to do," he said, and suddenly we were best friends making plans, "There is a vacant room left upstairs. Well, it's not actually vacant…it's mine…but I want you to have it tonight. Wash up, do your hair, the works. Girl, you need it."

"Where will you go? I didn't come here to kick anyone out of a room. I just needed a quick escape…"

"And escape is what you'll get. Don't worry about me, honey. I have it all worked out. There is an event up the way tonight I wanted to make an appearance at. Don't you see the glamour in this room?" I nodded, because he was right, it was the glamour I had first noticed. "This is *nothing* compared to the extravagance I'll witness tonight at the gala. Trust me, every bit worth it. Enjoy the room, you need it more than I do."

"Couldn't you get fired for this?"

"It's my room. I'm lending it to a friend. C'mon I'll show you to it."

He threw up a "Ring Bell for Assistance" sign and escorted me upstairs.

We stood in the elevator silently and suddenly, I was hesitant. This seemed too good to be true. His stature proved harmless, but I was then apprehensive on who to trust anymore. That's what happened when your ego became tainted, and in my case, you have to run for your life.

Then I saw the room and forgot all my worry. I was in awe. It was unlike any room I'd ever stayed in, let alone, seen before. It was a suite, definitely a suite, quite possibly nicer than any apartment or home I'd ever live in.

"Did you decorate this place? It's incredible." A full length mirror stood floor to ceiling in the corner, cultured decor filled the room, a stocked bar cart sat idly in the corner and there were more pillows on the bed than there most likely were in the rest of the place combined.

"I prefer fabulous, but thank you! Make yourself at home. I'll be back at the desk by 10:00 tomorrow morning. Oh, and complimentary breakfast will be brought to you around 8a.m., so if you hear a knock on the door and are hungry, answer it. Hope you like strawberry Danish, it's my Saturday staple." He patted the corners of the bed, as if a small wrinkle would deter me from the elegance of the room. "My first guest! I'm so happy you're here…"

"Sage."

"Sage! What a brilliant name! Buzz me if you need, darling. Sweet dreams." He clapped both hands in a fluttering motion, and I couldn't help but smile at the turn of events. He then slammed the door behind him as he left, no looking back. I took in everything about the moment and was grateful that there were still good people in the world. Good people, good intentions and good scenarios.

93

None of this would be happening if I didn't appear so helpless, I was afraid, but I knew the situations I was running into weren't by chance, but then by what? Faith? I had never been a person of prayer but it was difficult to believe that I had been provided so much from people who didn't even know me without God having a little something to do with it.

If I was lucky I'd be making it to Maryland in the next couple of days, which was much farther than I anticipated by that point. Even though I was out there alone, I felt that somehow my progress was a team effort, God included.

I could feel the transformation in me from the inside out, so I resorted to old habits when the opportunity allowed and I ate an entire bag of potato chips. Usually, I'd be ashamed to admit I did so, but not then. I used the excuse that I needed the carbohydrates to continue on and make me strong. I binge watched an entire documentary series, which probably last happened when I still lived under the same roof as my mother.

I relished every moment I got like that because as few and far between as they should be, I recognized I was surprisingly lucky. It goes without saying that I slept like a baby that night. Rejuvenated and refreshed, I hit the road the next morning after dropping the key off at the front desk, my belly full of salty potato chips and sweet strawberry Danish.

"So, how'd you sleep? You look good. *Much* better." Quite possibly an insult, but I took it as a compliment.

"Fabulously," I said, remembering he liked the word, and I owed him something, anything. "I cannot thank you enough."

"Don't forget about us back here. Safe travels to you, Sage."

I asked him if I could take his picture with my Polaroid, at which he struck a pose that made me smile ear to ear. I added it to the growing collection, used the restroom quickly and was on my way to trek yet another day of mileage.

Feeling like I took advantage of yet another situation, I left quickly and almost in embarrassment.

Although I never snagged a name, the desk receptionist made an impact on my life. I knew he had already gossiped about me to his friends. Not that I cared, I knew I was something to talk about, especially now. I was certainly a rarity. The thought was enough to make me stop dead in my tracks. I was constantly reminded of what could go wrong, instead of focusing on how I could make it right.

***

The day was crisp and alive. I could smell the fresh brewed morning coffee of those waiting at the bus stop, dew still rising from the small patches of grassy areas as people walked to work. Men in suits, women in pencil skirts, everyone seemed so official, and there I was, my feet wrapped in gauze, every second worth it. Good ventures and progress were in the air.

I looked back at the snapshots I had taken thus far. Although it was a cheap camera I bought in a hipster chic store, it was a camera that worked and that was all that mattered. It was considered an antique, but hardly anything special. Every great road trip needed some tourism, no matter how hard I tried to fight it.

I remembered going on a trip with my grandparents to Greece when I was eighteen years old. My mother never splurged on sending me on field trips while I was in elementary and middle school. She did the bare minimum when it came to extra-curricular activities or after school programs. I'd occasionally skim back through the pictures from that single trip, and to this day, I look at them like they were currency from a foreign land, holding them up to the light in fascination. I'd pretend I am back there more often than not, taking in the scenery and eating luxurious foods with names in which I would not even begin to attempt pronouncing.

All so elegant and fancy compared to the life I was accustomed to at home with my mother. Not that my grandparents were far off from her normalcy, but they decided for their retirement to treat themselves to an exotic vacation, as all couples should now and again. If you consider Greece exotic, for us it was. Especially I, an eighteen-year-old with dreams of busting out arms wide open after all I'd been through, ready to escape the corner lot my mother secured for us. Damn, Florida would have been exotic to me…

Moving forward, I made a pact with myself; no more complaining. I felt like an idiot talking to myself on and on, the random memories from my past popping up in my mind, but it was what I had to do to keep my body moving. There was no one to answer to, no one to hold me accountable out there; just me, myself, and I.

Then again, I had always been self-sufficient in a way. It's funny how everything has a tendency to come full circle in one way or another.

PHOEBE

It was a bright and sunny Monday morning post birthday when I decided to walk down to the river not too far from my grandmother's house. It was a peaceful place to regroup and catch the sunrise before heading off to school. I would do this sometimes just to clear my mind time and again.

Making my way to my favorite bench, I noticed it was occupied, not by someone but by something. It appeared to be some kind of book. I snagged a granola bar loose from my backpack, hopeful for some entertainment during breakfast on what I was about to stumble upon. The book surely didn't disappoint. I recognized it immediately upon getting closer. It was the sketchbook that belonged to my mystery crush.

I sat on the bench, looking left and then right. There were no signs of him anywhere, in fact it was eerily still, not even a ripple in the water.

Hesitant to open it, I sat with it there beside me until I couldn't maintain self-control. Skimming its pages could lead me to find out who the boy was, even if all I found was a name.

Caught off guard by the talent that covered the pages, I shuffled through them cautiously in case he was lingering somewhere near. All the guilt I had for invading his privacy faded when I flipped to perhaps the most intricate sketch in the book. By far the most detailed, was a scene of the party where I had met the boy who drew it. I was front and center of the portrait, a grim but not entirely unpleasant look on my face. It was flattering that the sketch portrayed me much more beautiful than I felt, but it was undeniably me. Every blemish, every crease and maybe even then some, were scattered across my face.

Most captivating of all, I was in color where the rest of the scene was simply done in grayscale.

My first thought was to tear the page out.

Somehow it felt that he had invaded my privacy; in a way, we'd be even. Although it felt entirely personal and almost that it had belonged to me, I left his sketches where they were and took the book itself. I figured he couldn't be too far since his book was found there, in a place I thought I shared with my grandmother and my grandmother alone.

I would add the sketchbook to the sweatshirt of his I already had, his things accumulating slowly and surely in the backseat of my car, I was bound to find him sooner than later.

Glancing at the tiny watch on my wrist, I decided it was time to head to class. I wouldn't skip any more if I could help it.

Brushing aside branches and twigs, I made my way out from the wooded area less gracefully than I intended. My car was parked just at the end of my grandmother's drive. I fiddled my keys in my hand, the sketchbook under my arm when I caught glimpse of *him*. The garage door of my grandmother's new neighbor's house slid up to reveal a weight bench and what looked like an assortment of other unpacked gadgets from the move.

Knowing the house next door to my grandmother's had been for sale for a couple months prior and sold recently, I couldn't fathom *him* being a resident so close to where I lived every other week. As if he hadn't infringed upon my life enough already!

I hid the book under my arm as best as I could while scurrying to my car unnoticed. For as much as I felt I knew about this boy, I didn't even have a name to call him by; it was almost embarrassing. I loved him and I hated him all the same.

First period flew by because my mind was elsewhere. I was thinking of the morning's discoveries. Walking to my second class of the day was when I noticed him yet again. He was in the main office signing some papers, holding a stack of books. Two other girls were ogling over him through the small window of the office. I felt a pang of jealousy, as if I had called dibs on him already.

I saw him first!

Following the jealousy came the guilt. I had Colin, the prime specimen in the high school dating world and yet, there I was hoping for someone equally as captivating for all the opposite reasons.

They were completely different in overall appearance. Colin was clean cut, and the type of person who always stayed clean. After working out, you could probably bathe in his sweat and it'd be cleanly. It was his personality that made him dirty.

The new and improved guy had a rougher exterior, which according to my theory meant a shiny interior, opposite of Colin, or so I hoped.

My next brief interaction with him came later that day and was perhaps the most confusing. I was at the red light in our small town on the way to my grandmother's when I saw him stumble out of the woods with nothing but rolled up jeans on. Near the river, I assumed he could have been searching for his missing sketches.

I hesitated for a second, but then rolled down my window and asked all coolly, "Need a ride?"

He stared, bewildered, his chiseled body caught off guard. I could almost see his heartbeat thumping out of his chest.

"No, no." He nodded and threw a single hand in the air.

He didn't seem to recognize me. How dare he. *After everything in my mind that we've been through!*

I felt briefly offended because I'd never been turned down before, even for just a ride. My reputation flawed, I stared straight ahead, rolled up my window and pretended it never happened.

I convinced myself he just didn't recognize me. After all, he probably didn't expect to see me in these parts. I settled on that rather than dwell on the fact that he didn't even say "no thanks!" rather, he reiterated his refusal with a second "no."

I stopped off for gas and treated myself to a candy bar. Sometimes it was nice to just eat your feelings when you couldn't express them.

SAGE

Dear God...

Instead of letting the loneliness overtake me, I turned to God, which reminded me of how often I didn't pray. I had a tendency to never seek help. I saw my mother pray in three different ways. As disgruntled as she was, she would pray before meals, when things went wrong and at night after she'd had a few too many to drink. I'd hear her from her room or couch— wherever she'd fall—praying aloud, asking for any sense of encouragement that the world was not all bad.

"The Lord has blessed us, Sage, whether you want to believe that or not."

I didn't go from cradle to church pew or anything like that, but I still felt a strong faithful connection even to that point in my life. So even if recently prayers weren't on repeat in my mind, I felt a sense of wholeness when I walked into a small, almost historic looking Catholic church up on a Delaware hill.

I wasn't far into Delaware by any means. Not even a mile at that, but progress was progress, no matter how small. I didn't sleep much the night before, which allowed me an early start. I ate at a Cracker Barrel, so if my stomach were a gas gauge, I'd be full on pancakes.

I remembered eating a salad with no dressing at work along with every other girl on the floor. It was nearly a competition of who could eat the least each day. No one in the suite wore above a size 3 pant and it was sickening. It was a small relief to not be badgered by societal pressures anymore. In addition, I walked off everything I put in my mouth before it even had time to be properly digested.

I hid behind the Cracker Barrel establishment while the workers trickled out. It was starting to rain and the awning overhead was doing its dutiful task at keeping me dry enough for the time being. The thick drops dripped off its edge, making the perfect shield.

I took out a small piece of string from a ball of yard I bought in a convenience store and made a clothesline for my laundry to hang. Very methodically I attached the string to the dumpster out back from one side to the other. Usually clotheslines allow clothes to dry, but I wanted to get mine soaking wet. The more the rain hit them, the cleaner they'd be. Although not ideal, it was all I had.

After draping the clothes over the edge, I carefully wrung each of them out one by one, a tedious task indeed, but it was getting the job done. And at some point, you had to admit to yourself that beggars could not be choosers, and I was a begging to diminish as much dirt as possible. Next, I'd work on the dirt that had caked itself under my fingernails. I was convinced it had found its home there and may never come out.

Like in any old movie you watch, I slid my back down the wall of the restaurant and let the tears fall, accepting defeat.

After all, there was no cry like a cry out in the rain.

My grandfather used to tell me "never let 'em see you sweat." As cliché as it sounded at the time, it was like all other advice we receive, useless until applicable.

A million thoughts swirled through my head. I focused on a drip coming from my underwear at the end of the piece of yarn; the yarn becoming ever more unstable with each passing minute, each passing drip.

I eyed the *drip, drip, drip* until I tried to doze off.

Thunder roared and lightning shot across the sky above me for a second too long. I was oblivious to think of sunny skies and seventy-five degree weather to accompany me during my entire journey. I was heading south, which was renowned for its warmer weather. Psychologically, that gave me some sort of solace. I sat cold and shivering until I was shaking uncontrollably, despite being cuddled in my sleeping bag that was relatively dry. I didn't have any dry clothes but one shirt I hadn't worn yet. I spared the shirt for what I believed to be ten more minutes until I fit it as close as possible to my body. It was a tight knit long sleeve, nothing special, but yet, I envisioned it a giant sweater, myself wearing that giant sweater on the most beautiful of beaches, attempting to convince myself it was all mental.

Last Thanksgiving, I went up to North Dakota with Tom to meet his family. They lived in your typical log cabin in the woods. A beautiful home with ungrateful guests. Tom got along well with his family but they were a boring lot overall. I remembered finally getting a spare minute or two alone with Tom by the fire. They were better times in our relationship.

We cozied up, he gave me his jacket and kissed me on the forehead while I looked up at him. I remembered feeling flushed all over. My heart was full in the moment of gushy warmth which I guess they call love. My body was roasting fireside and my hands were interlocked in his, swearing to myself I'd never let that moment go.

But then it came and went as all moments do.

Mindsets today are like that. We waste time trying to pass the time that we forget time is all we have.

Thinking back to that moment in his arms and to times when I saw a life with him made me feel smarter, stronger and freer without him, feelings I hadn't let myself yet feel. I didn't expect to ever have a change in heart. I was eager to marry him. I dreamt for nights on that trip of the ring he never got me, of the children we'd never have, running around the backyard of our two story colonial (we'd also never have) on the corner of a busy subdivision. We'd befriend the neighbors and have them over for wine and game nights. He'd have a big job, I'd have mine. In that moment that was the idea of happily ever after.

Fairy tales taught us as young children that happily ever after comes at the end of a story or phase, almost so we are brought up to believe that every chapter of our lives will end happily ever after but the reality of the matter is that people grow bored of each other, we quit jobs, our houses become too small.

My happily ever after kept being reinvented because I kept altering my perception of happiness and what it meant to me.

I never thought I'd admit it last Thanksgiving, but I was much happier without Tom in my life. I truly was. I thought about him thinking of me, and I thought about his wellbeing, but I didn't think of my life with him anymore, and that was healthy.

What was not particularly healthy, was sitting under the awning growing increasingly sopping wet. The rain seemed like it would pass in a few minutes as sunnier clouds passed through.

I was only a couple weeks into my journey and was feeling the struggle evident inside me, but I also felt refuge, excitement and borderline insanity. Lord only knows what type of woman I'd be when I meet Max again.

**

I hesitated to reveal the next letter from Max in the rain, because I knew I wanted to preserve every one he sent and soak in every word he wrote. I felt like he was there beside me when I combed through the letters.

I even caught myself gushing the other day while going back through the ones I'd already read. I could picture him writing them, his voice sneaking its way into my head while I read what he wrote so meaningfully. His mannerisms overwhelmed me, and I thought of the time when we'd reunite and all this was over.

Happier times.

Once the rain passed, I snagged the letter from inside my backpack. I read it diligently yet steadily not wanting it to end too quickly. He never seemed to have written enough. It could have been a ten page letter and I'd still be left wanting more, and that's just the way it was. It was like the worst cliffhanger to your favorite book where you're left hanging on, the suspense nearly killing you…

Sage,

I miss you. That's all there is to it.
When I get here and make sure
everything's all situated with my mother,
I'm going to get a job. I don't know
where yet, or what I'd even want to do
with my life, but I know, too, I need to get
back to you. I'll borrow my father's truck.
At least that'll be convenient.

'Bout time something is.

Maybe even one day, you can move here
and be with me too. We can get a house
together with a lot of land that I
can go hunting on and you can grow a
tomato garden or something. I don't
know, just thoughts. All I know is, however
you or I get to the other, I'm not
walking again. This is madness. Remember
that documentary we watched on that
guy who walked across the country?

It's not as glamorous as they made it seem.
Nothing ever is, I suppose. I was inspired
by him at the time, and now I'm just
envious of how effortlessly they edited
the episode. I probably am more upset
then I should be because I haven't eaten
much the past few days. I've been low
on money, as you know I didn't leave with
much to begin with. You get crafty out
here though, I will tell you that. I guess I
can't complain because I did catch a ride
on some public transportation today.
You may think that's cheating my journey,
but I consider it living large...

Anyways, I love you.

Don't you worry about a thing, my dear.

Max

It may just be my delusional and oxygen inept
mind, but I gathered from that letter that he too started
to change his attitude this time in his journey like I was
now. The Max I remembered was so carefree and
nonchalant all the time. The Max in the letters neared
sophistication, bestowing some wisdom on me.

It was difficult to explain exorbitant amounts of joy
and pain to someone else if they haven't themselves
been through it or experienced it firsthand. The night I
had just experienced was one such miserable moment. I

wouldn't wish such for a worst enemy. Glad it was over, I had no desire to rehash the memory of it, ever.

Like a child told not to touch a scalding hot stovetop because it'd burn them, the journey made me curious, and that's why it excited me most. No matter how tough, I was addicted.

Don't you worry about a thing, my dear.

PHOEBE

It was not until later in the week when I had already had a few encounters with *him* that he started to associate me as a familiar face. He rode his bike to school every morning that week. We'd make eye contact time and again and he'd smile.

His style was unique, like he at least tried to be fashionable. The last I saw him, he sported a white V-neck, jeans that weren't too tight but that hugged him in all the right places, and casual running shoes. I tried to watch his actions too obviously as he flipped his hat backwards, giving me a slight head nod as he spotted my car in the distance. A hoodie was tied around his waist and he was looking intuitively at his phone as he walked.

Then he did the unexpected. Good thing I hadn't blinked or I would have hit him. At the red light, my car rolled to a stop. He sped up to get directly in my line of vision, standing right in the middle of the road in front on my car as the light turned green. I was in no shape to pass or swerve around him, so I instinctively laid on my car horn, immediately embarrassed for overreacting.

He smiled innocently, then made his way to the passenger side of my car. He tugged at the locked handle as I glared at him, careful not to drive off.

"Want to give me a ride today?" he asked, like we were old friends. I didn't even know what were are at that point.

Before I could even respond, he had opened the door to my car and crawled inside.

"What was that about? I could have hit you! You can't just go around throwing yourself in front of cars and then act all relaxed about it!"

"I'm sorry, but I had to get your attention somehow. You're Phoebe, right?" he changed the subject, "Cliff, remember? We met at the party the other night."

He pointed to himself when he said the name Cliff. No wonder I couldn't remember the uniqueness of the name.

"I actually do remember," not wanting to make it obvious I already hung on his every word.

"Cliff's short for Clifford. It's a family name," he explained without prompting as if he had to often. I nodded, proud of myself for at least remembering the first letter, ashamed all the same.

"Where'd you move from?" I asked to break the silence.

"Pennsylvania."

"Oh yeah, and what brings you to the beach?"

"Your typical situation. My father's business transferred him here."

"Who'd you know at the party the other night?" I'm afraid I'm grilling him but I wanted to get to know him in any way possible.

"I didn't actually know anyone. I overheard some girls talking about it at the movies the other night, and it was a lame attempt at meeting some new people my age in this area," he said blankly.

It was a bold move for the new kid and I respected that. I would have been too self-conscious to arrive alone.

"And how'd that turn out for you?"

"Well… I met you, didn't I?" he said, looking at me deeply. It was all I could do to keep my eyes on the road.

"And this is your first week at school? I haven't seen you around." I changed the subject; it was safe.

"First day actually."

"Your first day of school? We need a picture."

"We need a picture?"

"Doesn't your mother take a first day of school picture every year? To map your progress and changes and what not?"

"Maybe when I was in elementary school…"

"Just smile."

He slid in reluctantly next to me and I flipped my phone around for a picture. Somewhat unlike me, I don't know why I brought that up, but I was happy to have captured the moment.

Awkwardness arose, so I decided to keep it going by bringing up that I had some of his belongings in the seat behind him.

"I found the sketchbook at the river," I said, gauging the ghostly look on his face when he realized I may have seen the picture of me in there. I continued, "I knew it was yours because I remember seeing you with it the night we met at the party."

"Oh, right," evident relief covered his face. "I had been wondering where it got to actually, so thanks."

He didn't ask if I skimmed his drawings and I didn't tell. Flattery replaced my curiosity, so I decided not to mention it.

"I see you've found my spot by the river..." I teased.

"You're spot?"

"Unofficially."

"Well, it's lovely. Next time I go there, I'll make sure to let you know I'm stopping by."

"You're welcome anytime."

All tension avoided, I got that feeling again that told me he and I wouldn't be strangers. Only this time, I could genuinely believe it.

SAGE

Something wasn't right when I continued my walk. I was visibly weak and growing more fragile by the moment. My headache pounded, and I could feel the insides of my stomach turning on each other in extreme hunger. But I had to continue. I had this unforeseen spark in me that I couldn't keep under control. I sat on the steps of an old, white church to simply regroup and I'd be on my way.

"Hiya!"

I was greeted by a petite elderly woman accompanied by her unleashed dog. As if my headache wasn't loud enough, she came along to remind me.

"Hello," I responded weakly, and almost rudely.

"Are you new to the church?"

"Oh, no. Just passing through."

"Well, welcome! What brings you here?"

"Not here for long," I was at the point where I couldn't even fathom producing a full sentence.

"Do…do you want to stop in for some tea? Have you been walking? You don't look well, darling. I just put a pot on the stove."

"That's okay. I should be on my way."

"To each their own! Just an offer. I saw you walk up to the church with all your bags and didn't recognize you. I just wanted to come introduce myself. I live across the street in the home right there," she signaled to a little ranch home across the way, a white picket fence in the yard surrounding it. Potted plants busted at the seams. It was the house I would have pegged her to live in. "But the church is my baby; my pride and joy!"

"It's beautiful. Truly," I managed a soft smile, followed by a sneeze.

"Oh, do come inside, darling. I see you are ill. At least to take a load off your feet for a bit."

If only she knew the severity of her words.

I promised myself that I wouldn't do that type of thing, but I'd landed myself here in this small town, with a sweet grandmotherly woman, how could I have

112

resisted? I could tell I wasn't well. Maybe she'd have some medicine or a therapeutic home remedy.

"I guess I could stop in for a little bit."

Little did I know that "little bit" would turn into three nights and four days. Over the course of the week, my health continued to get worse.

Melrose, the woman who took me in, cared for me like the daughter she never had. Her house was just as I expected: musty and cluttered with antiques of old bird murals, big clocks on the walls and outdated furniture. Through the mustiness, there was a scent of fresh bread in the air, supplies all over the counter, but no recipe to be found. Pictures of hand painted art covered the walls, but no photographs of people, except one portrait above the couch. It was of a young man, who I could tell by the wash and texture of the photo was no longer that young and in fact very much older. Everything had a yellowish-brown hue—the couches, the tables, the wallpaper. It was a small home, but plenty for little Melrose and her tiny pup, who more or less kept to himself.

"My late husband and I always wanted children," Melrose told me to break the silence, perhaps having spotted me eyeing the photograph above the couch.

"You never had any?"

"It just wasn't in the cards for us."

"What happened to your husband, if you don't mind me asking?"

"I don't mind at all. We were happy as could be until the very end. He passed after a bout of cancer. I admit, I should have been more patient with him than I was, but he was so irritable at the end of his life. Sort of

113

gave up on everything too soon. I knew he was in bad shape but I didn't want to see him go down without a fight. Don't get me wrong, we loved each other until the end, but it was rough those last few weeks. Then again, I do suppose I've always been a bit hard on him. I just expected the best, you know?"

I did know.

"Naturally." I felt tears welling up in my eyes.

"He was eighty-seven when he passed, so he did have a very fulfilled life, I'd like to think. I wish I had a daughter, though, or some living extension of him. Someone of your stature and poise, perhaps." She was kind to say that as I laid sprawled out on her couch with a warm rag on my head and my throat lozenge wrappers covering her floor, hacking up a lung.

"A crazy nomad, all sick and lonely out in the world on her own?"

"Oh c'mon, it can't be that bad. It's an adventure! You struck my attention immediately."

"You know what? You might be the first person to see it that way."

"That's what it is. I do wish you were a bit safer…" I had told her some stories.

"I am a bit too quick to trust aren't I?"

"You did come into my home, after all," she said in a tone mockingly malicious. I had to laugh despite how hoarse my throat had become.

I got to know her more that night, and as the nights continued, our dinner talks, porch swing conversations and red wine by the television gave me a sense of home. I had a feeling my presence in her life wasn't all that bad either, not that she was a grouchy old woman or anything like that, but doing anything alone can become cumbersome and, well, lonely.

Like any sickness, mine got worse before it got better. I contemplated going to the doctor but Melrose convinced me her home remedies would do the trick.

It's a trap how quickly we tend to fall into old habits, good or bad. I was suddenly extremely comfortable with home life. I could stay right there in Delaware with Melrose the rest of my life and quite possibly be very happy. That, of course, I knew I would not do. It just wasn't realistic in any sense of the word, but imagining it was needed.

The last night with Melrose, we sat and skimmed through old mementos she had kept throughout the years. Boxes upon boxes scattered her living room floor, overflowing with memories from "this event with my old friends," or the "summer of '62." So many emotions filled the air, stemming from both she and I.

"It's important to keep whatever you can from life. People say to rid yourself of the material things because you can't take them with you when you die, but I don't necessarily believe that. Just because I might die soon doesn't mean my things have to. There's something I want you to have," Melrose said, while scrambling for something at the very bottom of a box, as luck would have it.

I blushed involuntarily.

"It's a book I wrote back when I was young and seeking a profession I couldn't quite find. I kept up with a lot of the current world happenings and wrote a fiction piece in my free time between working down at the local grocer and helping my father on his farm. I was

115

about ten years younger than you when I wrote it, actually. I don't have anyone to pass it too, and I never got it published or anything, but I think you'll find it to your advantage. I can't bring myself to get rid of it because of all the hours I put into it and, oh the nights I victoriously conquered writer's block can't be all for naught. You might find something in there that helps you through just when you need it too. Or maybe just read it to pass the time."

"I don't feel right taking it from you, but I'll gladly give it a read at some point…"

"No, no, Sage, really. Someone of your mindset and ability is truly unique. There are not many young women your age that would have the courage to take off and do what you're doing. I like to think I was courageous in writing this. At the time my family was very poor, you see. My father particularly didn't support the idea of 'hobbies' if it didn't involve making money. But I was a determined young lady. I would sneak a candle into our attic where I made a makeshift desk out of old boxes that were going to be trashed at the grocer. I would sit for one hour every evening. Sometimes the words flowed from my brain effort-lessly, as easy as breathing, and other nights I struggled with what I wanted to say. Saying so little in so many words. But at the end of the day, I knew I had a message to send and words to preach. I knew when I met the right person, I'd pass the book onto them; someone who had been through some similar trials to appreciate it."

116

"Why didn't you try to get it published?" I didn't reveal to her that I worked for a book publishing company.

"Oh, I'd love to! I wish I did, but I don't have the means for all that business. I'm sure it's a whole process I know nothing about. Besides, I have plenty of business to take care of here and times were different then," she said, the boxes scattered across her living room floor little windows of her past.

"Well I'd love to read it through and see what you've got to say. Thank you for this gift, although I am embarrassed at how much you've already given me these past few days. You are so kind," Melrose reached across the table to clasp my hand in hers.

"The pleasure was all mine, darling. I enjoy the company time and again, not that I always take in people off the streets," I couldn't help but smile at her innocence. "And I want you to have the book, I know you're the right person to hold onto it. Read it when you're older, perhaps. But do me a favor, don't let it get dusty on some old shelf when you're through with it. There are good words in there I don't want to go to waste. That's what it's been doing all this time here."

I was grateful for the book, but all the same I was not. After all, I had just met the woman, then I had her moderately lengthy, amateur novel weighing down my pack. I resorted to just saying, "thank you," and not mentioning that not only did I get a novel to hang on to, but also a responsibility. Deep down, I did intend to glance over it and ship it anonymously to my old company.

She started to tear up, knowing my time with her had come to an end. I still had some symptoms of illness, but nothing compared to how I was earlier in the week. I may have been spoiled by Melrose tending to me bedside with a warm bowl of soup, or a spoonful of cough syrup, but I knew it was time to continue on. It was strange to think that just a few days ago, I was sleeping on a park bench with Julian, a stranger who I then considered a friend, to living the life of luxury in the classiest hotel, which then led me to Melrose in Delaware. Of all the places and things I expected to experience on the journey, none of it was what I expected at all. There were more people out there willing to help me than hurt me, I just had to find the right people.

I was prepped and ready for the venture ahead. Immediately, I regretted being so cooped up in the house for four days. I sacrificed a good sixty miles, at least, for the sake of my health, which some would say, is everything.

Constantly torn between what I should be doing with my life and what I was doing with my life, Melrose assured me there was nothing to worry about. I assured her in return that I could only hope that one day when I was older, I had as many memories in piled up boxes. Although, if I kept shedding things from my backpack to decrease its weight, there would be nothing left over from my venture at all.

I had Melrose write her address on a notecard and I promised to write to her when I completed my travels. Her eyes lit up at the idea.

"Oh, darling, I've always wanted a pen pal!"

I couldn't leave without one last home-cooked meal in my belly, as she insisted. Melrose whipped up chicken marsala sans mushrooms; our dislike for mushrooms something we bonded over.

She embraced me in a hug that alluded to the fact that neither of us got hugged enough. It wasn't awkward, but there was a sense of something unnatural about it. In that moment, I wished to stay there forever in Melrose's arms just feeling needed and overindulging in massive plates of pasta.

PHOEBE

I decided to go for a run later that night. It was out of character perhaps, but when at my grandmothers, I started to make up reasons to go outside in the off chance I might run into Cliff. I unpacked my car already, but went out a second time because I "accidentally" left something in there. Then I grabbed an old, dirt splashed watering can and started watering the plants on my grandmother's porch. Wishing she had a dog I could take for a walk, I opted for a run instead.

I had no such luck spotting him yet, but I wasn't going to give up so easily. Ideally, I'd march right on over to his home, knock on the door, and ask him to hangout.

Things just weren't that simple when you liked someone.

Thankfully, my grandmother was out playing bingo with friends to comment on my odd behavior. I hadn't watered her plants a day in my life, she'd certainly be skeptical.

The run was nice though. It cleared my mind. It was entirely too obvious I had spent my time eating from various fast food joints as the run did not come easy but rather welcomed. I stopped time and again, resting my hands on my knees as I hunched over to catch my breath, a small stream of sweat moistened the back of my neck in the process.

I didn't necessarily want him to see me a mess but took comfort knowing he rarely looked put together himself. The boy would either be missing shoes or a shirt, and his hair, a tousled mess. You never knew what you were going to get with him. In a way, it relaxed me. I trusted him because he made me feel comfortable to open up to, not that we have even made a dent in our relationship in the way I'd like.

I believed to have been a mile and a half out, as I was at Sam's gas station and convenience store. Using their location as a gauge, I turned back around to make my way to the house. Committed to do this more often, in hopes of it getting easier, and in hopes of catching a glimpse of Cliff, I couldn't help but smile at the positive life change.

I didn't plan on stopping, feeling invincible, until I caught sight of him on a bike wheeling towards me, as predicted a disheveled mess of beauty.

"Phoebe, hey," he shouted, "I didn't know you were a runner," he winked at me when he said it, and although I was somewhat insulted, I could tell he was completely joking as he circled his bike around me with ease.

I slowed to a walk.

"You want to give me a ride home on the back of that bike...? It's the least you can do after all the rides I've offered you..." I dished it right back.

"Hop on," he said through a smile he couldn't hide.

I did, suddenly self-conscious of what I must smell and look like, but this was ultimately what I wanted. I latched onto his black T-shirt regardless as he glided through the surprisingly warm fall air, the breeze blazing past him, hitting me softly in the face as I balanced on the back of his bike pedals.

He adjusted temporarily, putting his arms on the outside of mine, steadying me further. It was the closest I had been to him, which made my near stalking ways justifiable.

We got back to my grandmother's house, with his new home sitting beside it, entirely too quick. I hopped off the pedals as gracefully as I possibly could and thanked him for the ride. He told me anytime I needed, he'd be happy to come save me, in which he informed me he hated running and didn't understand why people thought it was enjoyable in the slightest. Currently, I could empathize.

We stood there eyeing each other for a little too long at the place where the driveways met, neither of us wanting to be the first to initiate parting ways. I didn't want to see him off, nor did he me.

"Same place 7a.m. tomorrow? We can ride to class together?" he asked.

"Sounds good to me," I blushed, but my face was already red due to the wind and the running, that I hoped he couldn't tell the difference.

"I'll throw you some gas money," he said.

"Don't even worry about it," I said, turning to walk away, because him being with me was somewhat of a favor in and of itself. Before I got too far, he snagged me back to him in one fluid motion. My heart fluttering when he touched my hand.

"Here's my number in case I'm late...just call me, I don't always wake up on time," he scratched a number into my hand with a pen he dug from the pocket of his jeans.

I never wanted to wash my hand.

He ran his through his hair, and released me from his gentle grasp.

"I wasn't sure I was going to like the move here, but it's not all bad, is it?" he said, taking in the cool September air, looking aimlessly in approval of his surroundings.

"I wouldn't say it's bad at all," I admitted whimsically, looking around noncommittal.

He turned to leave for good and I already wished he hadn't. He was so disheveled in a way that made me distracted. Walking back to my grandmother's in a forlorn manner, I convinced myself of all the reasons he was too good to be true. Already he cluttered my mind.

I put his number in my phone regardless, setting my alarm early enough to call him in the morning with enough time for us both to get ready. I stared out my window, hoping to catch one last glimpse of that perfect human being, a smile plastered on my face all the while.

SAGE

When I was younger, I made friends with everyone. When there was a new student in class, before the teacher even did their introduction I had made eye contact and smiled at them at the very least. Sometimes we already shared a minor memory. I guess it was true when they say that some things never change, although in the middle of it all, everything had.

When I worked at the book publishing company, I kept to myself. I was different than I used to be, and in the midst of it all, that's who I became.

The girls at work were different than those I was used to. They had prissy, annoying voices, probably due to the lack of air circulating through their lungs since their clothes were so tight. Their hair perfect and piled down with expensive hairspray, enough to cause asphyxiation. They found me bizarre as well. It was never spoken, but was seemingly obvious. Perhaps, I was just too plain.

A picture of a wolf was tacked to the bulletin board of my cubicle. One day, a six-foot-three model type coworker named Liz bothered to ask me about it.

"What's the meaning of all that?" she asked, as if there were some mural displayed behind me when rather it was just a five-by-seven. She flounced her pointer finger around the space behind me regardless.

"I don't know, I just like it. Wolves are different. They're almost scary and fierce. Very powerful. If you look closely though, it's so beautiful all the same." I attempted to describe with full knowledge that she wouldn't get the concept, nor did she really care.

"It frightens me," she said as she turned to walk to the cafeteria where she'd probably waft a piece of celery and call it lunch.

The wolf accessory may have been a bit much for our office setting, but my father took the picture and that's what I liked most about it. He went out with my Uncle Val (an old Army veteran and confidant of his) once when I was old enough to remember but young enough to not be invited on a ski trip in Maine.

It was a high quality photo that not only reminded me of my father, but also of everything the wolf stood for. There was a sense of adventure I had passed down genetically that was becoming more difficult to find behind that desk each day. The wolf's eyes seemed, at times, to be gazing at me dead in the eye, just watching me make every move, take every breath. Once, I turned it around to face the wall because I felt the condescension in its eyes. Maybe I've always been insanely paranoid, but I was forever my own worst enemy.

My picture of the wolf and the picture that had Tom in it were both flipped backwards simultaneously. I'd have to stop myself from sketching pointless doodles on the empty canvases they became.

However, for as many fictional characters as I would read about in the manuscripts piled on my desk each week, it was the wolf I empathized most with. In a way, we were always in this together.

One of the friends I made during the early high school years was a foster child, bouncing from house to house. Her name was Jane, and she taught me everything "cool" that was needed to know to survive high school. My mother let me have her over to our house unconventionally because we never had guests.

Typically, I was embarrassed to invite friends over, but I knew she had been in so many living situations that were not ideal through the foster program that I got over that thought relatively quick. The first time she came over, she dyed my hair jet black, like you'd expect from a rebellious teen. We pierced each other's ears with needles and apples, both of us holding back tears pretending to be braver than the other. We smoked cigarettes on the porch together after midnight and hoped my mother wouldn't come out and catch us. Then again, we were never that afraid, knowing my mother and that she would have simply joined the fun.

Jane did everything reckless with me, and it was the most carefree time of my life.

One night, she and I went down to an old bridge and brought some spray paint. We intended to graffiti one of the few spaces left vacant of others murals. We had some ignorant phrase we thought was cool at the time and we were going to try to emulate the other artist's work.

Thinking back, I struggled to remember what we concocted but I knew we whipped out our best calligraphy. I remembered clearly that Jane was disappointed it didn't come out as wonderfully as she envisioned it, myself feeling like I had let her down.

That night, we walked to a pizza joint located across the street, managing to piece together the change from our pockets to order a medium pepperoni and cheese. We took it back under the bridge, talking and laughing the entire night while eating our pizza and drinking the beer Jane had in her backpack, which she stole from her foster parents' basement refrigerator. No wonder Jane liked living with these folks, they'd let her get away with murder.

"They never look down there anyways," she would claim.

Once, I asked my mother when I was much younger what made a best friend the best. How will I know when someone is the best enough to be my best friend? She told me she never had a best friend, because "this day in age we have to be wary with who we trust!" she'd say, perhaps not the best mother-to-daughter advice. But I knew in that moment that Jane was my best friend and that I was lucky to have her, no matter how reckless she encouraged me to be.

We slept under the bridge we painted that night without a care in the world. We woke up feeling—and most likely looking—like zombies, but we didn't care.

It was but six months later that Jane started hanging out with a crowd I wasn't a fan of. She started taking her reckless abandon attitude to the next level, something I certainly couldn't keep up with. She was headed for a downward spiral, from which she wouldn't return, and soon, she moved away. When Jane turned eighteen, she was destined to take off on her own. She'd always said it since our middle grade years, but when the time finally came she actually did it.

I was envious of her for so many reasons from that moment on. There is such wonder and beauty in an attitude that does what it says it will. Some people come across all tough and strong on the exterior, but inside,

126

they are meek and insecure cowards just awaiting the day when they blow it and lose their mind.

Jane wasn't like that, though. She actually was a tough person, inside and out. Life had dealt her a tough hand of cards and she shoved that hand right back, showing it a clenched fist.

She had an air about her that didn't belong to anyone or anything. She would bounce around from house to house, having mandatory therapy sessions while in school. She'd always claim to be fine, and the teachers and everyone, myself included, believed her. She understood the meaning of life goes on and she did what she wanted to do when she wanted to do it.

I wasn't sure what made me think of Jane while in the midst of my travels, but it might be because I thought of her before I did anything the least bit rebellious. It might be the possibility of me potentially sleeping under a bridge again that evening. Or it might be because I just missed her and wondered if I would be passing through somewhere she might be residing.

Either way, I felt myself reach up to my neck to where my "best friend forever" necklace used to hang ages ago.

Mine said friend, but Jane's said best.

PHOEBE

I started driving Cliff to school regularly and taking him home at night the weeks I was at my grandmother's. Even when I wasn't staying close, we still found time and ways to meet up that I started forgetting about Colin altogether. Daily life became more enjoyable as memories grew more meaningful. It was all happening so fast and as blatantly terrifying as it was, I wasn't scared at all.

"Good morning," he said groggily as he picked up the phone the morning after giving me his number.

"Wake up, sunshine!" I was too peppy, and although I rehearsed what I would say to him when he picked up the call over and over in my head the night before, that was all I had. Now however, it was routine. I'd call him every morning to wake him up, and I never minded. I liked him being the first person I spoke with each day. On nights when I was back at my house with my father, I missed the convenience of picking him up.

I'd still call to wake him though, and then I'd wait in the parking lot until I saw him ride up on his bike, park it, and we'd walk in together. It was...nice.

Unlike me, he hadn't grown up in a world full of politicians and preachers, rather, he'd grown up more organically and I learned things from him because of it.

Oddly enough, we had plenty in common to carry a seemingly meaningful conversation to and from school, and even beyond that.

I could tell when he was in a subpar mood, too. One afternoon driving home, I sensed he was more down than usual.

"Do you ever get into any trouble, Cliff?" I asked him sort of randomly. He glared at me. Sometimes he had a way with condescension that made me want to forget about him forever.

"Not as much as I'd like...why?" he asked, becoming skeptical.

"Want to have some fun tonight? You seem to be in a mood."

"By fun you mean trouble?" It was then his attention peaked.

"Well... a couple of us are sneaking out to head down to Mr. Kline's house tonight."

"Your geography professor?"

"Mmhmm."

"Why would you do that?"

"Some of us are bringing eggs, others are bringing toilet paper...You get the idea."

"Sounds childish to me."

"It's more for the adrenaline rush than bad intentions. You in?"

"I only have shaving cream."

I turned amicably to him, smiling at the thought of him shaving what little stubble he had on his face.

"That'll do."

"See that basement window right there?" He signaled to a small window on the side of the house. I nodded.

"What about it?"

129

"Knock on it at nine tonight and I'll be there waiting."

I smiled again, this time more mischievously, like he let me in on some private and juicy detail. I have looked out my window at his house this entire time, never knowing he was a basement dweller.

"Ten. Be wearing dark clothes." My statement made me seem more in control, when really I just had to be sure my grandmother would be asleep before sneaking out.

He hopped out of my car as it was still rolling to a stop, already in a seemingly better mood.

***

It was 9:39p.m. when I quit pacing the floorboards of my room and decided to head over to Cliff's window. I changed outfits three times despite the night's activities revolving around darkness. Cliff was the one I was nervous to see, afraid he'd see too much of me and not approve.

Something inside me was more skittish than usual too.

Knowing my grandmother was asleep, I felt I deserved to make the most of the leniency at my fingertips.

I tiptoed downstairs and out the front door, just like that. In opposition, I began to bang on the window Cliff had instructed me to.

He opened it with urgency.

"Come on in. I'll help you down."

In the ten seconds that followed, I was scaling down the basement wall through the window as Cliff helped me in. I was very aware of his hands sliding up my body as he helped to guide me down.

"Why do you look like you're going to rob a bank?" he asked me when my feet hit the ground. He was standing freakishly close to me.

"Is my ski cap too much?"

"It's cute." He pet the top of my head and then retreated back. I instantaneously removed it as self-consciousness took over.

"Is this your room?" Of course it was, but the question just came out. His bike hung on a rack on the wall, paint cans relaxed on the floor waiting to be used, and rolled up posters peeked out from under the bed. I spotted a guitar too, not knowing he played, but wasn't surprised by it either. You can tell a lot about someone from their bedroom, so I was mostly just trying to take everything in.

"Yep. Still in the early stages, but it's becoming the man cave I've been dreaming of."

"I had no idea you had an interest in home décor and interior design."

It was dark in the room but he shot me a look.

"Mind if I finish this movie before we go?" he questioned, bouncing back on his bed, almost looking too comfortable.

"We're a bit early to meet the rest of the guys so I guess we can swing it."

"Come join me."

He was sprawled out on his bed so I took the place beside him. I laid there and took in the room some

131

more. He had a deer head mounted above his bed. You didn't notice it too much until you are in the bed incidentally, something he probably killed and stuffed himself.

He watched the movie, but I paid no attention.

Laying down, I realized how tired I actually was. It must not have been the night we anticipated having, because we woke up tangled up in each other when his alarm went off at 8:30 the next morning.

"Good morning, sunshine," he said, flashing me a smile so bright while spitting my own line back at me that he may as well have been the sunshine himself.

SAGE

Everyone has a niche and a tendency. That's what I believe. We all have something that makes us a bit more comfortable. My grandfather was the type (as strange as everyone said he was for it) that always knew what direction he was traveling, or standing, for that matter. I seemed to have inherited his sense of direction and interest for it.

He'd say, "We all have paths we must take in life. We have to go with purpose. If you don't know what direction you're going in, then you're already a step behind."

It made sense in a way. Then again, maybe I was biased.

"Oh Reed, don't be ridiculous," my grandmother would retort.

Knowing he peaked my interested, he spoke directly to me, blocking my grandmother out of the conversation, she tossing a hand in the air as if to say *I was done with this conversation anyway.*

"Take for example right now," At the time we were sitting on the pier overlooking the lake. "Right now we are facing the Northeast direction. Did you know that?"

I'd nod my head yes even if I had no idea.

"You can tell by looking at the sun…" He'd babble on about it for quite some time and I'd always let him. Most of the useful information I had stored in my memory came from my grandfather on days just like that. I quite enjoyed my talks with both my grandparents; their exchange always made me smile. They bickered, but you can tell they loved each other dearly.

They were so good to my mother too when my father left her for good. After he did leave, my mother became the bitter divorcee that contributed what seemed every negative character trait of mine on my father's "poor and unfortunate" genes. My grandparents would defend me no matter what, especially when I was young, despite her being their daughter.

Being out in the wilderness, just walking all alone, made me realize how many people were actually there for me when I needed them. Thinking of my grandparents, and even of Jane, I was sure they would be proud of me, no matter what. And that's what love is.

The time passed quickly thinking about them, and I was happy despite the phlegm that still hid in the back of my throat and my snot covered sleeves. All I could do was keep walking, because it was like when my grandmother taught me to walk, I watched her in a video explain, "You're never going to get to the other side without putting one foot ahead of the other."

Sometimes it was just so...difficult.

***

It was another long day. It had been a long, long time since I'd rested and ate as I properly should. At that point, I felt malnourished and over exhausted, but even then, that was an understatement. Although it felt that way, I still had plenty of money left to eat food that wasn't the most nutritional but fulfilled my humanly duties; I was breathing, eating and at times, sleeping. I couldn't ask for more.

It was the first of October, marking one month since I began this catastrophe. It had been thirty whole days and the only person who really doubted me was myself. Sure, everyone was in disbelief, but they didn't have a say in what I could and could not do.

It called for a celebration.

After putting in the required miles to get back on track, I ordered myself a chicken finger plate and picked up a six-pack of cheap, cold beer before scoping out the premises for a place to stay the night.

A little less than half a mile away, I sought out a construction zone. Tom used to warn me to avoid construction sites rivaling in sameness to the one that was before me. He'd tell me the men might hoot and holler as I walked by, but living where we did in a highly populated area, one of the downfalls was that crazy people were on every corner I turned. There were too many absurd personalities confided to one space that the likelihood of running into someone of the sort was great. Reminded of that, I got chills down my spine, but I decided to search the place anyways. After all, it was getting dark and the site seemed empty and absent of humans.

I slung my pack to one layer of scaffolding and met it in a short moment, leaping my body to the next layer. I continued to climb the scaffolding like that until I reached the top. I laid there for a bit, hoping that my honey mustard had not leaked all over my fried chicken dinner after tossing it from layer to layer, smirking that it was at the top of my priorities list.

Despite the sawdust that filled the air, I took one solid and deep breath. I was infinite in that moment. I was free, I was alive. There was no greater feeling than that of being free and alive. Above all, I was safe. No one could touch me up there. And if they made it up there, more power to them, that wasn't easy.

I reclined against the building using my pack as back support, popping open a beer and delving into the chicken, my eyes looking towards the sun as it was setting.

Every bite tasted better than the last, every sip more empowering.

It was a moment I had to smile. I was one of the crazy people, but I was also crazy happy. It wouldn't be too much longer until I found my Max. He'd laugh if he saw me up there unlike Tom, who'd say something like, "Get yourself down from there right this instant," in that overly formal tone of his, so doctoral and authoritative, like he was my father.

I drank all six of the beers, embarrassed by how quickly. I didn't ever want to come down from there, but I could feel my bladder busting at the seams. I thought maybe a heavier dinner would absorb most of the alcohol content of the evening, so I didn't realize how tipsy I was until I stood up.

Freaking lightweight.

I eyed the ground from where I was. It seemed to be the end of a kaleidoscope, moving farther and farther away. I gripped the rail to avoid going over the edge. I was suddenly nauseous and at loss, but aware enough to know I wouldn't survive scaling down the side of some hopefully sturdy scaffolding.

With no other option, I matched my eyes to the empty beer bottles lined up along the edge. Crazier things have happened. It wasn't the easiest task in the world and perhaps my most mortifying, but it got the job done. As soon as I committed, I felt eyes on me, but decided it was just paranoia.

How absurd. I have become a barbarian. The laughter hit me, or maybe it was just the alcohol.

Regardless, I busted out in a laughter I could not contain, the type that came from within that crept up in inappropriate situations.

One time in middle school, I got in trouble for passing a note. The teacher, as punishment, made me stand up in front of the class and read it aloud. I didn't know what it said until I got up there, so caught off guard at its hilarity, I let it out at the expense of the poor girl the note was referencing. The whole class was in on it then, which caused me to escalate.

I was given detention for two days where I had to write, as old-fashioned as the school system would have it, I WILL NOT BULLY THE OTHER STUDENTS IN MY CLASS, I WILL NOT PASS NOTES one hundred times on a scuffed up chalkboard.

Talk about a hand cramp.

I deserved it though, because I shouldn't have been gossiping. When I told my mother what happened, she bellowed from the kitchen where she was cooking dinner, as she did once a week to fulfill some sort of motherly duty. A healthy portion of Easy Mac was on the menu for that particular evening.

I was no longer a bully but I did still suffer from unwelcomed bouts of laughter. I should have felt more ashamed that I had just went to the bathroom in a bottle my lips had just been on moment's prior.

I eyed the ground, bottle in hand. Not a soul was to be found, and was getting dark. It must have been after 10p.m. and I had been up there for a few hours; just me, my thoughts, and I.

Tipsier than I intended for the night's festivities, I lined the empty beer bottles up one by one, aiming for the trash can that sat at the bottom of the scaffolding. If I really focused, I assumed I'd be able to land the bottles in the trash below.

When you've had the past month I'd had, it was the simple things that enticed you, but after all, I am only human.

I held the first bottle over the edge, the full one. I was about four stories high. Somehow my drunk self was fully aware of how stupid I must have appeared; I was worried to even wonder what my sober self would say the next morning.

I let it linger a few seconds longer, then I dropped the bottle. Five empty bottles followed.

All finally landed where an unfortunate incident would be had between the bottles and the hardworking construction workers who would be cursed to have stumbled upon them in the morning. Missing the trash can three out of six times, I had definitely left my mark.

There I went being an unintentional bully all over again, falling victim of some innocent fun.

Just as the glass bottles shattered when they hit rock bottom, I knew I had too hit rock bottom; yet somehow I fell asleep still laughing, the breeze in my face, and all my worries faded if for just one night.

PHOEBE

"Dammit!"

"What glorious first words to begin a Saturday with." Cliff looked over at me.

He was more attractive than ever before.

"I'm guessing we didn't make it last night, seeing as I don't remember a damn thing," I was acting more dramatic than I felt. I slept great.

"Hey, we still had a fun night. At least I did."

"Oh no, what happened?"

"Nothing happened. I watched the rest of the movie, but by the time it ended, you were passed out."

"Let me guess, I just looked too peaceful to wake up?"

"Something like that…"

I put the pillow over my head for some more dramatic effect.

"Also…your phone was going off like crazy, so I checked to make sure there was no emergency…"

"And…"

"Everyone who went to Mr. Kline's got caught in the act. Police busted the scene not ten minutes after they got there."

My eyes widened in disbelief.

"I'm kind of your knight in shining amour, saving you from a bad situation and all."

"Oh, shut up," I said, just before he kissed me and I let him.

SAGE

I had this one horrific dream where I'd wake up in a panic, my heart fluttering a mile a minute and sweat outlining my sheets. It'd recur and I would never understand it, nor did I ever try to. I wanted to let it go, just forget it ever happened altogether.

The forefront of the action was always where I belonged. I wasn't one of those girls to ever sit on the sidelines and look pretty. It made me entirely too antsy. This dream, though, had me in the center of its action and I couldn't take it. Something about it made me uncomfortable and full of regret.

Some dreams aren't our fault, though. We don't know why our subconscious takes us to such drastic measures, if maybe to prove a point to ourselves.

In that particular instance, I awoke from my recurring dream. By then, we had become familiar with each other, the dream and I. That didn't mean I liked it though.

I regretted drinking the whole six-pack of beer the night before, albeit too quickly, I should have known better. I stumbled up, rubbing my dirty face and eyes as if seeing the place for the first time. Gathering the current situation, I wiggled my fingers followed by my toes to remind myself that I was alive, unscathed and I was going to be alright, one day. Just not today.

If all this walking didn't kill me first, my own mind would. So much had happened that I regretted with Max and the way things ended. We needed each other more than we understood, but love is about balance in that way, I suppose. We were two people too imbalanced to level each other out. It was something we just couldn't help.

We blamed it on our age and inexperience and perhaps it was, but that's the beauty in it all. As disgruntled and scared as we both were, even so young, we'd always knew we'd have each other, and that was a once in a lifetime type of love.

As deranged as I felt for walking this alone, I knew Max would be proud. In more ways than one, that was enough to keep me going. Pushing all negative dreams aside, I reached behind me into the backpack I had transformed into a pillow, for a letter. Usually reading them at night, I needed something to hang on to before I approached the day.

Though tired eyes, I ran my hand across the next letter in the stack. His handwriting barely legible, it still meant everything.

Sage,

Things are neither better nor worse.
They are very much the same. I have so
much to tell you, yet so little to write about.
I blame my dehydration for my lack of memory
and focus, but I know it's more than that.
You are all I think about out here, and I know
I never want to be without you again
once this is all over. I wish you were here.
Well, now that I think of it, not really. I wish
that you are much cozier than where I
am right now. I wish I was with you there.

You know me, I'm always on the defensive.
I can hardly sleep most nights because I'm
watching my back. You can never be too
cautious, not that I have reason to worry.
And don't you worry about me either.
Nothing crazy has happened besides the
crazy I put myself into, I suppose.

Remember that time I took you to that
waterfall off 2nd and Willow? I found
one just like it. I went for a nice swim,
and you'll never believe it: I caught a fish

*with my bare hands. I didn't know what to
do with it at first, but when I recognized
there was a campsite nearby, I put it on fire,
sizzled it over the flame and ate it. It was
by far the best meal I've had out here
—although I guess not very well balanced in
nutrition. Like something out of a
movie, I'll tell ya! But still—the point of
the story is, I ate a fish I caught and
cooked with my bare hands.*

*You really don't have to worry about me,
because it came as a surprise to me too,
but it seems I can take care of myself.
It's crazy the habits you pick up when
you need them most. That's what I call
adrenaline. I have plenty of adrenaline
rushes out here, that's for sure. I
make do with what I have, and for
right now, that's enough for me.*

Max

I was in tears by the end of the letter. Not wailing,
but controlled. We were so young to find a love so
strong, but it happened. I just had to continue fighting
the feelings that reminded me that everything regarding
Max in my life was behind me, but rather a lifetime
ahead.

PHOEBE

"I should head back," I said, not wanting to leave his embrace. "My grandmother is out for her morning aerobics class, but she'll worry if I'm not back at the house when she gets there."

"Yeah, okay. When will I see you again?" he asked almost breathlessly.

"I can see my window from here, so if I run back, and you look hard enough, I'd say about four minutes."

"Hmm, okay I'll be watching."

"Creep," I smirked. He made it difficult to remain my stoic self.

I got up and gathered my things. I was afraid that him kissing me would make everything awkward, ruining it all, but he wasn't that type of person. He was far too nonchalant to make me feel uncomfortable.

I was about to leave when I realized I had no idea where I was going. I hadn't been introduced to the rest of house yet so I did what I thought was logical.

Eyeing the window, I implied, 'give me a boost.'

"You know we have doors…" he said. May as well be reading my mind.

"It's all good. I'll go the way I came, hoist me up."

As ridiculous as it sounded, he lifted me up and out the window. It was a much swifter process than I envisioned it being.

"Hey, can I take you to dinner tonight?"

I sunk down so I was eye level with him as he elongated his body to reach me at the window, giving

143

myself time to review my plans for the evening, which added up to none...

"I think I'm free."

"Great. I'll pick you up at 8:00 tonight."

"Throw a stone at my window," I spun around in the long fall grass as happily as could be, despite my dark, cops-and-robbers themed outfit from the night before.

"So romantic," he said rolling his eyes, although I wouldn't put it past him to actually do it. I smiled at him, and then to myself when he could no longer see, I smiled again.

SAGE

I didn't think I could, but I knew I must continue on. The sound of men's voices began to surround the area as I concluded Max's letter, in which the silence engulfed me. The sun had hardly risen yet but it was working on it.

My legs were like jelly; I could not feel them and they did not want to be felt. I could hardly see straight, the sun rising strong and effortlessly, as if kicking me out of the space I had rested for the evening with each bit it rose.

I was thankful for the life I had with Tom at times, mostly because Tom and I had couches to lay in and chairs to sit on.

To avoid being seen, I knew there was only one way I could escape without being caught. The workers were sitting below on a rail, four men, their backs to me, sipping some coffee.

Oh, the things I'd do for a cup of coffee, two creams, no sugar.

I had no time to think, just to act. Imagining a much cooler version of myself, I envisioned hopping the bar to the rooftop view, as if some undercover spy.

To avoid climbing back down the way I climbed up to bypass the men below, I knew up and over was the only option. I heard brief comments about the broken glass below. I threw a palm to my head, a headache briskly forming. Embarrassed was an understatement to how I felt when I saw the bottles splattered on the sidewalk pavement about ten feet from where they enjoyed their morning croissants and bagels.

Luckily, the roof was flat and it was easy for me to get my footing. Being on the fourth level of the scaffolding, there was not much I had to do, I was pretty much there. Hoisting over my bag ever so gracefully to the roof, my slow and tired body followed.

I was never afraid of heights, I knew that, but in recovery, I was overly cautious in the moment. One wrong move could reveal my identity to the workers below.

Weaving around some pipes, I steadied myself on a ladder that led to the lower level. I tried my luck with a door that was locked. Better yet, though. I would have hated myself for having access to the indoors last night and not taking advantage of it, no matter how nice a night it was.

Several other ladders protruded from the building's roof sporadically, but I deemed it too risky. With scaffolding on three of its four sides, the inside might be out of commission for reconstruction purposes as well.

In addition, I couldn't just walk out the front door like it was my house, despite calling it home sweet home for the evening.

My map had beer dripped on certain corners and I prayed they weren't important routes. At this point in the journey, I was so close, yet so far.

Scurrying down the side of the building, I was in a rush to hit the ground. It is easier than expected, but I still impressed myself. Like anything, the decline was always easier to fall into than the incline to adjust to.

***

It was a day like any other, except that there was a dog. I spotted him sorting through some trash when I hit the ground, hoping to find a morsel of food through the trash's belongings. I felt bad for it, because I too had been that famished out here and on my own. Although he looked mangy and without a collar, I knelt down to be eye level with the pup I oddly related to. From my pack I took out a sleeve of crackers. Having been there since day one, they were too stale for me anyways. I crumbled some up and cupped them in my hand. Dutifully, he sat and nibbled. I almost felt him smiling up at me.

When he was done, I stood up and said, "Goodbye, little buddy." My voice was scratchy. It had been awhile since I opened it to speak, only ever to yawn.

146

Except it wasn't goodbye, because he never left my side. I gave him one thing, and then I was his fateful owner by chance. He was pretty damn loyal and obedient, I will give him that. I'd tell him to sit, and he would. I'd tell him to lay down, and he'd do that too. He just wouldn't stay.

I could have used companionship out there, but a dog wasn't what I had in mind. It wasn't feasibly my best option. I couldn't bring him into other people's homes, fancy hotels, and he couldn't climb scaffolding, assuming all the situations I'd been in before happened again, albeit not likely.

We walked some time together, stopping for water time and again. Around mile five, I was afraid of pushing him too far, although I'd be fine if he stopped wherever and whenever. If anything, I was afraid I was bringing him farther from his home, if he even had one.

He was a sweet, little guy, of his breed I wasn't sure. I wouldn't want to cuddle up with him because he was definitely dirty, but completely harmless none-theless. Plus, if we bonded enough and he recognized me as his owner, he could be great protection. I could make him work.

I called him Niko. It was an instinctive name because my father had a dog called Niko that passed away when I was twelve. I loved him, but wish we had bonded better. In some strange turn of events, I felt this was my chance.

Niko and I walked thirteen and a half miles that day before I stumbled upon a Laundromat. We were making our way across Delaware and into Maryland one step at a time. I needed to freshen up the clothing in my pack at the Laundromat, so I was happy to have stumbled upon it, but first, I needed to eat.

There was a local barbecue type place around the bend I didn't have any other option but to try. Nothing was close enough to where I was, but it looked a good a stopping point as ever, and I mustn't backtrack. I told Niko to stay (or don't) as I made my way inside to ask for a patio seat.

Not twenty minutes later, I downed a whole rack of ribs, letting Niko suck the bones. It was while sitting out there I began to recognize how chilly it was. Days have come and gone out here and it was hard to believe it was already early-October weather.

A live band played cover songs, the lead singer's vocals subpar. A train whizzed by, a waiter stepped out on a smoke break and a young couple argued on the curb. There I was just taking it all in, salting my fries. I felt like a local and I had to snap out of it.

I brought Niko into the Laundromat with me. I decided I would until someone told me not to, but it was a twenty-four hour surveillance establishment, so no one was there to tell me otherwise, which made me want to push my luck and stay overnight.

Upon walking in, I avoided making eye contact with a woman standing on a dryer with her headphones in, singing a melody too far out of her vocal range. I assumed she wouldn't see me if I crouched down, so I sat on the floor with Niko's head in my lap and loaded my quarters and then my clothes. I set my head back against the washer as it cycled through its process. I could see the soap lathering and doing its job, almost mesmerizingly so.

148

Two others had walked in, but once they packed their clothes into baskets they were on their way again. I thought I was in the clear, but as luck would have it, the woman glided toward me with energy and jazz hands I was just not equipped to deal with. Niko had passed out on the floor, legs spread out behind him, and I wished she wouldn't be so loud because he truly was a cute, sleepy sight. Poor thing voluntarily had been through enough, I'd be surprised if he ever woke up, as horrible as it sounded. All I could do was assist along the way.

Maybe I needed Niko all along too. It was nice to feel needed and relied on. I nonchalantly patted him on the head as a sign of comfort we both needed.

"This your pup?" she asked me, all raspy and needing a lozenge from straining her vocal chords. She continued to dance through her inquisition.

I didn't mean it to be smart, I meant it be honest, but I couldn't help I came across as sassy, "No, he's not."

She didn't have a response, rather, she beat her head to the left, and then to the right.

"Oh, I love this song, here, listen..."

She shoved a speaker in my ear, and I cringed. The techno pop music coming from it made me anxious.

I'd been tolerating so well up until that point but I just could not empathize any longer. I was not ready to be taken care of or having her treat me like a guest in a place that didn't remotely belong to her, a safe assumption that she wasn't the owner.

I was raised to believe that everyone looks out for themselves in this world, that we live in an "eye for an eye, a tooth for a tooth" society. What happened to that world? Why does everyone want to befriend me? I'm not that interesting in the slightest.

"Do you want the dog?" I asked her, finally tearing the speaker from my ear. As fond as I was becoming of Niko, it was unrealistic and unfair for me to keep him under conditions I could barely survive in.

"Like to keep?"

"Sure," *whatever takes him off my hands.*

"What would I do with him?"

"He'd do whatever you'd do, I guess..."

It was then I felt bad for little, innocent Niko. I was pawning him off to this seemingly crazy woman, him unaware it'd be for the best.

"I'll take him. I'm sure Bobby'd want him. Bobby's my boyfriend. Here's a picture."

She showed me a picture of a guy that looked straight out of a magazine. An incredibly good looking model-type. Not that your significant other has to look similar to your style, but he was not what I expected from her whatsoever.

"He's handsome," I admitted.

"Well… he's all mine so quit looking! I'm Patsy by the way. I'm going to call the dog Bobby, so you can reintroduce yourself."

"Isn't Bobby your boyfriend's name?"

"Oh honey, you thought I was really dating that man?" she deep belly laughed, "In my dreams. Bobby's a character I concocted, but he became more like an imaginary friend. I just get lonely sometimes. You know, I don't have many friends." Her statement was very matter of fact, although, I had an inkling without being forewarned.

She was a rollercoaster of emotion and I wish I wasn't tall enough to ride. However, I had sympathy for her the more she spoke. Although I liked the name Niko better, if naming the dog Bobby made her happy, so be it. He was hers now.

For lack of conversation or anything else to do, I unraveled my sleeping mat and bag. I had clothes to sleep in but was ready for the washing machine cycle to sing me its lullaby.

Patsy was back up on a dryer singing me her lullaby instead.

"Well, come on now? Aren't you going to have a dance party with me?"

"I walked close to fourteen miles today, the last thing my muscles can handle is dancing. Plus, I'm a terrible dancer."

I couldn't have been worse than Patsy in her crop top, rolls of skin hanging over the edge of her ripped and faded denim jean shorts. I didn't lie though, I didn't have the energy to satisfy.

"No one's going to see but me and Bobby. You're already huddled away in the back corner. I remember the first night I slept here...Bobby kicked me out of the house, real bad situation."

I was having trouble keeping up if Bobby was fictional or not, but I decided it was best not to inquire. I wasn't trying to initiate a slumber party there.

"I'm sorry to hear that," was all I could muster out of politeness.

"We've patched things up since..."

Patsy continued to ramble on all night, at least until one in the morning, if not to me, to herself. She'd talk about her life, about Bobby, and the new dog. She'd break out in song, catapulting clothes she'd just washed.

Under garments too large for me, inside out pant legs and a large array of multicolored crop tops slung through the air time and again as the song crescendo.

You'd think getting some shut eye around here would be difficult, but both Niko and I were too exhausted to care. Something I discovered was that sometimes it was best not to open your mouth and let the world just happen around you.

PHOEBE

"Tell me something I don't already know about you," Cliff asked me from across the table. He looked really handsome, like he wanted to leave an impression on the evening.

I mentioned once the night we met, that I wanted to try the seafood restaurant on the Virginia Beach shoreline. At the time I didn't think he noticed, but there we were sitting across from each other in chic blue seats under an umbrella on the pier peeling back layers to get to crab meat.

"It depends on what you want to know…"

"Tell me about your family. What are they like?"

"Hmm…that's a loaded question," I hated talking about my family, mostly because I tried to avoid their abnormalities.

"I have all the time in the world." He sat back and made himself comfortable.

"My parents split when I was born, so there's a start."

"Oh, I'm sorry to hear that."

"No, it's fine. People always apologize, but they shouldn't. It's all I've ever known. I met a boy who was blind once at summer camp and we got close and he gave me that advice, but it's wise. I mean, everyone felt sorry for him, but he got around just fine, and probably had more fun at summer camp than anyone else because he didn't have to see Julianne Tifton in a bikini. One of those people who shouldn't be wearing one, you know…"

I was doing my absolute best to divert the conversation through irony.

"It was the worst when she attempted the rope swing," I smiled, and so did he, but out of confusion I'd assume more so than anything else.

"You're good at that," was all he said.

"Good at what?" I inquired all innocently.

"Making light of situations."

"It's not that I don't care, because I do. I mean, I wish things were different, but some things are simply the way they are. You have to embrace things, not accept them."

"But to a certain degree you have to accept it. You fell victim to your parent's divorce before you even knew what was happening."

153

"It wasn't divorce. They were never married. I was just an accident they tried to make work for a while before things went awry."

"Oh, okay."

"But yeah, I mean, now I just embrace the time I have with them separately."

I didn't want to mention my mother in depth, but it was difficult to talk about my family without mention of her.

"That's nice."

"So now I stay a week at my father's, and then a week at my grandmother's, and that's the way it's always been. I grew up in my grandmother's house so it was a comfort thing at first and my father travels a ton, so we use each other for company. My grandmother is more of a mother to me than my mother ever was anyways. I see my mother sometimes though when I want to, I just...don't...want to see her." I didn't mention seeing her only meant via the Internet, but I didn't elaborate. I sipped some water, my mouth recognizably dry.

I'm saved by the waiter, who appeared to have had a rougher day than he should have out there in the beach-like atmosphere. Food stains covered his clothing, a baseball cap hung on just barely to his red curls.

"Everything going well over here? Can I get you anything else?"

Cliff ordered a slice of pie for us to split for dessert, although I couldn't fathom eating another morsel of food, so full already.

"So tell me, what does your tattoo mean? Is it train tracks or something?" he asked, not skipping a beat.

"Train tracks? Does it look like that?" I felt my face grow flush, exposing the tattoo with haste to get a better view.

"Well it's hard to decipher. It might be more simplistic than that, but after all, it appears to be just two lines. Am I overcomplicating it?"

I pulled up my sleeve to better expose my wrist to him.

"It's just the number eleven."

"What's its meaning?" Out of everyone who knew about my tattoo, he was the first person to ask.

SAGE

To be honest, I could have been to my final destination in one day via motor transportation and it probably would have alleviated much distress, but Max had his own way of doing things, and I respected that. That's what I loved most about him.

Each day was a struggle, but I'd always been the type of person to work my way out of hard times. I am naturally positive. I was born that way. It was both a gift and curse because sometimes I just wanted to be realistic.

Realistically, I needed some food. I woke up to Patsy stroking Niko's fur before me, her eyes glaring at me like I'd crossed a line. I missed the dog's company already, but it was best he was out of my care. It seemed to have meant the world to her that she was his caretaker now. She may not have been mentally stable, but she seemed relatively caring.

I felt a rejuvenated jest despite the night I had endured. I wasn't just walking, I was prancing along. I couldn't explain how it was different than any day prior, but there was a crispness in the air I just could not deny.

It sprinkled a bit in the afternoon, but the cheeriness still hadn't left me.

It was nearing dinnertime and I'd put in some unprecedented mileage for the journey. I veered off in a residential neighborhood, off the beaten path with beautiful houses lined on either side of the walk. I figured it was my best chance of running into someone out on a jog or collecting the mail that might pity me and offer a place to crash for the night. It was wishful thinking, and unrealistic, but I had run into unknown acts of kindness before.

Instead, I spied on a family from afar. They were so typical. Two children, a boy and a girl, a Mom and a Dad. Although I couldn't see it, they probably had some Golden Retriever at the foot of the table begging for whatever dish Mom had put on the table, perhaps beef stroganoff.

Oh, I was wrong, I concluded as I saw Dad lift tongs of spaghetti and put them on Brother's plate.

I did something illogically logical in that moment. There are times in life you just have to think fast. I recognized that the family was just about settled in for dinner, all of them confined to one area for a minimum of thirty minutes. Naturally, I concocted a plan.

Waiting would be the death of me, but if I could make this work, I could consider myself wiser than I gave myself credit for.

I spotted a vacant swing nearby in the neighborhood park, not exactly hidden from view, but it'd do. I was adjacent to the bay window of their dining room. The brush of the trees allowed enough space to see them settling in for dinner. They'd have to look very closely to see me. A third child, a girl, emerged from upstairs. She was a teenager, a cell phone in her hand. She ripped the headphones out of her ears and took her place at the table, her hands expressing emotions almost I could feel from a distance.

A pang of guilt filled my chest for a solid five seconds, but the feeling was fleeting. They were so innocent, so *normal.*

Swinging for about ten minutes made me feel childish and absentminded. I must have looked utterly ridiculous, but I couldn't care less. I didn't know the people in that town, nor would I ever see them again.

Finally, the mother sat and the family grasped each other's hands, slightly bowing their heads thanking the Lord for their meals. My window of opportunity was gently opening. Slowly, I inched down off the swing, gathered my belongings and made my way to the back of their two story colonial. Birds chirped, but no other sign of life spewed about.

The window to their basement was easier to spot than I anticipated. I assumed there'd be climbing and hustling involved, but no. Nearly walking right past it, I crouched down and peered in. The job was almost done for me. Approaching the window, I noticed it was unlatched. I slightly pushed it open, but did not enter the home yet.

Entering the home would be a task for the morning when all the children were in school and Mom and Dad were at work, assuming those would be the roles they fulfilled. Thus far, they've done a flawless job of living up to their stereotypes.

Then, I had to continue waiting. Eyeing my options, I noticed a very well-built tree house in the neighbor's yard. It'd have to be cozy enough for the night. No cars were in their driveway, lights out all round, naturally my safest bet. Even if the family came home, what were the odds of them climbing into their tree house after dinner?

Still, it would be hard for me to get some sleep up there alone. The thought of being on someone else's property, the inkling of guilt and the off chance I was caught trespassing weighed heavily on my conscious. Then again, what other options did I have?

It started to drizzle again, but otherwise was a perfect night. Simply opening the gate latch to the next house was a bit of a struggle, but I managed after tampering with the lock I couldn't see from the other side. I began to make my way to the tree house when a little ankle biter barked his way to my feet.

Dammit.

For such a tiny dog, it sure could let out a cry for help. At that point, I was stressed because I wasn't certain that the family who resided there wasn't home, and I knew the house I just came from was busting at the seams with people.

158

Sprinting was all I could think of. When people panic, they run. When things get hard, they run. I ran, and I didn't stop, panicked at the situation I had put myself in. Intense and suspenseful music played out in my mind like it would if this were a movie and I its leading lady.

I didn't even remember climbing the ladder to the top of the tree house, all I knew was, I avoided the ankle biter. I was safe, no people surrounded the area. I eyed him from above as he from barked below, unable to make his way up the narrow ladder. My immature smirk let him know the battle was won.

There was a blanket folded neatly in the tree house that appeared unused, almost as if waiting for me. There was also a small bookshelf in the corner with a bug cage, all full of dead caterpillars. A magnifying glass, a torn up map of the world and some marbles in a Mason jar sat beside it.

The place reeked of neglect and I thrived on that notion. Cozying up under the blanket, I was thankful more than anything else. I had a montage of superhero collectibles to keep me company.

I never believed in luck, it was the last thing I believed in. It was a stupid concept, but as I drifted off to sleep, I dreamt sweet dreams of how lucky my circumstance had become.

For when I woke up from reclaiming my beauty sleep, I had a house to rob.

PHOEBE

"I had a really nice time, thank you," I concluded as we got back to our houses. I had never been on a date where his driveway was practically mine.

"I enjoyed myself as well."

He slid his arm in mine, sensing I was unsteady walking in heels, which I was. They were foreign to me and I appreciated his gesture and stability.

We sat on the porch and talked for some time longer. I don't think I talked to anyone ever as much as I'd talked to Cliff the past few days. I was not shy by any means, but he liked to have meaningful conversation. I could keep up because I spent many nights mediating debates between my father and grandmother about politics, religion and how to raise children. I would be an open book, he just had to ask the right questions.

"Phoebe," he said all nervously as we rocked back and forth on the front porch swing.

"Yes?"

"Will you be my girlfriend?"

Butterflies fluttered wildly in my gut.

I smiled and nodded. It was unexpected, but I like how old school he was by asking what I had assumed was implied.

"So is that a yes?"

"It is."

Then, he asked one right question.

SAGE

I had the kind of sleep you wake up from when you haven't an alarm set for the first night in weeks. I woke up naturally, and with the sun. A burly man let out the ankle biter from below. I was confident I could outrun him, despite how tired my legs were. I was also confident in the tree house I planned on sleeping in. He seemed like the type who built it sturdy with his own two hands.

Not sure of when he got home, I was arranging the cast of characters involved in this scenario as evenly as possible. I had never planned something as elaborate and sneaky, but I liked the game it allowed me to play. It was good variety.

All I had to do was time it out precisely, which I knew was easier said than done. I had two families I was working between; the family of five gathered around the dinner table would be the trickiest, and also the most crucial. It was their house I had propped the window open and planned to sneak through. The other family, who remained but a mystery, just provided shelter. Plus, I needed to get a move on, so I could hit my goal mileage for the day, which was sixteen. I wanted to finish the journey by the end of the month. That'd be one month shorter than Max's time out here sixteen years ago.

I'd always been the type to get things done efficiently, and he'd always been the lingerer. I used to get ready in all of twenty minutes, but he liked to take his time, filling what little time we had with menial tasks that could easily have been put off; but people are wired differently, I suppose. We all do things on our own time.

The burly man's wife walked out not ten minutes later in a pencil skirt. She was off to work, phew. One down, and from what I knew, six more to go. Burley man was spotted inside brushing his teeth from the top window. I needed binoculars for all this unexpected investigative work.

The garage door closed as her car emerged from the drive. About the same time, I spotted Dad from the house next door. He sprinted down the driveway after the minivan pulling out nearly simultaneous to their neighbor, a brown paper bag in hand. He was wearing a button down and a tie draped around his neck, but was not committed to the collar quite yet.

Mom rolled the window down and looked sympathetically at Dad, who passed her the brown paper bag. She tossed it to someone in the backseat. Were there one or two or even three kids in the car? I could not tell. The one in the passenger seat was for sure the teenage girl (probably mortified her mother had to drop her off at school), and from what I assumed, the other two little ones were in the backseat, one having forgotten their lunch. Assuming was never a safe assumption in that type of situation, I assumed.

My head was on a swivel. Attentiveness was key. I could not miss a motion from anyone or the plan would be all for naught, and although I hadn't left the place I was perched, I felt I had already come too far.

I waited what seemed like an eternity, but in reality was just thirteen additional minutes. In that time, I saw that burley man had retreated from the driveway wearing workout clothes with a matched gym bag in hand. If he was off to the gym, I'd only have about one hour to escape from his backyard, which was plenty of time as long as my other family cooperated and left accordingly as well. I had yet to spot a child in burley man's clan, so I wondered why the outfitted tree house stood so furnished and fun.

It was really just a matter of Dad from the other house. Once he finally emerged at the close of that thirteen minutes, with none other than one of the smaller children, I was ready to move. Perhaps an orthodontist appointment before school or something similar took place, but I had affirmed my assumption. Two children left with Mom, and one with Dad. All people I knew of had left the premises and I was on the prowl.

I relaxed as I made my way down the ladder. Although there were other neighbors in the neighborhood, I was tucked back enough in the wooded area of the yard that I was out of their line of vision.

Climbing through the window was when the nerves kicked in. I had successfully broken and entered with no external damage to the house. I was feeling reenergized from the night's sleep I had received, the best gift on a journey like mine.

I was in a very well furnished basement complete with a dartboard, full bar and an oversized ping pong table. You could tell the house was built on love, luxury, and credit card debt.

163

Making my way to the kitchen was my intention, though. It was harder than it seemed in a house foreign to me. I tried two doors before I found the one that hid the set of steps. I snuck up them until I realized I was in fact alone in the kitchen. I opened my pack and loaded it with canned peaches, granola bars, sticks of cheese, and helped myself to giant glass of sweet tea while I was at it. It tasted homemade, all the better. Boldly, I sat down at their kitchen counter and enjoyed the sweet moment.

I then made my way to Mom and Dad's room. It was never my intention to steal clothes. They seemed like hardworking people with three children. I could not take advantage or my conscience would kick in, but I was already there and so far felt little to no remorse.

Good thing I'd been walking all this way or I don't think I'd fit into Mom's size 2 yoga pant.

I took a pair of Lululemon athletic pants, two T-shirts that looked like they belonged to the teenager and a pair of socks that were still in the packaging at the top of a laundry pile.

A full length mirror stood about nine feet from the floor. I scaled my body, giving myself the twice over. Making my way to the pile of jewelry that shimmered on a nearby armoire, I considered taking some of that too. A real thief would. I decided against it only because I was taking things I thought I needed, not things I wanted. It was still nice to slide my hands across the crystals, holding every other piece up as if to try it on.

I spritzed Chanel No. 5 on my left wrist and met it

pridefully to my right in perfect unison. The scent was out of date, but that's what motherhood was, I assumed.

Feeling more glamorous already, I made my way out of the room. Just down the hall, I passed a bright pink room with the letters A-N-N-A hung over a bunk bed, pictures of kittens posted to a bulletin board in the corner of the room and a messy dollhouse had been put on pause as dolls laid helplessly all over the floor.

Beginning to make my way back to the kitchen, I was stopped dead in my tracks. A child's voice, and Dad. They were downstairs, back so soon!

I scurried back up the stairs after being at least halfway down, and made my way under the king-sized bed of the master bedroom, my pack crawling in behind me, triple checking that no strap snuck out from under the bed skirt. The room was most familiar to me, however, I never considered this scenario. There never was a plan B here. This *was* worst case scenario.

I'd have to lay there until they left again. And what if they never left? One million and two thoughts crossed my mind. What if he's a stay-at-home dad? What if they have family dinner and then Mom and Dad come back up to bed? What would I do or say if they discover me? I didn't know the house well enough to form an escape route. There was no way out.

Not possible, I convinced myself. It had to be but 8:30a.m. The day was young, there would be an option. I picked at the calluses on my hands to calm myself and for lack of anything else to be entertained by. I must escape my own mind yet somehow remain rational.

I held my breath as Dad entered the room, the child storming in behind him.

"And then they found the dog they had been missing because the poster's Nicole made helped. She must have made, like, a hundred gazillion of them and put them up around town. I saw one at our park. It's sad that their dog went missing, but they must be happy to have it back safe and sound," the little girl's voice said.

"They got very lucky," Dad said, "Come here, let me put your socks on."

The little girl hopped on the bed. The slightest bulge in the mattress appeared as Dad sat down beside her.

"Are you going to be a good girl in school today?" he asked her all condescendingly.

"I told Mom I would be!" she responded giddily.

"No more bad reports. And *no more* sitting next to Miranda at lunch. She gets you in trouble."

"Yeah, yeah, yeah, I know."

"Got your late note?"

"In my backpack."

"Don't forget to give it to your teacher. First thing you do."

"Got it."

She sprinted out of the room, and Dad lingered for a couple seconds longer before following her out. I hadn't taken a breath the whole time, hoping and praying they weren't the types to check for monsters under the bed when they left.

I laid under that mattress reminiscent of days my own father would tie my shoes and look out for me. I knew as I approached Virginia I'd need to look up his old friend, Uncle Val. He served two tours in the U.S. Army and was his dearest friend from that time in his life. I somehow started calling him Uncle Val, although he wasn't biologically linked at all. I intentionally threw a pit stop into my course because I know he'd help replenish my stash, happy to see me after all these years.

Uncle Val always had the best war stories of my father. When I missed him I like to give him a call, but it had been years since that actually happened, unfortunately. Although my father was the workaholic type, he had reason to be. Overall, he was a good man and the times with him were among my most cherished.

"It always saddened me you spent a majority of your time with that mother of yours," Uncle Val would say, and I had to agree.

I would go to my father's house every first weekend of the month up until his death, a trying time for us all.

I was brought back to reality when I heard the door slam. Dad and Anna were gone. Waiting three more minutes to make sure I didn't hear a sound, I made my way back to the open window. I didn't look back, I didn't grab anything else.

My first breaking and entering experience had been a success, although barely. Looking back at the house from the sidewalk, I waved and mouthed 'thanks' in the general direction, just because it eased my conscious.

I was just glad I didn't have to deal with that Golden Retriever, but the family of five no trouble at all.

PHOEBE

"So what? Do we not get to talk about this? Do we not get to talk at all? I mean, come on, what did I do?"

"Nothing, you literally did nothing, and that's probably the biggest problem."

"So you just leave me without telling me for another guy? A guy you barely even know! How could you even trust him? You're being irrational, Phoebe, and you know it."

I hated when Colin tried to make himself seem like the good guy when he clearly was not.

Plus, he knew I didn't like to make drama where drama wasn't due. I wasn't every other girl in our grade.

"It's not really up to you, you know," was all I could think to say. I wasn't too great with defense mechanism.

"You are…just…so…ugh!" Too distraught to even formulate a full sentence, he marched off down the hall, pounding a fist into a random locker on his way.

"I'm so done with you, Phoebe Harper!" he bellowed as he reached the end of the hallway. It was a spectacle that had a growing audience with each mortifying breath I took.

"What was that about?" Cliff was at my locker, sneaking up quietly.

I turned to him, every ounce of love in his bright eyes picked up the slack for the embarrassment in mine. Sometimes I looked at him and forgot just how strikingly beautiful he was. In that moment, it had never been more clear I had made the right choice in letting someone go and another in.

"Just hold my hand and tell me it'll be okay," I responded.

Cliff interlocked his fingers in mine, smiled, and said, "You are beautiful, Phoebe Harper. Don't you forget that."

We took off in the opposite direction of Colin. Girls snickered in gossipy cliques and guys eyed me, too, but I didn't care who stared because I was over caring about what they thought anymore.

SAGE

I was at mile seven for the day when I passed an outlet mall. Since I had replenished some of my stash from my breaking-and-entering saga, I discarded some rain sodden outfits that weighed me down. The miles were encroaching in on me, and I soon would be at Max's location. Every time I really thought about it, I simultaneously felt nauseous at the idea of seeing him after all these years, but I fought through, having no other option.

I had come entirely too far to turn around. Entirely.

Luckily, I hadn't spent nearly as much money as I thought I would at that point. I needed to buy a nice outfit I could wear when I saw him for the first time. Something that signified I'd been traveling, but also something that would still catch his eye.

I shopped for a bit because it was nice to experience some normalcy. My current outfit made me standout some, but not much. There were enough mothers there pulling off the yoga panted, messy bun, "I just dropped my child off at school, so I deserve a Starbucks" look, that I blended in just fine.

I splurged on a pair of new shoes. Trying to be savvy with my money, there were just some comfort objects you'd be willing to pay any amount of money for when you've been out on the road as long as I. They were a pair of olive green running shoes and I paid exactly $107.98 for them. Very chic, yet also applicable for walking. Fresh looking was key, no matter how many days without an actual shower the truth warr- anted. I tossed my old shoes with no regrets, feeling bad my shopping spree followed my thievery, but what was done had been done.

I used to hoard things. Not in the repulsive and overbearing way they made documentaries about, but I'd hang onto things I didn't want to forget. In a box under my childhood twin bed, I had old receipts, gum wrappers, certain pencils. Some things I forgot what meaning they ever held, but wouldn't toss them for the world, because at one point, it had significance to my life. Now, I knew that every little gum wrapper or extra receipt was just a small piece of a forming mound I must conquer. I couldn't have excess baggage of any kind along for the ride. Typically, the old Sage would hang on to those shoes, admirably seeing the dedication and miles they trailed on pursuit, and although it should have phased me that they were gone, I was not the least bit remorseful, gradually becoming better with letting things go.

As with any conclusion trip to the outlets, and for the sake of fulfilling a role I was quite good at playing, I had to grab a Starbucks and was on my merry way.

PHOEBE

Colin had avoided me for an entire week. I didn't mind, and neither did the other girls in the grade. Colin was free for their taking now.

I left my class and began to walk down the halls. It felt they were narrowing in on me as piercing stares came from all directions. Why all eyes were on me, had me worried. Cliff typically met me at my locker so we could walk to lunch together, hand-in-hand all cutesy. Maybe he could bring some clarity to what was happening. When I saw him progressing towards me hands flying in the air tragically, I was on the defensive.

"Don't freak out, you cannot freak out," he told me.

"What're you talking about?"

I proceeded to my locker and it was there the problem was revealed to me. I knew the source, the culprit. It was Colin and his gang. Despite his famous last words to me "*I'm so done with you, Phoebe Harper!*" he sure did linger around. Profanities and other obscure innuendos were etched and carved into the side of my locker. It was difficult to tell what anything said, rather it was a jumbled mess.

I breathed in, I breathed out.

"It's out of your control, you know. At this point, there is nothing you can do about it except consult the authorities," Cliff kept talking but I couldn't hear him, "They want to get a rise out of you."

"Cliff, it's not some competition. This isn't a war. I know what it takes to be the bigger person. We're going to lunch now," I told him because ultimately he was right, what's done was done.

"Phoebe Harper. I'd like to see you in my office. NOW."

Principal Williams was standing behind me. He said "now" with some dragged on emphasis, like I didn't perhaps know how to spell the three letter word and he was sounding it out for me. *Noooooow.*

I was starving so I pulled the half sleeve of crackers out of my lunch and crunched along the way to the Principal's Office, the place in middle school we'd all be afraid to go, but in high school the place we'd hope would get us our fifteen minutes of fame. From the lunch room I already saw Colin and his posse of meatheads glaring me down because they thought they won a war I never agreed to fight.

SAGE

It was getting old, the journey and all of its parts. Even Max's letters weren't that riveting anymore. It wasn't that I was losing interest in them, it was that he was tired and frail when writing them that they began to look like notes a friend would pass from an opposite desk in grade school. They were shorthand, had little advice and his storytelling skills were lacking. And I swore if he told me not to worry about him one more time...did he not know me well enough to know I would do that regardless?

My new shoes were great, so that was at least working in my favor.

Only two miles left and I'd be at Uncle Val's home on the Virginia border. It had been a long ten days leading up to that point since waking up in the tree house. I slept under a bridge or two, bargained with a woman over some money in exchange for her coat and ate a meal of leftovers someone gave me out of pity as they left a fancy restaurant. The idea of a home gave me hope and a sense of comfort. Although I didn't plan on staying too long, it was familiar to me and I liked that.

"Sage, get all your things together, we're going on a road trip," I could hear my father's voice saying to me, now a distant memory. Even though I only ever got one weekend of the month to spend with him, I never minded sharing it with Uncle Val too. The two of them together made my smiles much wider.

We had our father-daughter alone time on the car rides anyway. New York City to the Virginia border was just long enough of a trip for us to stop and grab a Happy Meal and sing along to whatever country songs were popular at the time, his favorite.

Uncle Val would be there to meet us with outstretched arms, not ones that hugged though, ones that carried a huge turkey through the kitchen to the outside fryer. I definitely ate good with those men, that's for sure.

Uncle Val never married, and my father would spend so much time alone himself that they often thought and talked about living together. It made sense, and although never said directly, I knew I was the reason my father would never move out to Virginia on a whim. Few and far between as they were, even he looked forward to our weekends together. We'd often kayak, hike, and he taught me the ramifications of hunting; the ins and outs of all outdoor activities.

Then I'd return to my mother's house and all those memories seemed to fade away.

She'd act all flustered and say, "You smell like fire. Don't be bringing that scent into this home. It'll get my allergies going," as she'd light a hypocritical cigarette, letting it dangle freely from her fingers as if taking control of the room.

I never knew she had allergies, but with all the dirt and grime encrusted into every nook and cranny of her unkempt home, I never felt she had the right to speak. I obeyed anyway. I'd scurry upstairs to shower and wash off whatever remnants of fun and good memories the weekend provided.

It was strange walking the streets of Uncle Val's neighborhood. The numerous childhood memories I had there were unreal. I had my first kiss with an acne covered bully in a game of truth or dare in the basement of the house adjacent.

My worst nightmare happened soon after stepping foot on Uncle Val's driveway. A middle aged man not much older than myself was loading or unloading (I couldn't tell) boxes in the garage. He seemed to be doing a whole lot of shuffling around and it seemed to be stressing him out in the process.

Ergh. He grunted, all the while, having no idea I was standing there.

"Excuse me?" cracked my hoarse voice.

He jumped a mile. If only it were that easy...

"May I help you?" he said, but not in a rude way.

"I'm looking for Val, is he here?"

"So you haven't heard?"

"Heard what? Probably not."

"Val recently passed. It was somewhat unexpected. Were you close with him?" He wiped sweat from his brow but never broke eye contact as he revealed the news.

"Were you?" I was suddenly offended, of course *I* was close with him, who even are *you*?

"Not as close as I probably should have been."

"But you knew him?"

"He was my father."

"Val didn't have a son."

"None that he probably talked about, but he had two. Myself and my twin brother, Jeremy," he said, wiping his hands on a rag before extending a hand to shake in my direction. "I'm Warner."

"Sage."

I extended a hand to meet his, all at once noticing Val in every other one of Warner's features. Warner was much more fit than Val had ever been, even in his Army days, from the pictures I'd seen, at least. The more I looked at his face, I realized he was actually very attractive. He was tall and lean. He didn't even lose points for having a farmer's tan because it suited him so well. He had dark hair and wide blue eyes, just like Val.

I studied him quizzically as he did the same to me.

"Would you like to come in?" I knew what question was coming next, and then he said it, as if on cue, "Did you walk here?"

"Not the final destination in mind, but, yes, I am on foot."

"I was just about to put some skewers on the grill. I've had them marinating in this sauce I concocted all day. Just something new I'm trying out. You look like you could use some and I made plenty."

How could I turn down an offer that tempting? Besides, I had lots of questions for him.

And just like that the vicious cycle began again, and I was following a man I had just met across the foyer of a home. This time though, it was different and all too familiar.

PHOEBE

"I really don't know their endgame, Principal Williams," I stated my case and claimed my innocence to no avail.

"I'm worried about you Phoebe. Your grades have dropped since starting high school, you quit volunteering, have dropped your extracurricular activities, and now you're involved in the biggest campus crime we've had all year."

"It's just vandalism," I said, because that's what it was. Things are only as bad or as good as what you compare them against, and at the end of the day, the defaced locker could be replaced.

"See, Phoebe, this is the exact attitude I'm talking about," Principal Williams said expectantly, "Is everything all right at home?"

"Everything's just peachy."

I grabbed a lollipop from the ceramic bowl on his table to suck on as he ranted.

"I don't see what's holding me back from giving you two weeks detention."

"Two weeks? That seems entirely too lofty," yet I was surprisingly calm. I'd never been to detention, but it was not the end of the world. Even yet, two weeks was a greater chunk of time than I would have expected, even from the irrational and power-hungry Principal Williams.

"Let's make it one."

"For falling victim of others bad decisions?"

"There must have been some instigation, Phoebe. I'm not buying the perfect angel card you're trying to play."

I took a vow of silence because I knew people and oftentimes silence was the deadliest weapon. Not enough people know how to use their silence to their advantage, but it was something I'd been practicing, and I could see it was working. Rather, I rolled my eyes with authority and saw myself out.

I was done there, anyways.

"One week then! Sending the pass to your homeroom..."

But by then he was just a voice in the distance.

I was in the middle of the lollipop, where the gum was. I took it out and stuck it on Principal Williams mailbox on my way out, because if I had a week's detention, I may as well earn it.

SAGE

"So tell me, how did you know my father?" I had to watch him cook the skewers, although he was right, most of them were already skewed and prepared. I just had a strange phobia about other people's baked goods. If I didn't watch them bake it, then their grubby fingers might dip themselves in the saucy marinade between flips and that just didn't sit well with me.

Assuming I was intimidating him with my gaze, I looked away, taking delicate sips of the ice water he provided me in a Pittsburgh Steelers beer mug, Val always a big fan. There were signs of him everywhere I just couldn't maintain focus.

"He was a friend of my father's. I used to come down on weekend trips and hangout with the two of them quite often actually. I practically grew up with the neighborhood kids and spent many nights in this very house."

"That's more than I can say."

"Like I said, Val never did mention he had a son." Was it rude of me to rehash the fact? Rub salt in old wounds...?

"That doesn't surprise me in the least. I'm sure he was a good guy, but left when I was very young for reasons I still don't know."

"That's awfully nice of you to come down here and sort through his things anyway." The house hadn't changed one bit. Val and all his "things." He called it a hobby, but I called it clutter. Warner had over half the house cleared out already. For a one man job, it was certainly impressing.

"Someone had to do it. If my mother did, all his things would be burned out on the sidewalk, so I looked at it from that perspective and I took it upon myself. It's doing everyone a favor."

"Are you getting anything out of it?"

"Not as much as I'm sure you're getting out of your little venture. Tell me about it."

Before I could have controlled it, the tears came. I didn't know why I started crying, but they came strong, like little floods from my weakening eyelids.

Uncontrollably too. I took my stance from propped up against the edge of the kitchen counter to my hands catching the stool below, hoping it'd provide me some sort of stability from the nausea I was experiencing between heaving sobs.

Warner didn't say anything but I noticed he walked to the outdoor fireplace to start it, signaling me to follow. My father, Uncle Val and I used to sit around it a similar fashion, me roasting marshmallows, them drinking scotch.

"Come sit with me."

I joined him with no hesitation. He wrapped a plaid blanket around me. It was the first night I had let myself admit openly and to someone else that I was not as strong as I led on. He made me feel so comforted there. I just met the man, yet not only did I feel like I'd known him forever, I trusted him.

Starting from the very beginning, I talked for a total of thirty minutes before I asked him anything about himself, but he let me talk, nodding his head appropriately, letting me know he was tuned in.

He said he did construction, a job I figured he'd hold because he was built for hard work. He lived just forty-five minutes west and although he always had good intentions of meeting his father, he could never build the courage to do so.

"The way I saw it was if he never wanted me, what would vying for his attention do? I didn't need him then either," he explained, my turn to nod.

"Touché," I didn't necessarily agree with his logic, but I understood it.

Everything about being there was reminiscent and obscure. Combine that with being weak, sick and tired, the tears just keep flowing.

"I promise I'm not always this emotional," I had to preface.

"I understand."

Although he didn't say much in response to my stories or reveal as much about himself as I had, I knew he did understand. He seemed like Val in that way.

"Will you keep talking until I fall asleep?" I asked him blatantly, his invitation to stay coming amidst him wiping my large tears away.

My eyelids were growing increasingly heavy, like little weights were suddenly attached to them. I yawned twice in a row and realized I needed sleep.

"I packed up the bed frames and all earlier today, but I have the mattresses up on the floor. I planned on staying over tonight. You can go claim the one in the guest room, unless of course there is a room you're accustomed to staying in. Wherever you're comfortable, really. You definitely deserve it." A wiry smile flashed across his face as he stood up. He extended both of his hands toward me, still wrapped in a blanket on the ground, the fire dwindling down.

"Come with me," It was more of a command than a request, but I abided, grabbing his extended hands to assist in lifting me up.

It was too convenient being in a place that was so familiar. Now I knew what it meant when they say home is where the heart is. The night with Warner, my heart was wholly there, and I was tempted to never leave it behind.

I cried all night in his arms while talking about drywall, and it was the best night I'd had in a really long time.

PHOEBE

Cliff was waiting outside the door with a poster that read "Freedom for Phoebe" in his chicken scratch handwriting that Friday evening as I served the last of my detention sentence. Blushing with embarrassment, I clawed my hand down the center of the poster, nearly tearing it in two. Cliff just laughed maliciously at his little success.

"Hey, I worked hard on that," he said through laughter.

"Yeah, I appreciate it...just put it away and let's go eat."

"Where to tonight, my lady?"

Although he was joking, I still got flushed when he called me his lady.

"Something through the drive thru, I need to get home and finish this project. It's due Monday and I'm so close to finishing it."

"Well, you certainly don't seem like the girl I thought I knew. What did they do to you in there?"

"Quit it," I nudged him playfully, "I can be sophisticated too..." I continued half-jokingly.

"Yeah, right…"

It shouldn't have offended me that he disagreed but in some way, it kind of did. I wanted him to think highly of me, of course.

Out of the corner of my eye, I saw Colin propped up against his too expensive car when we open the double doors to exit the school, as if waiting for someone. Was it *us?*

"Phoebe and Clint," he said as we approached.

"It's Cliff," I retorted for reasons I was didn't know, simply wasting breath.

"Whatever," he didn't seem to mind, "where you two lovebirds off to?"

"Back off, Colin," why was I even responding at that point? Talking to Colin was like feeding fuel to a

182

fire. He thrived on just a simple reaction, awaiting to ignite.

"You happy now Phoebe? Now that you have a new man..." Colin didn't finish his sentence, distracted by Cliff's body hurling in the air towards him rapidly and fluidly. Colin glared at me before contact was made. Before I could say anything in my defense, Cliff was already doing it for me. He had pounced in the air, his backpack soaring a good five feet away from where we were standing to complete the act. He had rolled Colin off the edge of the hood and was mounted on top of him on the cold, hard cement.

He wasn't punching him though. He was controlled and strong. With Colin in his grasp he stated, "She said back off."

"What're you going to do about it pretty boy?" Colin asked through a roaring laugh before wiggling a hand free and cleanly punching Cliff across the face. It was then when Cliff didn't hold back. He punched right back, repeatedly, still maintaining that steady control.

I could not take the sight any longer. It got increasingly more violent as the fight progressed. I'd never seen either of them fight, and I honestly didn't think they had it in them, so I couldn't be more uncomfortable as an onlooker.

Out of instinct, out of sorrow, or out of defense, I climbed on Colin's back, who had then managed to lay Cliff face down on the pavement. He always did watch too much wrestling.

Where was everybody at this time? Was *no one* around to watch this? Where were the ever-present authorities, a teacher, anyone...?

Colin, surprised and caught off guard by me on top of him, whipped around quickly. I flew off his back, hitting the ground forcefully, by face scraping against the concrete as I slid.

I saw the rage in Colin's eyes start to fade when he realized what he'd done. My nose dripped beads of blood, or maybe it was my lip. I was too dizzy to tell.

Cliff stumbled up, swooped me up in his arms, spit in Colin's general direction without hitting him with his bloody saliva, and carried me to my car. Colin knew he was wrong and retreated. He even managed an apology aimed at me but I was still too baffled to take it into consideration. Plus, he had a list of things to apologize for, I was unclear as to which he was referring to.

Resting me on the backseat, Cliff stroked my hair. Catching a glimpse of myself in the rearview mirror made my stomach churn, although Cliff looked far worse, taking the brunt of the beating. It was reactionary on Colin's part, who had a much stockier build than both myself and Cliff put together. Doubled with the adrenaline pumping through his veins, there was no stopping him.

"This is all going to be all right," Cliff muscled out, "we just need time to regroup. We'll go to my house and clean up."

When I didn't respond for a while, Cliff turned to me and said, "Are you okay? I guess I should have asked that before anything else, huh?"

He smiled through a fat lip. He dabbed my face softly with the end of his shirt before relaxing into the backseat alongside me. I was more in shock than anything else.

"I think I need to be asking you that."

"Nah, I won that fight," Cliff said all masculine and proud, "I'm sorry it had to come to that."

I couldn't help but blush. "It's okay. Like you said, it's *all* going to be okay."

SAGE

Sleeping on old mattresses on the floor gave me that new home vibe. In that moment, it wasn't the first time I missed my home. I had felt feelings of defeat on my journey in the past, but never that strongly. I told Warner everything. He was not in the bed with me when I woke up and there was no sign that he slept there, but I did remember him rocking me to sleep as I wept in his arms.

We live in a world of oversharing. Technology has made us that way, perhaps. It'd been a long while since I'd been behind a computer, whereas I used to sit for eight hours (on a good day) staring at the screen in front of me, sending one message after the next, hoping to gain some sort of reprieve from the norm. Although I'd dread returning back to work, because often you need a vacation from your vacation, it was nice to sit behind a computer for the first time in months. I logged in, surprised I had more unread emails than I had money in my savings account. Half would be trash, but it was relieving to log out with no responsibility of needing to

185

know and needing to do. Instead of investigating the web any further, determining I'd seen enough, I made my way downstairs to find Warner chucking logs into the fireplace. He rested his arm on the mantel before catching glimpse of me. I had yet to find an imperfection in that man.

"Morning," he said scratchily.

"How long have you been awake?" I was standing in an oversized T-shirt and underwear with a blanket sprawled around me while he was dressed from head to toe in plaid and jeans. Very mountainesque.

For a minute the crackling fire was all that sounded, the realization that we were still strangers settling in, yet I didn't mind.

"I made breakfast. You can't be a vegetarian hanging around me."

Of course he had time to make a hearty breakfast in addition.

"God no," although the deliverance on his line made me reconsider for a moment.

I followed the smell of bacon omelets all the way to the kitchen.

"What time you taking off today?" he asked seeming genuinely concerned, as if no time was late enough.

"Are you kicking me out?"

"Quite the contrary. I was going to extend the invite and ask you to help sort through some things today. I should be done and on my way soon, but there are some things that might be beneficial to you. I'd hate for you to miss out. The house will be put on the market by the end of the week, I assume. Hopefully it'll sell quickly, because I can't miss much more work."

"I'll help you sort through some things," I said more to the bacon I was biting into than looking at him.

"You don't have thirty some miles waiting for you?"

"Oh I do, don't get me wrong. Way more than thirty, but they'll get done one day later than expected now and it'll be worth it," I smiled, reading the genuine guilt that consumed his facial features as if he shouldn't have asked, "I don't really have an agenda to be honest."

"There's one box you might particularly be interested in labeled Craig Riley."

My father.

All I could do was smile. I started woofing down my breakfast without a care in the world.

"I'd like that," I said remorsefully, "and sorry for all the tears last night, by the way. I appreciate you being so... consoling."

"I grew up with a lot of stepsisters. I'm used to it," he stood to walk to the counter, "Mimosa?"

A cleared plate in hand, "I'd love nothing more."

He passed me a mimosa in a beer mug, claiming half the kitchen supplies had been packed already. I was impressed by what he made work with what he had around there, and could only hope that one day when all of this was over, that every Sunday morning would feel this way; this jovial, this relaxed. Maybe not with him, but with Max.

Cheers.

***

We reminisced well into the day. One thing after the next. Every new piece that got pulled out of my father's storage box chilled me to the core. It'd been so long since I'd even seen a picture of him; it was almost frightening.

Surprisingly there were no more tears. I shed enough to last a lifetime the night before, I suppose.

I told Warner the stories behind the photographs, as much as I knew anyway. Most of them were taken before my time. He knew so little about his father, and my Uncle Val, it was disheartening.

Looking at the photo and then up at Warner, it was a spitting image, no denying that. He had his mannerisms too, and it was refreshing. He stood to pose the way his father was in the picture, which turned into him posing goofily several different ways as I cheered him on. I hadn't laughed with a friend in a while, so I let him indulge me.

"It's a shame you're selling the house," I stroked my hand along the banister, making my way down back to the living room after escaping upstairs to freshen up. We had photographs spread out all over the floor, no particular order about them.

"What else would I do with it?"

"Live in it, of course," I was appalled he'd give it away so easily, "If you only knew the time and energy your father committed to this house. It was his pride and joy. That's why we'd always visit him rather than he coming to us. There was always something new to see here, or some project he was too glued to, that he couldn't leave. Not till it was done and everything complete would we be able to make our way over. He was such a perfectionist."

I could see the range of emotions in Warner's face as I talked about his father in the past tense.

"What happened in the end? Did he pass, you know, peacefully?" I had never been good at dealing with death, not sure anyone ever is, but it was different for me. My father's death set the tone and since then, I'd dealt awkwardly and unbearably.

I had to know about what happened to Uncle Val though. It was beginning to eat at me. For as much as Warner and I talked, we had been dancing around the blatantly obvious fact that brought us together.

"Just his time to go. I imagined he was very much at peace when it happened. He was sleeping from what I heard. Just never woke up..." His voice trailed off, rightfully so.

"Good, good. That's reassuring to hear," I saw the look in his eyes shift from me to his hands, where he fidgeted with an imaginary hangnail. I said, "I'm sorry. I shouldn't be saying all this. Obviously you have a life elsewhere, you don't need to keep the house," I was rambling because I felt his objective was tainted and I had to do damage control.

"I thought about it," he interjected, "Staying here, I mean. It'd be logical in a sense. Plus, all the history. Although I never knew my father, he built this house with his bare hands and there is something to be said about that. He couldn't have been all that bad, you speak so highly of him, and you seem to have it all together."

"Can I ask you a question that's kind of personal?"

"You can ask it, but I'm not sure I'll answer it," he snickered.

"Would you wait for a girl you once loved?"

"Explain..."

"How long would you wait for someone you loved without giving up on them. Say they went off the deep end and had to reevaluate life through their own self revelations. Say it was really bad, and she totally screwed you over, but deep down she knew you couldn't stay mad at her for too long because you really loved her. How long would you wait for her to heal?"

"I think it totally depends on the person and circumstance. A ton of factors go into that scenario you just described." He let an unsure laugh escape from under his breath as he took a swig from the beer bottle he grasped, totally ambiguous.

"But what if it's been ten years or more. Would you wait that long?"

"Personally, I'd probably move on...but I'd hate to think this story's about you."

"It's entirely about me," I said, putting my vulnerability aside.

"Please don't tell me you're walking all this way for a guy."

"Please don't judge me when I tell you that I am."

I felt outlandish and bashful, having never admitted it aloud.

Maybe it was a stupid idea after all…

PHOEBE

We picked up a stuffed crust pizza on the way back to Cliff's, blotting off some blood from our face with the given napkins before heading inside, where we'd blot the grease off the pizza. Luckily, his mother was helping his little sister with her homework, so she just shouted out a quick hello by throwing up a wave, not even looking over her shoulder.

I pulled him into the bathroom to clean him up and he went along with it. He sat on the closed toilet lid and motioned to where he had a first aid kit. He didn't say anything but twitched here and there as I tenderly pushed on a sensitive area. Once cleared up, the damage didn't look as horrible.

"I'm so sorry this happened to you." I looked him square in the eye, noticing he may need a butterfly bandage over the hearty bruise on his left one.

"It wasn't your fault," he was looking at me too, never breaking gaze. I continued readily aiding his needs in attempt to heal him, but before I knew it, Cliff had stood up, backed me up against the wall and had managed to kiss me with every ounce of energy left in that boy's body.

In his bathroom...with bloody gauze in the sink, how romantic...

But somehow it was. Somehow I was so consumed with this human being in a way I never thought possible.

191

He finally surrendered to his aching body, and muttered, "sorry," although the look in his eye was anything but apologetic.

We retreated to his room where we laid on the bed in each other's embrace before his stomach growled in interruption. I grabbed the pizza, which was cold by then, but Cliff claimed it was better that way as he grabbed the biggest slice.

***

The next week was full of inquiries from people in our classes. By then, word had spread quickly that Colin and the new kid had gotten into a fight over Phoebe Harper. Luckily, I had no sign of cuts and bruises on my end. Cliff and Colin both had some battle scars that fueled the rumors. People would walk by Cliff in the hallway, girls would throw their hands tightly to the mouths appalled when they passed as if they were monsters instead of immature boys. Others simply gave sad eyes, like any of that made it better.

The only one who made *me* actually feel better was Cliff.

We snuck out after the final bell and headed to the stadium, putting off parting ways for a while longer.

Empty, except for one corner where the baseball team was taking laps, we had the place to ourselves with the empty soda cans, marching band playbills, and cigarette butts.

"This is torture," Cliff said, "I hate having the school know that *Colin* did this to us."

We sat there for thirty minutes more, not bringing up Colin's name again. Cliff twiddled his thumbs aimlessly, obviously his mind and mine somewhere else.

"I love you, Phoebe," he said out of nowhere.

I was surprised and flushed.

"I mean it, I love everything about you," he leaned in and kissed my still lips, "I'm sorry if that's too much. I didn't mean to take it there. To frighten you. The last thing I want to do is scare you off."

"No...not at all," why couldn't I speak? "I...I love you too, Cliff."

He smiled that smile he always did, like he was up to something and everything, and maybe he was.

SAGE

"Let me come with you," Warner pleaded as we prepped our goodbyes, "to complete your journey. You'll need help out there."

"What? That's absurd!"

"Sage, I want to do it."

"I don't need your help," I said more defensively than I meant it, deep down I knew the additional company would ease the burden.

"Look, my estranged father just passed, I have a crappy job to return to, it's only getting colder outside and I need a sense of adventure. If that's not enough to

193

convince you, I'm not sure what will," he laughed throatily, persuading himself more than I. "Besides, what are the odds that we stumbled upon each other?"

"Don't give me this 'meant to be' nonsense," I laughed, knowing he didn't have to convince me any further, I was sold on the idea, but it was cute to watch him try.

"Hey, I'm just saying it could be fun."

"I don't think you can handle it."

"Give me three days. We'll do a trial run and see how it goes."

"Hmm okay...I can shake on that."

We shook hands to make it official. Somehow, it felt entirely too formal.

Three days didn't seem like a long time in theory, but when all you do is walk, it can become an eternity. He had a lot to learn.

I smiled and said, "You're trouble."

"Let me just get some things together and we'll be on our way," he was entirely too giddy for his own good and it was adorable.

He threw a change of clothes, two cans of soup, a toothbrush, and a comb in his bag before taking the soup back out, realizing there'd be nowhere to cook it.

Instead, he burrowed through one of the boxes in the garage and passed me a pair of gloves and a hat before finding some for himself.

The innocent process continued for about ten more minutes until he decided he had everything he needed. Time was not of the essence anymore, not when traveling in groups, or in our case, pairs.

"We're doing twenty miles today," I reminded him.

He was not good at hiding his shock, although he played it off well.

"Yeah, great," he said, "I'm ready for it, excited actually," The sad thing was, I could tell that he was actually genuinely looking forward to it. Being more than over it, it made me despise him. I wished I could face anything at that point in my life with similar energy.

He ran back inside, took a swig of cold coffee and returned with the biggest grin on his face. More bundled up than I was when I got there, we took off.

This just got a whole lot more interesting.

***

Warner fared a lot better than I anticipated he would on day one. He complained a total of four times and stopped to catch his breath only twice. His favorite word had become "regroup."

He was far less troublesome than I thought he'd be. We talked and laughed and wanted to cry even, but it was better together. It made me feel less psychotic when he was by my side feeling the same way, if not worse.

"I'm hungry," Warner said, making that his fifth complaint.

"I'm actually starving too now that you mention it."

He eyed a can't-miss-it type of billboard that read *Jo's Bed and Breakfast.* It was just four miles ahead.

We then eyed each other with a look that read "let's go," although neither of us wanted to waste our breath actually confirming it.

Moving along in silent agreement, we made a four mile trek through the cold. It was a lovely feeling to know a warm bed awaited you, though. Warner received a lot of inheritance money from his father, so traveling with him might present more financial luxuries to my benefit. It was comforting to know that even though I didn't know Uncle Val ever had children, he still looked after them by including them in his will. If he didn't exemplify the best character, at least he attempted to be decent.

Not a word was said that entire four miles. I snapped a lot of pictures, more than I'd ever need. As Warner posed discreetly here and there, remembering it had made me smile in the past.

Jo's was everything I expected it to be, almost to the point of a cliché. It was a gorgeous white building with columns, yet still possessed a homey feel, complete with red shutters on the windows, flowerpots draped over the ledge. It certainly made it feel like springtime rather than on the verge of winter.

Warner opened the door for me to lead the way to the front desk. A crackling fire was the first to greet us. Next was who I assumed to be Jo.

Low and behold, "Hello, welcome, I'm Jo," greeted the elderly woman, "Room for two?"

"Yes please," Warner spoke up. He was always in a good mood.

It was only 7p.m. but it appeared to be midnight outside. I was grateful it was a night I wouldn't have to sleep in the cold, damp weather of the outdoors. Although, I warned Warner not to get too comfortable with the bed-and-breakfast lifestyle. I was going to make him sleep outside one of these nights so he could know what I'd been enduring, that way someone—anyone—could commiserate with me. Plus, I seriously doubted that with Warner as extra baggage, others would be as likely to take me into their home and pity me, leaving us no other choice.

Jo ran Warner's debit card as he brushed his hands together hoping to generate warmth.

With the widest smile, she said, "You two make a beautiful couple."

Although she meant it as a compliment, a feeling of awkwardness enveloped immediately.

"She's a keeper, ain't she?" Warner smiled, playing along, throwing an arm over my tired body, the little weight he put on me feeling like a ton of bricks.

Jo came around the counter, key in hand, and led us to room 319 where there was one king-sized bed, the smell of small peonies in the air and a breakfast-in-bed menu tacked to the wall.

"This'll do just fine," Warner chimed.

"Darling!" Jo replied, "I'll be downstairs another hour or so should you need anything. Breakfast is served tomorrow from six to eleven, unless you opt for the breakfast-in-bed; the true experience," she tapped a knuckle solidly against the menu on the wall. "I think that covers it all. You folks have a good evening."

"We will, thank you," Warner said.

I was happy he took the reins on negotiating our room because I was too exhausted to care. I trusted the bed to catch my body as I let myself fall onto it. The mattress was hard and the floor struggled to hide stains, but it would suffice.

The first day back after a few days of rest was always the hardest groove to fall back into, but for the first time in a long time, I had a sense of ease. Jo never asked if we were wandering by foot, she didn't even seem to suspect it. She just treated us like another normal couple, although, we didn't look too rough after one day. Windblown if anything, but I was content with my life in that very moment, and sometimes that's all you can ask for.

***

He brushed his teeth religiously after meals in makeshift ways while we were out walking. It was just one of those little idiosyncrasies I had picked up about him. Despite his bizarre tendencies, for some reason I trusted him more than most people, and it was those same tendencies that made me like him only that much more.

As Warner and I crawled into bed that night, there was no awkwardness. Rather, he called in for some beef and broccoli with a side of lo mien, and had room service bring up a bottle of champagne, to "celebrate the completion of his first day."

Everything was going really well, I had to admit.

We stayed up later than we should have, talking and laughing until we fell asleep. I told him of stories of far-away lands I'd read as an editor, of times when I was a little girl, and of Max, because everything circled back to the journey whether I intended it to or not, especially after a few drinks made their way through my system.

With Warner in my life, I had been distracted. I had felt childish and carefree. The best thing to bring me back to reality, or likewise to seek escape in a fantasy, were always Max's letters. I mentioned that I needed to use the restroom and Warner just nodded, his lazy, tipsy eyes begging me not to go, even for just a second.

My heart melted a little bit as I walked to my belongings and shoved the next letter into my toiletry bag before making my way to the restroom.

It was as if I couldn't open it fast enough. My fingers were suddenly pudgier and stickier than I remembered, as I struggled to break its seal. Finally:

Sage,

Although the days grow ever longer,
know that I have thought of you consistently.
You are still in the back, front and center of
my curious mind. I said I'd always wait for you,
but that just seems unrealistic. The thought of
leaving you haunts me but I can't have you
grasping onto a love I cannot return...

The letter was crumpled, as if he had intentions of tossing it in the trash instead of sending it, but then continued regardless.

Additionally, a dirty smudge of a faint fingerprint stained the top left corner of the note. I touched it longingly and urged myself to keep reading, old, raw emotions deplorable still.

> *I'm sorry, Sage—for leaving, for what*
> *happened, and for what I'm about to do.*
> *We can't be together. You know it isn't*
> *right for either of us. We're only sixteen*
> *after all, with full lives ahead of us. We*
> *can't be in a relationship where we're*
> *thousands of miles apart, writing a letter,*
> *time and again. I have lots to look out for*
> *here in Virginia. It's a whole new experience,*
> *a whole new life. I hope I am getting my*
> *point across, Sage, and that this is*
> *closure enough. I may be making a huge*
> *mistake, actually I know I am, but it's for*
> *the best.*

> *As much as I love you, please don't ever*
> *come and find me.*

> *Max*

I was shaken up and torn all over again. Fumes of anger enraged my mind and body despite already knowing the ending to the story. Yet, there were so many questions left unanswered.

During the time of our break up, cell phones and computers weren't as prominent as in more recent times. The long distance wasn't as simple. It hurt to hear him admit his feelings even after the passed years. They were explicit then, and they held true now. We had the stop everything and cater kind of love that for so long was completely and utterly limitless.

I walked out of the restroom to return to Warner. I had been hiding out long enough, hoping he wouldn't see any sign of disparity in my expression.

He laid there restlessly, making room for me.

"I laid on your side to keep it warm while you were gone," he said.

I had possibly the sweetest man laying beautifully in a bed before me, and yet, my heart ached for a love that was no longer. A modern-day disaster.

Oftentimes, I forgot Max was only going on seventeen when we parted and I remembered thinking that sounded so *old* and even mature. Looking back, it seemed that was just the beginning for us.

I kissed Warner warmly on the cheek, "Thank you," I said, "perhaps we should go to bed?"

"Ah yes, big day tomorrow," he said, putting his glass down on a bedside coaster before turning the lamp off.

"Thank you for everything, Warner."

"You're welcome," said his scratchy voice, "Where are you? Why are you so far away?"

He jokingly made his way over to me in the massive king-sized bed, unaccustomed to sleeping in something so large.

The next thing I knew his hands were crawling over my body, pulling me into him. Without thinking, and without regret I kissed him, and I meant it, but I slid away quick. It had been a wild night, and I just wanted to sleep.

Forgetting Max, forgetting what brought us here and forgetting the world, I drifted into sleep, thankful it was Warner by my side. He was one of the good ones, and when you find people like that, you have to stick with them.

Max brought me this far to reiterate telling me to never come find him, but in the back of my mind, I knew he sent the letters because he still wanted me to. I was determined to gain something from seeing him.

My little consolation prize.

***

I woke up feeling sore, my mind in tatters. Warner, being the gentleman that he was, put a halt to all confusion and awkwardness "the kiss" created.

I had pulled away abruptly from him, but there was more passion in that room than any I had ever experienced in a minor moment. We didn't act upon our lust, still feeling out where we stood with each other.

"Sage," I felt Warner poke my arm hesitantly before I awoke that morning.

I opened one eye, and then the other routinely.

"Good morning," I said too cheerily for the sake of masking emotion.

"So you're not mad?" He kept feeling like he was crossing a line, but if he did, I was be glad. I needed him to cross lines so we could always be on the same side.

"I'm not mad at all," I said.

He smiled and looked down at his watch. It read 7:05a.m.

"Breakfast, shall we?"

I smiled, stood briskly, and got ready and so did he. Just a short time later, we are making our way downstairs.

We loaded up on carbohydrates and protein through eggs and bagels.

We don't leave without telling Jo how much we appreciated our stay. Despite it all, Warner wasn't weird about anything that happened. I thought he'd look at me differently, or treat me strange because I was weak, but if anything, he was more affectionate, and that only made him all the more attractive. Sometimes there were advantages to not making light of your fragility.

"Please do sign the guestbook before you're on your way!" Jo exclaimed.

"Gladly," Warner and I said in unison.

We made our way over to the book, skimmed through the untold stories from years ago, every entry just a blurb into the traveler's lives.

"I encourage everyone to sign it. Dates go back to twenty some years ago when I opened the place," Jo explained.

"That's wonderful," I was taken aback by the recordings. I snapped photos of some entries I liked before leaving one of my own. It was a generic "thank-you for your hospitality" message, but it was signed: *Sage and Warner 11/16/16,* which had a ring to it. I could tell he felt it too and for a split second, we are just a normal looking couple.

Warner was beaming as we strode out the door, hand in hand.

PHOEBE

Blood, sweat and tears make a person tough. I was young, but I was wildly mature, and dare I say tough for my age. I'd never known what true inexplicable love was because I had never seen that with my parents, but I had a feeling what I felt for Cliff was more than infatuation.

This past year was my toughest yet. I did quit a lot of things that made me better, but those things were just part of the facade that made me just like the rest of them. I wanted to find myself. I never expected to fall in love in the process.

It was a night like any other, where I'd pick up Cliff and we'd head to dinner. I scribbled my father a note on the counter letting him know my whereabouts before heading out.

I tried on roughly twenty outfits before finding one that appeased me, a tight crop top with high-waisted pants. My hair flowed down my back, freer than freedom itself. It was unruly, but after spraying it with some heavy duty product, it was a tangle of beach waves even I had to admit looked out of a commercial.

That'll do, I thought.

Cliff had yet to meet my father or see our home so I lit a candle and did some shuffling around in attempts to make the place presentable so he could knock off one of those two things.

After he knocked on the door, I opened it to see his face covered in an ambush of roses. At least two dozen.

"Come in," I said, "These are beautiful. Let me get a vase."

Leaving him alone in the foyer I scurried off. It had been a long while since we had fresh flowers in the house, let alone ones to call my own.

"You look wonderful," he said with confidence, as if he knew he was going to say it all along. I could have worn a trash bag for all he cared.

He looked good himself though, so the feeling was mutual.

"Thank you," I hoped he could hear in my voice that I meant for everything—the compliment, the flowers, for existing...

"Shall we?" he asked, extending his arm to loop mine in.

"We shall," I simultaneously nodded my head, overcome by warmth.

Opening the door arm in arm, we hesitated to avoid being caught in the rain that hadn't been there just a minute prior. As if on cue, the skies opened into a torrential downpour on the great hair day I was having.

Instead, I scurried to grab an umbrella sheltering us on the way to my car before heading to the high-end burger joint on the far side of town.

Cliff sang rather terribly to the pop song blaring from the radio. Everything was perfectly ideal.

But, I thought that preemptively.

It was 8:43p.m. when we rounded a corner, admittedly a bit too quick and all too distracted.

Although it was nearing the end of November, it was relatively warm outside, the roads not particularly icy but rather my vision skewed from the rain.

Before I could blink, the front half of my car was smashed flat against what looked like the largest oak tree I'd ever seen. Little flames and sparks erupted from just below the windshield.

Rattled, I managed to stumble out of the seat belt I thankfully had clasped on. Seemingly unscathed, I heard something in my body pop, but all I felt was shock, disbelief and total numbness. There was also a strong ringing in my ears that made me instinctively bring my hands to them, letting out a groan as I regained my orientation.

Blood dripped from somewhere as it hit the steering wheel. My vision blurred, I turned to face Cliff.

Not considering the fact he could be worse off than me, Cliff's condition caught me off guard. He was supposed to be the strong one, the healthy one, the one who was always safe and unfazed. Who would protect me if not he? Cliff, however, hung his head off to the side, the airbag serving as a pillow for his unconscious body.

I knew I had to get him out of there and I had to do it quick, so I attempted to scurry to the passenger side of the vehicle. I let out an eerily sinister scream when my door wouldn't open. It wouldn't even budge. I felt trapped on all sides, as if the car was closing in on me, my breath irregular.

Cliff was definitely unconscious if he didn't react to my scream; it even perturbed me.

Cursing at the car and at life in general, I slithered my way to the backseat to escape that way. I was not against busting out a window if I needed to, but thankfully it didn't come to that. After all, it wouldn't have mattered because the car was damaged beyond repair anyways.

I stumbled, my equilibrium clearly off as I made my way to him. Blood dripped steadily off my head and onto Cliff's arm as I pugnaciously wrestled the airbag out of my way.

This had never happened to me before, so I didn't quite know what to do. I never even considered something of this caliber occurring.

I just had to get him out. That's what I did know, and all that kept replaying in my mind. *Come on, Cliff.*

Expecting him to be heavier, I tossed his dead weight over my left shoulder, avoiding the sharp pain I felt stabbing into my rib cage on the right side of my body. I let out another yell. I had no control over my limbs, I just kept grunting and somehow, it helped me not to focus on the reality of the situation. Hot tears rolled down my hot face, burning small wounds on the way down.

I could hardly breathe by the time I made it to the curb, he barely on my back.

Not a soul was out on the road. It was a back road, but damn, it was never usually that desolate.

I propped him up against another tree, as my worry set in. As much as I wanted to sense a pulse of his, I was afraid to check. All color and life that used to be

207

his face, I watched disintegrate with each passing second. It was so cold outside, so cold in my heart, just so cold. I was numb, but through icicle fingers dialed 9-1-1.

"There's been an emergency," I muttered when the call was answered on the first ring. My voice was not my own, but I was coherent enough to know this was our only hope and possibly our only solution to survival, "We're on the corner of..." I squinted at the street signs, the letters blending into words and the words a mess of letters. My vision was hazy, and I had to sit down, barely catching myself as my elbow gave out to break my fall.

It was not ten minutes later when the ambulances came whirling through, their light bringing me back to the senses I had lost control of. Parked not far from where I was, they diligently and knowingly strapped Cliff's limp body to the stretcher, placing a tourniquet around his temples. One woman held a flashlight to his face, while another man tucked a blanket over and around his body. I was shivering, but Cliff was motionless.

I quit fighting and surrendered my body to the darkness that was calling my name so loud and clear.

Blood...sweat...tears....

***

I awoke to a heart monitor by my side hours later. What I assumed was a heavy medicine dosage trickled from an IV opposite the monitor. My father and grandmother hovered around like lost birds in flight, the look in their eyes clueless.

The IV dripped slowly and steadily that watching it nearly lulled me back into a sleep I never wanted to wake up from.

"Phoebe," my father said, tiptoeing near extra cautiously, as if I'd pass along a disease he might catch if he came too close.

"Where's Cliff?" was all I could muster, the memory of what happened coming back in flashes all too distinctly. My throat was so dry it pained me even to breathe. Let alone speak.

"Cliff's going to be okay," he said.

My chest hurt alongside everything else, but a pang of despair made it worse.

"But where is he?" I slouched to sit up, the pain stopping me right there. I winced despite not wanting to show any discomfort.

"He's down the hall, you'll be able to see him this afternoon," my grandmother said, unveiling despondence in every word.

"I'm going now," I began to stand.

"No, Phoebe, please just rest!" my father insisted, "God, you can be as stubborn as your mother sometimes."

I glared at him. He rarely talked about my mother, but when he did he knew he'd struck a chord. Then, more so than ever, was the worst possible time to bring her up. My cheeks reddened as I felt my blood beginning to boil.

At least I had feeling though, it meant I was alive. I took a forgiving deep breath because I knew my father was alarmed like the rest of us.

"I'm sorry, I really am, but please Phoebe, you need to rest up. You're a ghost." It was subtle, but the reference to death made me cringe.

A nurse too perky for my liking pranced through the door with a handful of equipment I wasn't ready for. Her nametag read Naomi.

"Phoebe, Phoebe, Phoebe, I'm Naomi," she smiled as she jotted down something on her clipboard, "Let's see here, age 16, 111 pounds, 5 feet 4 inches, all vital signs seem regular. Your heart rate seems a bit high, but you feeling any better? All that information sound about right to you?"

"Yes and yes," I was in no mood, rightfully so.

"I'm going to give you a dose of some pain medication, and we'll let you get the rest you need," she continued, "I'm sure you father has told you, but..."

"Haven't gotten there yet, Naomi, thanks..." My father interjected.

Before I could ask what they had yet to clue me in on, I was out. Wanting to inquire more, I retreated and let my weakness decide for me. I'd rather have one last sleep in relaxation in case what they told me was so horrible it would provide me a lifetime of sleepless nights. It was a selfish move, but I needed to escape the moment and I needed to do it quick.

I didn't remember everyone leaving the room, but when I woke up thirteen hours later, everyone was gone.

***

Two broken ribs, a fractured collarbone and a minor concussion. That's all I got.

A coma. That's what Cliff got.

I hadn't left the hospital even though I had been dismissed two days prior. When his family came to visit daily, I sat in various waiting rooms, eating from vending machines whatever I could stomach, but otherwise I never left his side. I tried to regain my stamina and strength, but I found I was only weaker with each passing day without Cliff in full recovery.

My father called my cell nonstop until it finally lost its battery. He had a phone but I didn't think he knew how to turn it on. It sat hidden away in a desk drawer or his glove box, one of the two, just collecting dust.

He'd come down to the hospital looking for me, but understood after little debate I had unfinished business left there. He was usually much more strict, but was afraid of what I might do if I went home with him.

Broken people are often the most detrimental.

"I have to be here when he wakes up," was all I needed to say for him to understand. I was fragile, and he always treated me like I was about to break anyways.

I'd never had to deal with a situation like this before. You never think it can happen to you, until it does.

Well, for me it had, and there was no way of stopping it.

I would visit Cliff's room each day, not sure of the protocol. I tried speaking to him the first few days, but I

211

ended up sounding idiotic asking questions that couldn't, and wouldn't, be answered.

I flipped through a magazine I found in the outpatient waiting room after crawling into the hospital bed alongside him, hoping that whatever ounce of warmth I had in me would channel off to his body.

Other days, I'd sit in the chair beside him and turn on the TV, pretending to hear his laugh ringing in my ears at the funny parts. It hurt my ribs to laugh still, so maybe I imagined for the both of us. I felt guilty smiling in a time like that anyways.

When the nurses would come to check on him, I'd make my way out of the room to give them their space. I'd still be waiting though.

Waiting, waiting, waiting.

I wasn't sure of what, however. Waiting for some miraculous turn of events where he came out of this unscathed? The odds were extremely unlikely. Waiting for my guilt to fade, so I could stop blaming myself for what happened? I don't think I'd ever fully get to that point. Or lastly, waiting for him to die? I couldn't stomach my pessimism, but it was the one that kept me up at night.

On days my guilt took over and I couldn't fathom facing him, I'd sit in waiting rooms on different floors pretending I was here for something or someone else, trying not to think too much. At the end of the day, I'd force myself to return to him, though. I had to. If he did come out of this, as people do, I wanted him to remember me for all the good that was our relationship.

I was reliant on his company. I couldn't imagine my life without him. It just wasn't possible.

***

Eleven days. It had been eleven days and ten whole nights since I found out Cliff was in a coma. It was then the new news came.

Sleep came and went when I was at the hospital, and as I laid awake just after midnight staring up at the ceiling, my hand rested on top of his, just thinking, a beep from one of the machines keeping him alive broke all serenity of the moment. I leapt from the bed in one fluid motion and clamored to the hall.

"Help!" I shouted for lack of know-how and sensibility.

A nurse dropped everything and hurried over to me from down the hall. Another was quick to follow. Attentively, they injected him with different needles.

After fifteen minutes that felt like five hundred, the first nurse approached me and said, "Looks like you caught us just in time, Phoebe. He just might be okay." She rested her hand on my shoulder reassuringly.

His eyes. His bright eyes. They looked lifeless, but they were open, and that was all that mattered.

The second nurse backed away after making mention that she was going to go grab a doctor. Alone with an awakened Cliff, I made my way over to his bedside as gently but swiftly as possible.

I hovered directly over his unrecognizable body. With open eyes, I could see how sunken in his gaunt face had become. Tears streamed down mine uncon-

213

trollably as I watched him extend and flex fingers on his right hand only.

Careful to not touch him, I let him come to me. In much confusion, he reached up to touch my face very slightly. The back of his pale, white fingers brushed my skin, giving me a rush like never before. "Phoebe," his hoarse voice spoke. I couldn't decipher if he called out to me in question as to ask what was going on and where was he or if he said my name just to say it, but regardless, he *knew* my name. His jaw quivered uncontrollably as my tears fell on his face, warm and yet so, so cold. He started having a seizure.

I stepped back, my jaw now the one quivering as a nearby nurse scurried back in, interrupted by the doctor seconds later. He did a quick examination.

Atrophy obviously had taken over Cliff's weak body, but the doctor looked hesitant as if it were much more than that. From the expression on his face, it seemed something still wasn't right.

I waited outside the room in a chair the steady handed nurse had provided me. She recommended it, as it was better for me to relax. They weren't sure what was going on and in a way, I didn't want what they were going to say to hinder the moment we had just shared.

On the eve of that eleventh night, the doctor came out to where I was at 2:18a.m. and knelt beside me like I was a child incapable of tying an untied shoe.

"I'm so sorry, Phoebe," he looked forlorn and sounded defeated. "Cliff wasn't able to make it."

"But...I just..."

"I'm sorry, again."

214

The tears didn't come immediately. Had I not just seen him with open eyes? Hadn't the nurse just told me he would be all right? I couldn't wrap my head around the situation.

I called my father despite the late hour from a phone I found downstairs in the lobby. I met him at his truck just eight minutes later, not having the strength to return to Cliff's room with how things had turned out.

With tears dried to my face when I saw him, it was all my father could do to turn the truck off and help stabilize me. I collapsed in his arms, an exhausted and emotional mess. He checked on me sporadically the whole ride home as uncontrollable sobs took over.

Cliff was dead.

"They did everything they could..." he said as we made our way out of his truck and into our home, thankful it wasn't my grandmother's house I was at, the memories of the past two months written all over the house beside hers.

"...it just wasn't enough." I finished the sentence for him.

I looked down at my tattoo instinctively because eleven had always been a number that followed me. I vomited up every ounce of hospital pudding and crackers I'd eaten in the past few weeks, wanting to scratch the tattoo right off my arm. It would forever hold a new meaning.

As much as I was expecting the moment over the course of the week and was well aware of the glum possibility, there was no way to ever prepare. As the bruises from the fight with Colin were healing, new ones from the accident were taking their place. There

215

were always going to be scars, always going to be bruises, but there was no replacement like the bruise on the heart after someone you love leaves you forever.

Death was the worst bruise of all.

SAGE

It was getting colder and colder, but we were getting nearer and nearer. Growing old had become increasingly more tiring.

Warner had surpassed his three day trial with me and was going on one week. He had lost weight, mostly seen in his face if it wasn't hidden behind a full, dark beard that had seemingly grew in overnight. Where he was once burley and extremely masculine, his features had softened, even in just one week. Yet, he was still just as good-looking.

There was something so enchanting about the morning. The first moment you open your eyes for the day. Waking up next to Warner had felt all the more magical. He was charming, enthralling, and more than anything, he intrigued me. In a way I felt like I'd known him forever, and in a way I didn't know him at all.

He'd surprise me constantly and I found myself catering to what I observed he needed.

I suddenly felt entirely too insecure about my unshaved legs and overgrown eyebrows; my personal hygiene in general. Promising myself a day of upkeep before seeing Max again, no one ever wanted to look as tired and worn out as they felt.

Warner was too put together, too clean for what we were doing and it made the insecurities I had brewing more prominent, even despite his changes.

Even though I questioned his motives when it came to how he viewed me and our relationship, walking with him never felt tedious. It never felt like a chore, whereas by myself, I certainly struggled to find that motivation. With him, it was fun, our sense of normalcy skewed from the start.

"Let me ask you something," Warner turned to me and said nine miles in.

"What's that?" I inquired.

"Why'd you wait for the coldest time of the year to do this?"

"When it's time, it's time. And it was time," that's all I had. I didn't really have an explanation, although I had contemplated this tragedy myself.

"Huh. I wish you'd elaborate," he said blandly, tiring out, perhaps tiring of me.

He always got perturbed about me not sharing my feelings enough. It's not that I'm not an open person, it's that I'd rather not waste my time on the fluff. I'd tell him when things really mattered to me but I'd rather say nothing at all than something I'd potentially regret.

"I had to escape my old life or I would I would have self-destructed," I hoped he would appreciate the abbreviated version of the elaboration I could spat out, "I didn't like who I was becoming and I needed to get out before I dug myself a hole much deeper. Plus, I'd always needed to do this, and I'm not getting any younger."

"You needed to do this?" Of course he had follow-up questions.

"It's complicated," was all I could stomach.

"You already told me it was all for a guy, so I think I've heard enough, although I don't necessarily approve if I do say so myself," he eyed me smugly, "You seem different than that. How old are you anyways?"

"I'll be thirty-three in March. March 2nd."

He nodded, as if approving.

"I'll be thirty-five next year," he stated.

"Thanks for the sharing," I teased smugly.

We both laughed at how disheveled our situation was. Here we were, digging deeper into Virginia with each step we took, mocking each other for comic relief, if nothing else.

"I've been having a really great time with you, Sage," he began. "Thanks for letting me be a part of this with you."

"I'm happy to have you join. No one wants to experience these different walks of life alone," I reassured, hoping it wasn't too insightful to ruin the moment.

"It's almost fun trying to survive out here, isn't it? Sore and tiring, but that's expected, so I just look past it, and there lies the fun. I would have never thought," he said in awe. I could relate to the breathtaking feeling he was experiencing.

"Everything I do in life I like to make fun. I'm walking over five hundred miles through different states and at the end of it all, yeah, I can say it's been great. Really great."

There was no dejection in his expression when I asked if he had two more miles in him, whereas he used to complain. His body heat warmed me on cold nights and his company kept me motivated. I too often underplayed the time we shared. I didn't voice it, but initially I thought he'd be extra baggage. I got to a point where I couldn't imagine doing the trip without him, despite the majority of the miles completed solo.

It didn't need to be said to be understood that we enjoyed each other. I was even afraid he was going to tell me he loved me, the look in his eyes confused, but instead we walked in silence.

It was colder during the nights so we planned to stop off at a hotel again if we could help it. It was crazy how people were so willing to aid a selfless woman, nomadically making her way across the east coast, but add a man to the equation, and all those people disappeared.

I never believed in fate until I met Warner. What were the odds that someone so prominent in my past would somehow make a return through his son? It was like I had an angel watching over me, sending companionship I didn't know I needed. Although things had changed, it wasn't necessarily for the worst.

It pained me to think of the conversation Warner and I were inevitably bound to have. The one where we go our separate ways, and I stay with Max and he does God knows what, with his life.

He grazed his hand against mine, and I knew he wanted to hold it, yet I didn't let him. He talked constantly, to the point where all I could do was nod through my tiredness and try not to zone out. I did appreciate his conversation, but the guy never even paused for breath. I started to believe he was saying a lot about nothing to avoid the conversations we really needed to have. Perhaps it was just me who was worried about it, but what would Warner do when we got there? Where was he headed next? Would our paths *ever* cross again?

"It's almost 9p.m." he said through stories.

"I have to reevaluate the map tonight but...we shouldn't be too far off now." I had my map out, twisting it to provide a new perspective.

"Let's just stay here," Warner signaled to a hotel off to our right, changing the subject, as he did religiously every time I brought up how near to the end we were.

"It's entirely too rundown," I said as if I cared, like I haven't slept in worse conditions as of recent.

Wind chapped and rosy, I smirked as I caught Warner's eye. Why was I so drawn to him?

"Although, that bar does look excellent and I can use a drink," I said.

"Now, how could I deny that?"

We dropped our things off in a room with a squeaky bed and floral wallpaper from floor to ceiling. I couldn't look at it for too long without straining my eyes. It was cheap as dirt, so I really had no complaints. Besides, most girls would consider themselves lucky to be cuddling up with the likes of Warner, setting their morals aside on this rickety bed. I rolled my eyes at just the thought.

He walked into the bathroom, did a once over on his hair and called, "You ready?"

"Would you mind if I showered first?"

220

"Oh yeah, absolutely, I'll wait here and watch TV or something."

"It's weird that TV is such a hot commodity, isn't it?" I could see the light in his eyes when he decided to watch a basketball game, almost relieved, I requested a shower.

"I wouldn't mind skipping the bar and staying to watch all night," ...*because the last time, we were nearly too preoccupied with each other to turn the TV on*, but I finished the thought in my head.

I started to take my top off and I could feel his eyes on me through the adjacent mirror, lining my half-naked body up perfect with his eye line.

Why was I playing the game so aggressively? For his sake and mine, weren't things complicated enough?

Self-conscious, I closed the door abruptly.

I could be such a tease, but the thought of leaving Warner behind soon scared me more than I cared to admit. I didn't want to get too close. It sounded shallow and elementary, but it was nice having Warner around in case things with Max flopped tremendously. He was insurance in a way, although I knew I viewed him as much more than that.

After all, why should I be holding out for Max when he technically already broke my heart years ago?

I finally shaved my legs and washed my hair before I examined my body in full. I heard a crowd of fans cheering during whatever game was blaring from the television, the applause feeling all mine. I had gotten so thin, not even looking like myself, and I didn't have much weight to spare to begin with.

When I walked out in my towel, Warner focused his eyes on the TV, daring himself not to peek. I could tell that he hadn't been with many women just by the way he looked at me and communicated. His innocence was refreshing and willed me to want him all the more. It was rare to find a man like Warner and I was going to be the idiotic woman to let him go.

"I called room service and sent down our clothes to be laundered while you were showering," he said, eyes glued to the screen.

"You are impeccable, you know that?" I said. His blushed face made my stomach turn with butterflies. "I'm surprised this place even has a washer and dryer."

"Can't promise how clean it'll actually make the clothes, but one did exist downstairs."

I hadn't heard anyone come to the door, but I was craving cleanliness, so I was grateful he still had enough energy to think of things that needed taken care of.

I changed behind closed doors, not wanting to be the tease I had been known to be.

"And you...you look...beautiful," he pieced together, once I had reemerged, my hair drying wavy.

"I clean up well," I admitted, because that particular evening it had been true. I was feeling more confident than I had been in the past two months.

"Let's drink," was all I could say to break his gaze. It was as if he'd never seen a woman before.

"Let's," I followed his lead.

I walked into the bar with an all new air about me, ready to mingle with the locals and hopefully learn

222

something new. It was relieving to know that my temporary best friends were just strangers in bars.

***

582 miles. 102 days. Three entire months and eleven days. I had leftover letters from Max I wanted to catch up with before seeing him, odd that I finished the trek a good deal of time before he did. From the earlier letters, I had his lousy address on a note burning a hole in my pocket. Paranoid, I'd check to make sure it was there every other moment.

"What're you going to do when I get there?" I asked Warner as the days closed in on us. Tomorrow would be the day of arrival. It'd be a thirteen mile trek, but what was one last half marathon after what I had put in already?

"Get a hotel, do what we do. Maybe get a flight to somewhere else, continue exploring. There's so much of this world I haven't seen."

"Walking while exploring can lead you to potentially hate the land we live on, because it always seems to be against you. The weather, the terrain, the soreness…nothing works in your favor," I said, almost lackadaisically and to myself, not even sure I was making sense.

"It wouldn't be so bad if it wasn't this cold," he said. The wind chill had definitely picked up, comparable to the northern winter weather I had grew up with, although it had been abnormally warm for this time of year. Call it global warming, call it whatever you will, I wasn't complaining.

"Would you do it all over again? You know, if Max has moved on, would you walk back?"

"I've thought about it, but I've become extremely lucky in my travels...I mean, abnormally lucky. Most people die doing things like this. That's why I've put this off for so long. I knew I wanted to walk it, but now that I have, I have no desire to walk back," he and I both laughed.

"I'm sure Max will embrace you with open arms," he tried to sound reassuring, but I could see his heart wasn't in it.

"I don't let him keep me up at night. After all these years, I've grown to be my own without him."

"Well, know I'm always here for you if you need."

"You're sweet, Warner. I can't thank you enough for staying with me these last few weeks."

"The pleasure has been all mine," he smiled genuinely.

This fling, albeit short, was coming to an end, and it hurt more than expected. For some reason, I fell for this guy and his spontaneous spirit, which was crazy to think because I was doing all this for *another* guy. I'm a selfish woman, but at least I can admit to it.

We stopped into a bar and grille type place for a parting meal where we continued to talk and reminisce on the walk of a lifetime, myself carrying the conversation, as he was still new to it all.

"Let's sleep outside for your last night, you wanna?" Warner suggested.

"Mmhmm, I guess for the sake of tradition," I said.

We had been there talking for about an hour about the best and worst times of this trip, like a highlight reel, when a man in his late twenties interjected.

"I don't mean to eavesdrop but I couldn't help but overhear a bit of your conversation. I'm a reporter, and I was wondering if I could ask you a couple questions. I'd love to run a story about you."

Warner eyed me skeptically, almost protective. As a used-to-be-editor, I knew the importance of snagging a good story when you heard one. The girl the reporter was with introduced herself as Carly and apologized for the dinner interruption. She rolled her eyes as if this was a common occurrence for her.

"I'd be honored," I said. It is then Warner eased into conversation too.

"Great! I'm Brian," he said as he untucked a pen from out behind his ear, "I'm just going to take some notes if you don't mind."

"Not at all. I'm Sage Riley."

"Warner Dixon."

"Good to meet you both. Let's start with some easy questions, shall we?" Warner, Brian, Carly and I exchanged handshakes and pushed our tables of two together.

He asked why, how and where this all came about. Although, I wasn't doing this to gain any sort of popularity, I never had a column written strictly about me and it was nice to know that people were interested, even if they simply would skim the article.

We stayed at the restaurant for another couple of hours discussing my biggest struggles and my greatest successes. Carly *oohed* and *ahhed* expressively as Brian jotted down direct quotes and smaller tidbits. She rested her hand on her chin and said, "This is all so romantic," nudging Brian on the arm as if to say 'step it up.' He knowingly responded aloud, "Don't even think about it."

We all giggled and grabbed yet another drink. I wasn't going to be able to answer many more questions coherently if the drinks kept flowing.

As if reading my mind, Brian said, "One last question should do," I nodded, ready for anything, "Even if things with Max don't work out, will it all be worthwhile?"

I was taken aback by the obviousness of the question, but answered what came to the forefront of my mind, "Of course it will. I've had some challenges to get through in life, some more difficult to recover from than others, but this was definitely a challenge worthwhile. It taught me that life is comprised of different walks and different people in each phase. There is kindness in this world, I mean, true and utter kindness. There are good people, and I just try to be one of them. There's no complicated explanation for any of it. I'd sum it up by saying that yes, it taught me to enjoy each different walk of life and to pass along the kindness given to me, because life's too short to be challenging."

I got more passionate than I should have, perhaps, and it wasn't much of an answer but still, everyone was silently taking in the moment. Warner was staring at me with love in his eyes, Carly was sipping her cosmo-politan, trying to mask the tears in her eyes, Brian just wrote away before breaking the quiet atmosphere with, "Perfect."

That moment clarified that I had done it. I had actually done it. It was enough to make me emotional, but I held it together through quivering lips.

We talked about how wonderful it was to have come in contact with them, and I snapped a Polaroid of the couple. Carly apologized yet again on behalf of her intrusive boyfriend, but she didn't seem to mean it. Our conversation spoke to her too.

"Sage, you are an inspiration," Brian concluded, and I blushed at the compliment. No one had ever said that to me before, and although flattered, I found it hard to believe.

For a debatable night out, it sure did present the unexpected. Soon, I knew, these random encounters would begin to cease. I'd no longer be the helpless woman on a mission. I'd go back to being uninteresting, and therefore, myself.

We headed back upstairs where I threw on one of Warner's oversized shirts to sleep in. I unmade the bed, remembering how I used to military tuck every corner of my California king. Missing the discipline I had in making a bed every morning, unmaking one seemed ironic, and also oddly satisfying.

Before I knew it, he had me wrapped in his arms, his lips on mine.

"Because soon I won't get to..." he said between breaths, although he didn't need to give an explanation; I already knew. We cared for each other more than any two people should after knowing each other for a handful of weeks. I too was hoping for one last night with him, because soon things might be different. *Would be different,* I had to keep reminding myself.

I never wanted to give up something and someone so sweet. But, Max...and the curiosity that loomed over our history would eat me alive if didn't try.

In my heart, I tried to convince myself that Warner was my back up guy for Max and not the other way around, but in moments in his arms, where I was wrapped in his warm embrace, his lips on mine, I didn't need to convince myself of anything. Warner couldn't have been more fitting.

Too bad it was terrible, and absolutely horrible timing.

PHOEBE

How did we get here? Where are we going? We ask ourselves these things too often that it forces us to miss what's happening in the moment. And life is full of moments.

The only picture I had of Cliff and I hung by a thread from my shaky hands. The picture we took that first ride when we were still unsure of each other.

Have you ever thought back to the time when you first saw someone? First spoke to them? And then wonder 'how did we get here?' and 'where are we going?'.

I had already endured many sleepless nights since his passing. Cliff was dead and I felt like dying too.

I couldn't say anything, couldn't form words. All I could do was cry until the tears ran dry.

Fortunately for my mental wellbeing, Cliff's family chose not to press charges or investigate the accident that caused his death any further. My tattered state made them fully aware this was an accident, plain and simple, but a horrible one at that. The police involvement was limited and I was left to lead my life as I would, although the guilt of what happened made it seem I didn't deserve to be treated so kindly after what *I* did to their son.

"There is nothing that could bring my baby back now, Phoebe. They did all they could, and it's not your fault," his mother said to me through teary, tired eyes.

My father hesitantly left on an overnight business trip to Seattle after I urged him I was going to be all right on my own. Twenty-four hours had passed, so I assumed the worst was behind me. Like a bandage that had just been ripped off, the hardest part was over. In fact, I preferred to be alone at that point. As much as I appreciated him caring, the constant checking in on me over the past day and night had started to wear me down. He didn't need to miss out on important meetings and opportunities because his sulking teenage daughter needed him to stay. If I couldn't be with Cliff, I just wanted to be alone, so he left, promising he was just one call away.

Being alone, I had to force my wobbly knees to lock. I hadn't eaten anything since coming home from the hospital. It was all I could do to take care of myself. A small twist in the wrong direction, I was made aware

229

of my healing body, as well. My abdomen ached, my head throbbed and my heart broke.

Putting Cliff's picture down to focus on something else, anything else, I decided to go for a walk to clear my mind. Lacing up some tennis shoes, I stepped out into the December air. A coat too large for me, my father's, enveloped me in protection.

I wiped unavoidable tears onto my sleeve as they'd trickle down. It wasn't a long walk, but enough to make me hate the antsy anxiety that crept up and the hot, salty tears that wouldn't stop coming. In frustration, I turned to head back home in the slight drizzle of the rain. I must have looked straight out of an old horror film.

There was one cigarette left in the pocket of his jacket, the lighter coupled with it. I lit it and took in the smoky pull. I could almost feel the nicotine creeping its way through my bloodstream, making every stop. My father didn't smoke much, but everyone had their vice when life encouraged a smoke break.

I was losing my mind and I had no idea what to do with my body either. I had nothing else to do but head home. I saw the house as I rounded the corner and was immediately struck with how much I longed to be comfortable, wondering if I'd ever be happy again.

There was someone on the porch of the house as I approached. I slid tears out of the way, so I could better see who it was.

She turned around and waved awkwardly. Were those tears in her eyes too?

"*Mom?*" I whispered scratchily, as if she could hear me.

How did *she* get here? Where is *she* going?

PART II

AFTER

December 11, 2016

SAGE

I'm convinced I'm going to hell. At least I could admit it, though, and sort of be prepared, right? Isn't that the way it worked?

There were some things in life you just couldn't mess up, some people you couldn't let go. As hard as I tried to rid my mind of Max, Phoebe was the one I could never shake. Your own *child* was one person in life you should never abandon, never forget, and I did that to mine. So for that, I'm going to hell.

The thought of her sent a strange pulse through my body, unnerving every ounce of me. I had been putting her out of my mind, out of my thoughts, like I'd been her entire life.

But she was always there in my subconscious. She'd creep up in recurring dreams, I'd see her in the face of another teenager and I'd wonder what she'd think of me.

As hard as I tried to erase my indecency, there was something in my every day that reminded me of her. I thought about her more often than I'd like to admit.

I knew it was guilt. Guilt for the way things turned out, guilt for how unfair I'd been to her, guilt for being so selfish.

Now there she was, before me.

It's difficult to prepare for the biggest day of your life. It's best when those type of days catch you off guard.

Rather, the day had been full of rearranging. I shuffled around and wasted time procrastinating, pampering myself to appear prettier than I was, walking begrudgingly while rehearsing every word I wanted to convey when I got there. But as time does, it snuck up on me. It was already well into the afternoon before I arrived on Max and Phoebe's front porch step, the biggest day of my life already halfway over and yet barely begun.

I rang the doorbell of Max's address twice, both going unanswered. There were no cars in the drive and one totaled one out on the street. Not all hope was gone, he just wasn't home. The thought of waiting any longer had me squirming, but at that point it was out of my control.

And then there was Phoebe. It was only a matter of time before I had to face her and to face the past, no matter how ugly.

Standing a good distance away but having spotted me, I observed her eye the totaled car, approach it, and kick the tire, letting out a rambunctious scream.

Somehow, despite the scene, she was the most beautiful thing I had ever seen. Even after witnessing the current outburst, I could tell Max did a good job with her. There was a part of her that looked so wholesome and kind. I could see it mostly in her eyes when she narrowed in on me standing helplessly on her front steps.

Looking at her was like looking at myself when I met Max. I was innocent, but wanted to be edgy, sweet but put on a sour facade, and meek even though I claimed toughness.

233

"Phoebe," I said as she walked up the steps. I couldn't help the slow roll of tears that were forming and falling, seemingly a new trend I had started.

"What are you doing here?" she said lifelessly, "I just want to be alone."

"I know this is all so confusing, but I'd love to talk to you. And your father."

"After what? Sixteen entire years? Now is really not the time, I promise you that."

"But...Phoebe..." It almost hurt to say her name out loud because it made the girl from my dreams so real, "I walked here from New York City to see you."

I didn't mean to make her feel guilty, but I had come too far to not at least explain. The gold trophy now dangled teasingly before my eyes. It was all I could do to not lash out and pounce to reclaim what was mine.

"You walked?" There was no masking the disbelief in her voice. It sounded that with the next breath she'd take she'd be laughing in hilarity and condescension. Instead, she just grew more serious and whispered, "That's impossible."

"Yes, to see you, to see your father. I have...I have this stack of letters, I'd love to explain."

"You can come in, but just until my dad gets back."

"Okay," I said as she turned the key to open the door to their house. Max and Phoebe's house. Always a concept, always an illusion.

Not that I expected it, but I scanned for a trace of me anywhere. There were none, but there was also no trace of another woman either. My emotions were all over the place and I had no intention of hiding them.

234

The house was nice enough, decor up to par. It was tidy, almost like they were expecting a guest all along. Either that or no one was ever there long enough to dirty the place. A couch was neatly arranged by the fireplace, a place I would have liked to cuddle up and hide from the rest of the world right about then.

Milestone pictures hung scattered across the walls: Phoebe holding first place medals, Phoebe with missing teeth, Phoebe hugging a small canine. I mentally noted each, but didn't spend too long reflecting in fear I'd miss out on some other aspect of the home. The four walls around me were suddenly sacred.

"Are you okay? You look like you've been crying a lot more than a few tears," I said, motioning towards the couch, pretending I was not on the verge myself.

Phoebe filled up a glass of ice water. Although I'd like one too, she didn't offer and I didn't ask.

She came to sit across from me on the adjacent couch.

"Do you really believe I'm going to tell you anything about my life?" She was so forward, yet so unthreatening.

"I suppose I don't expect you to, but I'd like to hear if you'd let me," I was trying to sound as pleasant as possible, even though the emotional breakdown she was trying hard not to make evident was exactly how a touch of me was feeling too.

"Well, if you must know, I have recently returned from the hospital after watching someone I love pass away, and possibly being the only person who is responsible for his death, to come home to find my estranged mother on my porch. That's the kind of week

I'm having. That's what I'm working with here, so my apologies for not being all welcoming and accommodating."

"There is no need to apologize. That's a whole lot, and I'm sorry that happened to you," I said in dismay, "Are you hungry?"

Her demeanor changed, as if eating was a foreign concept. Hearing about the week she had, she might indulge in the idea of eating her feelings if nothing else. Plus, I could tell she was curious about me. How could she not be?

"Starving, and I know I good place. You're paying."

I wanted to touch her face and tell her it would all be okay in the end, but like anything else, this relationship would take steps. But I was not worried. I more than anyone was no stranger to steps.

PHOEBE

My mother wasn't the way I remembered her. Not that I had any memories of she and I, but from what I had seen in pictures. I looked her up online several times, much to my father's dismay. There was quite a bit of information on her too, being a big time editor in New York City and all. She seemed like the type to have her signature latte being six words or longer and her heels never less than six inches tall...not someone who walked several state lines, for reasons that were still unexplained.

236

I don't think I've seen anyone in my life who could actually wear the double zero sized jeans they sell in trendy stores and pull it off, but my mother could. Not in a malnourished sense either, she was entirely glamorous and her beauty was all encompassing.

I guess I looked more like my father.

Not that that was such a terrible thing, it was always evident I had his light, curly hair and olive complexion. Her eyes were bright green and alive, and mine were much more sullen. It was her personality and mannerisms I saw myself in most. At times, the uncanny resemblance was frightening.

Her voice had a sultry rasp to it that I didn't expect and her long, braided dark hair was unkempt, but fitting.

I took us to my favorite diner. We walked to the bus station not far from our home. I had zero intentions of leaving the house the rest of the day, yet there I was.

It was awkward at first, neither of us making a peep. A wall of a million thoughts stood between us. I second-guessed why I even agreed to do this. I had business to attend to back home—alone—like pitying myself.

My father used to tell me that when I was younger, I got to pick the place we'd go for my birthday dinner. It was always "breakfast for dinner" when I had the choice. Waffles always tasted better after 6p.m.

When I was turning ten and young enough to air innocence but old enough to know better, I questioned him about my mother for the first time. We were sitting in the diner; it was just he and I.

Oh, the irony.

He was immediately taken aback by the inquiries but told me that one day, he was certain my mother would come crawling back to us, that she had to find herself first and that I needn't worry. I didn't assume he meant that she'd *literally* come crawling.

So I didn't. I didn't worry, but I always thought about her. I'd see kids at school having their mothers come in to read to the class on Friday afternoons, other's coming in to instruct crafts once a month.

I envisioned a woman I imagined to look as my mother prancing about my elementary school classrooms, being the one to greet us for volunteer recess duty, but not knowing what she really looked like had proved a more difficult task with each passing year.

When I was twelve, I thought about searching for her on the Internet, but computers and their wealth of knowledge still scared me. Maybe it wasn't the computer, but the idea of accessing her and not liking what I found being the haunting thought. What if I didn't like what I saw? It wasn't like I'd reach out to her anyways.

It was my thirteenth birthday, just a year later, when I regained the courage to sit behind that keyboard and search for Sage Riley. Birthdays always proved to be a weird time for me, as I'd think of her considerably more and more the older I became. After all, my birth very much involved her too.

I thought she had been beautiful immediately.

I had skimmed through different social media profiles of her in the past, learning more and more about her in the process, so much so that I envied her. And resented her. And was infuriated by her.

The feelings she brought up scared the hell out of me.

In person though, she had a way about her that just made you fall in love with her. You could tell she was adventurous and bold. She had her life together.

There was a cute looking guy with light eyes and spotted freckles in lots of her pictures, her job seemed wonderfully professional, and her friends seemed like a down-to-earth lot.

Even though it appeared she had it all together, I couldn't help but think that she was missing one thing.

Me.

I was missing.

Did she think of me at all? Did she tell these glamorous friends about me, her *daughter*? Did the boyfriend/fiancé/husband know?

There were things I wanted to know about her that I intended on finding out my entire life, so much so that I stopped mentioning her completely after looking her up. Deciding it was best to presume she never thought about me, I'd give her the cold shoulder as well. I made my father promise to never make mention of her, and at that he only recommended counseling, but only few and far between was she brought up, and even then briefly.

She was a figure, but not a being. As she sat before me in the diner, I had a feeling everything was about to be different.

SAGE

"So I bet you have a lot of questions for me..." I began to ask, as a strawberry-blonde handed us menus. Phoebe didn't even glance down at the menu, already knowing what she was going to order.

I asked for two decafs, not realized she may not even drink coffee. I eyed her quizzically, and as if reading my mind she told the waitress, "Make that one decaf, and one regular."

I braced myself for whatever questions she had. I knew there must have been a list that covered a lifetime. Literally. I was ready for whatever was thrown at me.

"Why'd you walk here?"

The tone in her voice was bordering condescension, but easing into questions like that I could handle, so I just shook it off.

I pulled out the letters from my backpack. I should start at the beginning.

"Your father and I were so in love, Phoebe. That's the first and most important thing I want you to know. We were your age, maybe a bit older. You're sixteen now right? Turned sixteen this past September?"

She nodded simply.

"Let me ask you something, have you ever been in love?"

She nodded again.

"Good, so even though you're young, you know the emotion that comes along with it. And from what I do know about your past relationship, the pain..."

She's was staring at me impassively, but I could tell she was hanging by my every word, so I had to choose them wisely.

"I never wanted to leave you. Ever. You have to believe that. It's just, everything was so tragic. I know you know about the events that happened the day you were born. God, it made history books."

She gave me nothing but a poker face, "Tell me about that day. The day I was born."

"It was September 11, 2001 and we were in the suburbs of New York City. I had just turned sixteen years old myself. I had dated your father just about a year at that point, so you can imagine the news of a baby was something surprising to us all. I couldn't be happier though, even that young, believe it or not. My mother at the time had been through lots of up's and down's. Always in out of rehab, you know, the runaround. I see a lot of myself in her sometimes, and it's my biggest weakness. My father was a phenomenal man, but I didn't see him much at all. He worked a lot and lived in the heart of the city. He had his own agenda. I felt that my baby was the one person I could do right by, that wouldn't leave me, and be all mine," I paused to wipe a tear as she sipped her coffee stoically.

"Your grandmother on your father's side was supportive to an extent, although she never could quite figure me out and I her. But Max was amazing in every way. He guided me through the pregnancy when he could, when he was there. We were so scared, Phoebe. So, so scared. I was three months pregnant with you when he left to take care of his mother. She was very heartsick at the time. Is she still alive?"

241

"She is."

"Good, good. Always a sweet lady, but struggled immensely when her husband passed. Max just felt like he needed to be with her. He had no car, no money, no anything for that matter. He lived with a cousin for a few years at the time his father was ill up in New York, where we met. His mother wanted him to remember him as a good, loving, active man. She didn't think it'd be years before he passed, but it was and Max had established a life in New York that he didn't want to depart from. When he did die and she was all alone, she clung to Max and he recognized her needs outweighed any of his own. Neither of us were ready financially for a baby, so he needed his mother especially then too. You were the one thing in his life that put the fire under him to get a move on, to do better. As much as I tried to be that for him, it was always you.

But his mother was high priority, too. And of course she was out here in small town Virginia. So he walked. He came in the room I was in, and I remember it like yesterday, he told me he was going to 'walk to her if I have to!' with such authority that I believed him. I understood, but I made him promise to be back for when the baby was born. He promised me he would, and he kept that promise, but in the meantime he walked. I watched him leave and half expected him back the next day, and maybe that's really why I was so comfortable with him leaving on a whim to begin with, but he just kept walking and walking. Once he saw his mother and that she was going to be okay, he borrowed his father's old truck and he and your grandmother drove on up to me just four quick months later to be

242

sure not to miss the birth. It was September 11, 2001 at 5:12 in the morning when you were born. It was 8:53 in the morning, when the first attack on the Twin Towers occurred. Everything that happened in those three hours and some odd minutes in between were pure and beautiful, and I need you to know that they were the best of my life. It was when the attack happened that something in me changed, a heart string was plucked a little too hard.

My father was on his way to see me in the hospital, but was leaving at noon so he'd miss my mother and let her have her time with me. They couldn't be in the same room since their separation. They knew the day was important to me though, and that I didn't need their problems overshadowing the birth of my child. They planned to come in increments...except he never made it. I don't know if you know this, but my father was a firefighter in New York City. He died in the mix of it all. We know nothing more. We don't know if he was in the building, if he suffered a painful death, if it was immediate...nothing. We didn't find out he passed officially until five days later, but I had a terrible inkling when he didn't show up, like I knew all along the worst case scenario had found him."

Our waitress could tell we are in deep conversation as she tiptoed around making sure we we're alright on refills. "I think we're ready to order," Phoebe said, although I had yet to look over the menu.

"I'm ready when you are," the waitress got ready to jot down our order.

"Two waffle platters please. Eggs over easy for me, and for my mother here..."

"Scrambled," I finished, my heart skipping beats at her mother reference. She was the only person in the world to be able to acknowledge me with the term and thus far, it was…unusual.

"It's the best plate here," Phoebe informed me.

The silence lingered a second too long before she said, "I'm sorry about your father. I didn't know that happened."

"I panicked, Phoebe. I panicked. There was no other excuse or reasoning for it. It was all too much for me at the time. Your birth, my father's death, the tragedy that shook our country, and there we were, not far from any of it and unknowing of the next big crisis. In that moment, though, all that made sense was giving you up. Breaking up with your father was never an option in my mind. I mentioned to him my idea of giving you to a family who'd raise you right, and he refused, trying to talk some sense into me. My mother was in the corner of the room making ignorant and uneducated comments and yet, even after his death, still badmouthing my father. I didn't want to be her. I didn't want to be that to you. So I panicked.

Shortly after I had you, I was institutionalized for a few months in a counseling facility. I...umm...I've never actually confessed that out loud to anyone. The stresses of the world coupled with my postpartum depression scared a lot of the doctors that came to see me in the weeks to follow. I remember feeling so trapped by cruelty, feeling ambushed by all my insecurities. Everything happening at once, in the span of a few hours even. Max, your father, was infatuated with you though. Even though he decided to leave me, I never

244

worried about you once. He packed up everything we accumulated for you and loaded it into your grandfather's truck, which I suppose became his at that point, and he brought you right back to where he came from. And now here you are. Here *we* are!

I knew he'd do a great job raising you, and he has. I can just tell by looking at you. In a way, I felt like I did give you up to a family who'd raise you better because he was no longer my family, but yours. That doesn't mean I regret not being there though. After he left with you to come back up here to Virginia, I was so alone. It wasn't until my late twenties I whipped myself into shape and changed my life around.

Your father, in between all that and the years of not hearing from him or seeing you, sent me the stack of letters I have here, urging me to take my own journey at some point in time, to walk and never look back. I had already walked away and turned my back on the things that should have mattered most in my life, but he encouraged me to walk in the right direction this time.

The funny thing is, it's like he knew all along, like he somehow predicted I needed this, because I was still pregnant with you when he wrote these letters, before it all got too crazy. He broke it off with me in the letters before I even had you, I just didn't know it yet. He planned to leave me all along, but your arrival and the tragedy of that day just sort of masked it all, I guess," I gazed at her as she took a bite of her waffle, my cue to continue, "I know I'm talking a ton now, and I shouldn't be, because there is so much I want to learn about you, but you need to know this.

That's why I walked, because I believe that people hang on to the sliver of the off chance...the long shot idea that I would see your father again after all these years, the idea of having a relationship with you potentially and if you'll have me. And of course, the off chance that there is hope for ourselves and our world."

PHOEBE

I thought immediately of Cliff and why I stayed at the hospital so long while he was unresponsive. It was my own sliver of the off chance.

I had never heard this story before, just pieces of it. I knew nothing of my grandfather's death, the letters, nothing. As much as I wanted to hate my mother, I empathized with her more than anything else. She needed help and she sought it, which not enough people do.

"I met some wonderful people on my journey, and was very blessed considering how dangerous a lot of these scenarios could have been. I took these pictures throughout," she handed me a stack of Polaroids, very old-timey of her. "I want you to keep these. Just like your father passed his letters along to me, I wanted to pass my pictures along to you. You don't need to walk hundreds of miles either, but one day you're going to need to do something different, and do something for you. You may even need to do it now, but keep these as a reminder. There is a story behind each one of these I'd love to tell you one day."

She said things like one day, insinuating there would be a future where she and I held hands skipping through sunflower fields. Not that I didn't want her in my future, because it wouldn't be the worst thing happening to date. We'd just have to take things slow, but I think that's something she and I were both on the same page with.

"You know, I have the number eleven tattooed on my wrist right here," I showed her and she started crying immediately, "The number has always been some type of omen for me. Good or bad, it's always been relative to my life. The tattoo also reminds me of you and where I came from."

And now the eleven days I waited around for Cliff to revive.

This made her cry harder.

"You are such a beautiful soul, Phoebe." She then took out her Polaroid, "May I?" she asked, and then snapped a picture of me to add to the collection.

SAGE

I felt relieved. I felt better. A lingering weight, heavier than I knew, had been lifted from my shoulders. There was still just one thing. Max.

Will he be there when we got back from our meal? What would he think?

I didn't tell Phoebe everything. There were things I was holding back. Perhaps it was my newfound motherly instinct, but I wanted to protect her. I didn't want to make it seem like her birthdate was a big of tragedy as it was. I remember seeing people on the TV in my labor and delivery room roaming the streets aimlessly in herds. Bridges were packed full of people walking in silence. You could hear the prayers recited in their heads if you listened close enough. You could feel the fear and sheer terror radiating from each person, potent in the air even through a television screen. *What would happen next? Would it be me?*

When there was so much chaos in your own mind, coupling it with chaos from the outside world makes something in you snap. I snapped that day. It was truly a time unlike any other. As much as I tried to set aside the conflict in my own mind, that day will always remind me of things brutally lost.

"Are you trying to get back with my father, what's your objective here?" Phoebe asked, snapping me out of my horrific daydream.

"We'll just see how things go. It's been years since I've even spoken to him. Does he have a girlfriend, a wife?" I hated that I asked, but I had to know.

I noticed she wore the opal necklace around her neck and it made me gush. That used to be mine. She twirled it around a finger as I questioned her.

"He's been on dates occasionally, none that he likes me to know about. I never get to meet the women, I mean. He shields me from them," at this she threw up air quotes, "but I'm sure if he had something serious he'd inform me of it, and I don't know of anything happening currently in his love life. What I also don't know is how he's going to react to all of this..."

The thought crossed my mind that he could realistically walk into this diner at any given second. I had seen him in phantom faces on the street plenty of times before, but to know that we were actually in the same town was unreal. The address worked! I couldn't even fathom the thought.

"Will you walk back if it comes to that?" Phoebe asked.

"I've done enough of that for a while. After all, he was back and forth, but your father only walked one way. It's only fair," I joked.

With so much to talk about, there seemed to be nothing at all to say. Her tearful face from earlier now attempted to smile alongside me as we ate together, shoveling waffles into our mouths unattractively.

"Tell me about your life," I urged her as we walked back to the bus station together. The diner was not far from their house at all, maybe a handful of yards outside their neighborhood. Just long enough to squeeze in a good conversation but short enough to not feel like you were overcompensating.

Phoebe went on and on about her life. About her boyfriend Cliff, who hard to believe, died that same week. Although she saw it coming, my experiences with Phoebe thus far have revolved around the circle of life. The day of her birth, and today. I couldn't help but feel the symbolism, and that the rebirth in today would be our relationship.

She was so strong for feeling so weak.

I heard about school, or maybe the lack thereof, what her aspirations were, what interested her.

And then we were back.

No car was in the drive but that didn't mean one hid behind the garage door. Phoebe did mention that Max was on a business trip and that he was due to return later that evening, at what time she didn't know.

I was feeling queasy after my waffle special and at the thought of his face. I would potentially be seeing all of him in the coming minutes.

As if clockwork, the door swung open to the front of the house and Max came running down the porch steps, "Phoebe, I was nervous when I didn't find you here..." his voice trailed off.

"Sage?"

***

We embraced as two old friends who were apart awhile would. It was an odd sensation, clasped tightly together for thirty seconds too long.

Max looked different in a way I couldn't pinpoint. He was obviously older than I remembered him. Framed glasses sprawled across his nose, which made him look sophisticated and wise. Not that he wasn't, it was just little alterations like that that made him appear as someone I never even knew.

He took a step back, clasping a hand to his mouth in disbelief.

"The letters..." I said, but the tears forming in his eyes caught me off guard.

"I always knew you'd return..." he said breath-lessly.

We stood in silence before he invited me in. Sitting on the couch, just the two of us, neither knowing where to begin.

"You look great," he said.

"Considering..." I should have just thanked him and moved on, but I was jittery and anxious.

Rather, we made small talk until I proposed one week. Just as I had given Warner a trial run, I'd do the same with Max and Phoebe. It was unrealistic to believe I'd come here and expect to blend my life with theirs in perfect unison.

Somehow though, I had to make it enough. Max hadn't entirely turned me away, but he was still skeptical about me and it was obvious. Why I had walked now, how after all those years I hadn't reached out to my daughter, what I had done to the family we could have had that September of 2001?

God, that man could hold one hell of a grudge.

But, one week was one week. I had time to prove myself. To prove that I was worthy of them, of their presence and their lives. Giving Warner initially three days ended up changing my life. I certainly could do some damage control in one week if I needed to. I was confident in that.

It was so laid back there compared to my busy city life. Max went to work and Phoebe went to school, but as high speed and distracting as my life was where I came from, their lives here screamed contentment and nothing more. Maybe they did need me more than they'd like to admit. I could be their breath of fresh air.

Or it could end up a total flop. Only time would tell. In the meantime, I called Warner.

I had slept on the couch I first spotted when I got there, and it may as well have been the most comfortable place on Earth. I was at my final destination, no more walking. A permanent smile plastered to my face; I couldn't help it.

"Hi," he said in a manner he didn't mean to be seductive.

"Good morning. Did I wake you?" My voice was still raspy.

"You didn't. I just got back from a jog."

"Of course you did."

"So, how'd they take it?"

I told him everything, "I'm on their couch now," I ended with, as if it was the most relevant and exciting piece of information he'd ever receive.

"So a week, huh?"

"Seven whole days," it seemed like an eternity, when in reality it may as well be six and three-quarters of a day. Time kept ticking. Every minute I spent away from Max and Phoebe was one less they get to know me and I them.

"How are you feeling?" Warner asked half-dejectedly.

"I'm refreshed. I'm happy. Which is more than I can say for how I've felt for the majority of the last year," I said honestly, because there was nothing that melted my heart more than someone asking me how I was doing and genuinely meaning it. It was one of those three word groupings that had become so overused and understated. Warner was that way, always putting me

252

first. I had never known him not to care. Turns out he took my advice too and didn't sell his father's house, but instead decided to live in it.

"Well great! And thank you, Sage. For everything. You've been an inspiration to me, changed my life even with the walking and all."

"You're sweet, Warner," and although I was laying comfortably where I knew I wanted to be, I would have done anything to be in Warner's company at that very moment. It was safe there and I would remain untouched with him. It was all so inconsistent.

"If at the end of the week it doesn't work out with them, you know where to find me. And Sage, you don't have to walk to me."

I giggled.

"I love you, Sage," he said simultaneous to me hanging up the phone, which was so typical of me, running away when I had everything where I wanted it and everyone where they needed to be after it all.

It was early yet, so I turned over, opening a novel off the shelf in their living room and waited for Max and Phoebe to wake up, because if you don't know how to manage true love, the least you can do is read about it.

***

The reading didn't last long. It didn't last long because I felt guilty. There I was supposed to be proving myself in their home as I didn't even know what, maybe an active and participating family member, so I needed to at least attempt that.

I just didn't feel at home there. Not yet, I expected it with time. Everything about Max was enchanting. There was no better way to describe it. Even his house was pristine. I couldn't clean if I wanted to. It was not completely unlike how I remembered him. I wondered if he thought I grew up just as much as he had.

Doubt it.

My father once told me that if you want to take things to the next level, you have to want to go there bad enough. I wanted things with Phoebe and Max at the next level, and I had never been more sure of anything.

I heard scurrying upstairs. Someone was awake. I scurried off myself to freshen up in the bathroom before they too made their appearance. Having a shower and bathroom readily available made this easier than ever before. I had a newfound respect for the process of beauty preparation and I was not ashamed of it.

Pretending the night hadn't kept me up tossing and turning, I hurried off to the kitchen, pulled six eggs out of the refrigerator, and fumbled around until I found a skillet and spatula to whip up some breakfast. Or attempt to anyways.

Sage and domestic were two words rarely found in the same sentence, but there was an exception to every rule. Baking was that exception for me.

Talking to Warner first thing in the morning had me shaken up. Being there had me weirded out, it was so surreal.

My body was bruised and blistered, but beyond everything, stiff and sore. I could not fathom taking another step at certain points in the day. If I sat too long, I convinced myself I could lead a happy life from that very spot for the rest of my days.

But then there was Max and Phoebe. I couldn't let them see me weak. I had been weak for them entirely too long, but somehow, they managed to make me stronger than ever before.

PHOEBE

Both my parents, together, under one roof. An anomaly at best. I often dreamed of that feeling of completeness, a sense of love and maybe just a glimmer of hope that we might end up all together. Instead, all I felt were the weight of my grievances. They grew heavier with each passing second. I knew Cliff wouldn't want me to feel embodied by his loss at a potentially crucial turning point in my life, but I couldn't help it.

I hadn't yet let it all out. I cried silently face down in my pillow for two minutes, before retreating to the shower. Even I could admit the sight of my current state was nothing short of pathetic. I didn't even shampoo my hair until minutes later, preoccupied with regrouping my thoughts. It felt good to get clean, but I hated the idea of starting fresh.

The last thing I wanted to do was go back to my classes. Even the ride there would remind me of all the times *we* carpooled together. You never realize the simple things you did with certain people until you know you will never have the opportunity again.

I had been granted time off though. For everything that Principal Williams and I had been through, he told me to "take as much time as needed with no repercussions."

I was trying not to blame myself, but it was difficult not to. Through my tears, I attempted to rationalize. Sometimes things just moved so quick, it was difficult maintaining control.

I heard the faint voices of my parents from down below. I couldn't make out any words, but no one was screaming yet, so it couldn't be all bad. I decided to head downstairs to them, refusing to face the mirror as I passed, afraid of the lifeless bags under my teary eyes, the mourning written all over my face and the godfor-saken hope in my eyes.

"Phoebe," my father said calmly upon first seeing me.

I didn't imagine myself in a robe in my first ever meeting with my mother, but under given circum-stances...

"Come. Please sit," my mother said. I did.

The walls felt like they were going to cave in and crumble bit by bit. I should have just stayed upstairs.

"So what's the move from here?" I asked.

"Getting down to business," my father said, typical of him to lead with a joke to silence the awkward tension.

My mother grabbed my hand, feeling foreign and unnatural. She must have felt it too because she let go shortly thereafter. This was when they revealed to me she would stay one week.

"It's just a very busy time for me with the funeral and all..." My stomach growled as I said it.

"We'd thought you could use the support, see how things go," my father said, all accepting.

"Okay," was all that became of the one thousand thoughts streamlining my brain.

***

I'd never been a dreamer, but rather a realist. It was not that I didn't believe lofty dreams weren't possible, I just admit that they're lofty and deal accordingly.

That's why I gave my mother a chance. I'd seen her, confronted her even, in dreams too many times. I needed to know her story. I knew she wasn't perfect going into all this so I didn't have high expectations.

The night before, upon not being able to sleep, I crept to the steps from my room so I could eye her wrestling the pillows on the couch in attempt to get comfortable. I couldn't imagine walking the way she did. There were so many ways that would have been so much faster and much easier. Was it principle? At the end of it all, I settled on the idea that maybe my father was right, she and I were both just *that* stubborn.

I wanted to love her, but I didn't think I could yet. I thought of all dances she didn't help me get ready for, all the awkward to say the least conversations I'd had with my father about bodily changes and functions, and all the times I'd spent in this home alone while my father was away on business. All the times she was supposed to be there, to step up and raise me.

I wished I could have used the excuse that I'd gone mad to escape from reality for fifteen years like she did at my age. That sounded pretty damn accurate right about then.

SAGE

It was Phoebe who came down first.

"Good morning," I said.

"Hopefully it's all right," she responded, making my greeting a question.

"I made some bacon and eggs," I said as she made her way to the cabinet to preemptively grab a plate.

"Also, I was thinking that I take you shopping today. Maybe pick out a new dress for the funeral, and also get you something nice for yourself. Something happier."

"So now we're going the retail therapy route?" she asked.

"Not therapy, no. Just something we can bond over," I hated the fact that I was trying to bond with my daughter after so many absent years over a funeral dress, but I had to start somewhere. It somehow felt very forced.

"I despise shopping with a deep-rooted passion, but I do need a new black dress so yeah, we can go," she said, forcing a piece of greasy bacon down her throat.

Sometimes she said things that made me question if she was my daughter at all, if she had any traits that replicated my own. Yet, she escaped upstairs to get ready for the day's festivities, my attempt at putting some pep in her step seemingly doing its job.

I waited for Max to come down before I made myself a plate.

"I still can't believe you're here, Sage. Thank you for making breakfast," he said evenly.

I invited him along to go shopping with us because even though I was ultimately comfortable being alone with Phoebe, she still scared the hell out of me. When there was nothing to say, it was obvious I didn't know how to raise a child. I didn't know the right things to ask her, and I was constantly walking on eggshells making sure not to offend her in the slightest. I was hoping Max's accompaniment would give me some insight into her teenage life.

Warner called again in the same morning to let me know his plans for the house. He was putting a shed in the back, one that he'd build himself, making Val proud. I tried to hide my excitement for him because Max was in the other room, and even though there should be no secrets between us, since I was trying to alleviate and altogether avoid any blurred lines of our communication, I still didn't want him to know about Warner. Even though somehow he was an open book when it came to being vice versa. He talked to me like any old friend would, and I envied his maturity.

"Ready to go?" Max came in wearing a denim shirt and khakis, his light, curly hair perfectly combed. You could see his obvious part and his attempt to mask where his hairline had started to recede.

"I am," I said as evenly as possible through unsteady breaths.

"You look nice," he said to me, and in that moment I wanted him to touch me. I wanted him to walk over and grab my waist, pulling me into him so I can smell the hint of cologne on his body. I just wanted him to hold me, nothing more. It didn't seem like too much to request, but I would have to settle just being in his presence alone.

He just stood there, and I didn't blame him. He didn't owe me anything. I hated that after everything we'd been through, our relationship would always air on ways of complication.

"*Phoebeeeee,*" he called up the stairs.

We heard boots hit the floor as she started scurrying down the stairs. It made us both smile.

It was forever hard to believe that we *made* Phoebe. We made that human being together, when there was so much love between us that it was palpable.

And yet, there we were, held together by ties that were barely bound, connected by only a brief amount of time in our past, when we thought everything was easy.

Until one day it just wasn't.

***

Max drove. It was a bizarre sensation being in a car. I tried to think of the last time I was in a car and I concluded it might have been when the police officer pulled me over for walking along the interstate. The confined space felt nearly intimate. I told them about all the people I met; the homeless man in the city, the kind hotel lobbyist, the elderly woman who housed me for multiple days, the college band nerd and I briefly mentioned Warner without giving too much away.

I told them of the places I'd slept, leaving out anyone who accompanied me in that slumber. I touched upon my trials, secretly reveling in the shock on their faces with each passing sentence.

"You must be dramatizing," Phoebe butt in.

"Surely she's not," Max said, grateful that he defended me in a way, but also knew from experience the brutality of the situation.

"I'm incredibly sore and trying not to show it," I smiled weakly, making them laugh.

We chatted casually until Max's phone rang. Faintly, I could hear an older woman's voice on the other end.

It was a brief call. Upon hanging up he stated, "My mother wants us over for dinner tonight. Sage, of course you are invited, although I did fail to mention to her that you were here..." Max let his voice trail off.

"I'd love to see her again, of course, but if it's a problem..." I couldn't tell if I was supposed to take a hint that this is a 'he and Phoebe' thing or not, so I waited for him to elaborate. Times and tempers were sensitive with everything going on.

"No you should come," Phoebe interjected.

Max looked immediately hesitant, but he couldn't say no, so I just smiled and thanked them for the invite as politely as I could.

261

"It'd be pointless for you to stay at our house alone while we're enjoying a dinner," Phoebe said, perhaps having said that out of personal benefit just to watch me squirm.

"It'd be lovely," Max said out of obligation.

Hearing the word *lovely* leave his lips made me tingle. It used to be his favorite thing to call me. I wondered too if he picked up on the coincidence.

"I'll have to get a new dress myself now," I said, in hopes of making light of the seemingly cumbersome situation.

It would be the first time seeing Max's mother in years. As much as I would have preferred avoiding the confrontation, I knew I just couldn't, my curiosity always getting the better of me. What would her take on all of this be? She was always a gracious person but I didn't even see her after I had my meltdown that left her with a broken son and an abandoned granddaughter. I could understand she might have pent up frustrations.

I tried to set it out of my mind. We had a lovely day at the mall; Phoebe and I both got a dress, hers black, mine a long-sleeved burgundy number.

It took us six stores and some jumbo pretzels later before we decided to call it a day. It felt more comfortable as time was passing. Max would hold our bags, and we would grab piles of things to try on. Only one would work out (if we were lucky) and we'd move on. Everything felt normal for that piece of time.

There was always just that one thing tugging at the back of mind that made me uncomfortable overall. Something about my days with them were so forced.

Too, as much as I'd been putting it off, the passion Max and I had was not something I felt anymore. He was extremely distant, making it hard to get to know him. It took me seeing his face again to come to that conclusion, as much as I didn't want to believe it. The morning's comment about my appearance was the closest I had received in ways of a compliment that even suggested a slight interest I sparked in him.

He was never one to be entirely too serious or talk about his feelings, and I always found it easy to accept that because I loved him and that was just a small part of who he was. The letters were as emotional as it got with him. I couldn't complain though, it could have been so much worse; all his good qualities oversha-dowing. We just didn't seem to have that much in common anymore. Time may heal all wounds, but time also created barriers.

Phoebe held us together, though, and that was just one of the million reasons I could think of, as to why I needed her in my life.

PHOEBE

Dinner was sure to be comical. If anything, it'd be an enjoyable relief from the dread I'd been enduring.

The funeral was the next morning, so it was good to be engaged, putting "everything Cliff" off for a few hours.

Originally, I offered his parents help with the funeral arrangements, but once they found out my

263

mother was in town, they wouldn't let me assist the slightest, claiming I needed all the time I could get with her.

After all, if there was one thing Cliff's death taught us, it was to hug your loved ones tighter or something tacky like that. I, in denial.

My mother arranged some flowers I would have deemed weeds from the yard and made them into a beautiful arrangement for the dinner tonight, as only she could. She was so effortless, always. I could tell my father was itching in nervousness with each passing second.

He made his "famous but tasted by a maximum of nine people" sausage lasagna as we got ready to go. The ride seemed longer than usual, as we passed the time listening to classical music and discussing the weather in hopes of not overstepping during the emotional time.

Small talk sucks, always.

I was the first to ring the doorbell, mainly because the sight of Cliff's house next door made me feel just as I assumed it would, almost queasy and ill. My grandmother didn't answer on the third knock so I dug to the bottom of my purse in search of a key and wrestled it into the door.

"Anyone home?" my father said awkwardly as we entered the foyer, "We've brought a guest!" He sounded just like a dad. He was usually cooler than that.

My grandmother emerged from a cloud a smoke in the kitchen.

"Sorry for the hold up, I nearly burned what I had in the oven and, oh my..." my grandmother caught glimpse of my mother. I thought she might lose it because she certainly looked like she was about to, with her hands clasped to her mouth and her eyes wide enough to see through to the back of her head.

Instead, she walked over and in a warm embrace she took Sage in her arms, a single tear trickling down her right eye.

I'd never seen tearful emotion from her, minus when I awoke in my hospital bed, so it was bizarre and out of character to see her tear up again, and so soon. She was the one always able to maintain her woefulness.

"I always knew you'd come back," she said all choked up, "Come, let me take your coat."

My mother smiled warmly and tears filled her eyes as well, meanwhile, my father nearly cried because the lasagna pan was burning his skin as we lingered with reunited jest.

We made our way to the table where the aroma of food was overwhelmingly intoxicating. There were only three place settings, but my grandmother was quick to fix a fourth with utensils that hadn't been touched in years. It was always us three, always had been.

The food was wonderful, which allowed us to ease into the uniformity usually present. That, or it might be the fresh bottle of merlot that was already running low.

"I'm just so glad you chose to stop by, and on a night Max made his signature lasagna! Do tell me how you've been. It's been what, fifteen years?" my grandmother said, not meaning to imply any subtle jabs at her absence, but doing it anyways.

"It has been an eternity," my mother said graciously as she began to tell the stories of her walk.

Although it was interesting and unique, I was afraid if she hadn't walked here there wouldn't have been much for us all to talk about.

When she finished, my grandmother asked me the question I was hoping to avoid all evening..."Now, Phoebe, are you all ready for tomorrow? How have you been holding up?"

"I'm okay," I said, shoveling a forkful of lasagna into my mouth so I didn't have to elaborate. If there was one thing about being a lady my grandmother had taught me, it had been to chew with a closed mouth. I now used it as a silence mechanism.

She just looked at me with sorrow in her eyes and disdain in her voice, "Well I'd be happy to come with you tomorrow if you need."

"I think my mom's going to come with me, right?" I turned to her.

"Absolutely," my mother smiled, the mother-daughter moment all too much, it made my grandmother cry all over again.

We stayed until the evening news came on at 7:30, something my grandmother hadn't missed in twenty years. We said our goodbyes quickly before my grandmother made mention of the funeral tomorrow as if I wasn't coexisting alongside them hearing every word, she sometimes forgot I wasn't as adult as I appeared. Instead, my father kept it light and asked, "So who wants ice cream?" My mother nodded and I forced a smile.

The three of us made our way to his truck, looking like an actual family.

SAGE

When I found out I was pregnant with Phoebe, I knew I was foolish to think that Max and I would become something more. Some sort of *family.* I supposed the word itself seemed foreign to me because I never had a firm example of it. We were *so* young, even though we didn't feel like it. I know Phoebe felt that way now. She thought Cliff was all she'd ever know, but she's *sixteen.* Entirely too mature for her age and wise beyond her years, I did understand it because I was the same way. She'd been through so much, just like I had around that age. She was more like me than I at first assumed. I never did give her enough credit where credit was due.

It was after dinner and I was cozying up on the makeshift couch bed. Max offered me his room, but I denied, not wanting to put them out more than I already had.

Phoebe had gone to bed too, emotionally exhausted. There was a faint and flickering light of a TV coming from the cracked door of Max's bedroom. Surely he was not lying in bed watching without saying goodnight, but his peculiarity made me wonder how much I ever knew about him at all. Not needing it to be as severe as to tuck me into bed, it would have still been nice to be acknowledged by him. The journey had me oversensitive and keen to every minute detail.

I lugged my toiletry bag into the bathroom, brushed my teeth, washed my face and took two deep breaths.

267

Finality had never felt so uncomfortable.

Unpredictably, Max was sitting awkwardly on the corner of the couch when I returned, a book in his hands. He acted like a trespasser in my territory, when the couch actually belonged to him.

I smiled when I saw him and he smiled back. Not a toothy grin from either of us, but enough to acknowledge contentment. Neither of us said a word, I just went to sit beside him, leaving some space so we didn't touch. I heard his breath sync with mine, his one breath, two of mine. Soon to be three if he decided to slide any closer.

"I must admit something," he said.

I nodded, the moment so serene.

"I knew you'd be on your way to me." He continued.

"How would you have known?" I asked rhetorically, not thinking of one single clue he could have obtained that I was on my way. Instead, he answered an answer that caught me completely and entirely off guard.

"A letter..." he started, "It came in the mail maybe a month ago. It had your name on it, but my address. I'm sorry I opened it. Curiosity got the best of me."

It was then I noticed he had anything in his hand at all besides the novel. Who would address a letter to me there? Confusion and embarrassment swept over me.

Pure disbelief, and even a bout of rage, filled me as I was handed the letter. There was no mistaking the doctoral handwriting on the outside of the envelope. I'd recognize it anywhere. *Tom.*

"I wasn't going to ruin your night with it at first, but it was addressed to you...so here you are," Max said, sounding like a prepubescent teen who didn't yet know quite how to talk to girls.

He must have seen the wondrous stare on my face when I unfolded the envelope's contents and scanned the page because all he said was, "I'll give you a minute. Would you like some coffee? I can put a pot on."

I didn't need coffee at that nightly hour, but I wanted him to leave and come back soon, so I said, "I'd love a cup," and started reading:

Sage,

I know what you're doing, or what you may have done at this point and where you've walked. I found the letters from Max long ago in a shoebox in the closet with the address enclosed. I made note of it because I knew you'd leave, and without a goodbye. I never meant to invade your privacy, but I was drunk and curious.

I didn't came after you because I know you, Sage, whether you want to admit it or not. You're as stubborn and persistent as they come, and you wouldn't have listened to me anyways.

I knew this moment would come in some way or another, and I guess all I have

269

to say is that I'm happy for you. I also don't know why I'm writing to you even now after everything, but I guess I wanted to wish you the best and say the times we shared were at one point very pleasant.

We never did get a proper goodbye, so in a way, I thought this would help. Don't hold it against me for copying down his address and going through your things, I guess I just wanted to know where you'd be. But this'll be the last you hear from me. I hope you find what you're looking for in Max and I hope your daughter is a beautiful as you.

Have the best life, Sage Riley.

Tom

There had never been a time when my emotions just totally leveled out. I was indifferent as far as Tom went. I never assumed he knew about Phoebe, but in a way, I was glad he did. If closure was all he wanted, I was happy to give it. That was Tom just being Tom. I always admired a person who thought they knew everything about anything. It took extreme confidence to be that cocky.

Max peeked around the corner, and after verifying to himself that I had enclosed the letter securely back in the envelope, he handed me a coffee mug that had

270

Phoebe's name etched along the bottom, a cup she made in a pottery class I assumed some time ago.

"You okay?" he asked, sounding genuinely concerned.

"I haven't been okay for a while..." I let myself be completely vulnerable in the moment.

He simply laid a hand on mine. A solo tear trickled down my face. He turned to me in one fluid motion and swiped the tear gently, transferring it from my face to his hand. I looked at him and my body wanted to crash into his arms, have him tell me it would all be okay in the end and that we'd live happily ever after.

But that's not the way everything turns out sometimes, and for us, it appeared to be too late.

"I'm sorry I did this," I said. "I'm a stupid person for even thinking..."

"Shh... It's okay, Sage. I'm happy you're here," he eyed me quizzically then said, "Tell me something about you I don't already know."

His demeanor shifted, and mine echoed.

I rambled for ten minutes about Tom, my job, my friends. I didn't miss the part of me that lived for making more money and eating fewer calories, but I took pride in the fact that I pulled my life together in nearly every regard since the last time he saw me.

He cut me off midsentence, not with words, but rather a peck on the lips. It was quick, but meaningful. I lost my train of thought and didn't attempt to regain it.

It was the type of moment I had been waiting for since I arrived there. He said, "Sorry, I just had to," and smiled bashfully, tucking a strand of loose hair behind my ear.

The eloquent moment was brought to a halt when a bloodcurdling scream was heard from upstairs. Phoebe.

In one movement, Max was off the couch and headed up the stairs, myself following. He did the stairs two at a time, not able to get to Phoebe fast enough.

Through heaves, Phoebe took sporadic breaths. She had awoke from a nightmare, the sheets covered in sweat and sobs. Max embraced her, her arms falling limp around him. I stood in the doorway and watched, tears flowing from my own eyes.

"It's going to be okay. Just breathe," he reassured.

If I hadn't noticed it one hundred times already, that moment solidified it. He was a wonderful father to Phoebe. She needed him now more than ever. Her life was only complicated by my presence in the home; her comfort space.

Max gently wiped tears from her eyes as she gathered her breath.

"It was horrible, Dad." She said. In the moment, I saw what she must have been like as a toddler. She seemed so innocent and scared, a bad dream waking her up. Only this time, it was amplified. It was real life.

"Always about a car crash," she hissed tiredly.

He stroked her hair tirelessly until she fell back asleep in his arms. I dared not take a single step further. It just wasn't my place.

He rested her head back on her pillow, gazed down at her lovingly, and said "I love you, Phoebe," even though she had fallen back asleep and wouldn't say it back.

You're never formally welcomed into adulthood, it sort of just happens when things start to catch up with

272

you and everything becomes more complicated. Phoebe was in the midst of it all.

***

The night that followed was one that was hard for me. I tossed and I turned as I realized the family I could of had didn't need me. The time I had to prove myself was not enough, but it was unrealistic to think I'd live on their couch forever. I had to get a job and move on with my life.

I thought the kiss between Max and I would complicate things for me, but it happened and it was special, and we moved on. I found it strange how little I thought about it, considering just a month ago I would have flipped head over heels to know *my* Max's lips were on mine, if just for a moment.

I tossed and turned for a bit, and at the end of it all, I decided I'd leave after the funeral the next day. I'd be making my exit, but hopefully not out of their lives forever. I didn't regret walking there and I didn't regret my journey. They just had their lives, and I had mine. They just happened to remain separate.

I'd leave then if I could, but I couldn't fathom leaving Phoebe at a time so delicate. I decided to roll over and do my best to fall into sleep. It'd be the first time in days if I did. You'd think someone who had walked as much as I had in the past few months would be able to sleep well, tired muscles and all, but it was much more difficult when your mind wasn't on the same page. I concluded that there would never be enough time for us to do all we want to in life. I had high expectations for what my time with them would be, but at the end of it all, no time would be enough for me to be what they wanted me to be.

***

It was drizzling outside the morning of Cliff's funeral, as luck would have it. It let up some on our way out, but was dreary enough to keep the morning ominous.

"You look beautiful," I attempted to make her spirits rise, "Cliff would be proud of you."

She half-grinned out of sympathy for trying, of which she owed me none, and had even less to give.

We drove in silence as I expected to, but Phoebe was appreciative I was there. Some things didn't need to be said to be understood.

The rain evened out, thankfully, as we stood outside, post ceremony. We joined in prayer and hymn about passing into a better place. About a dozen other high school students attended the event, something they should never have to be experiencing so young. It was evident the ceremony meant something different to Phoebe than the rest of them. Some shoved their hands in their pockets, while others tore away pieces of tissue they never got around to using to wipe their snotty noses and teary eyes. Phoebe held back tears, but I saw some trickle down through slits in her hair. She recited every prayer aloud and even sang the songs through crackled voice. Her black dress was gorgeous on her, almost like she could pull off hitting a runway afterwards if she got her makeup back intact.

It took the congregation forty-five minutes to properly clear out. Silence filled the area as he was delicately lowered into the ground. His mother, God bless her, attempted to say some words through her own teary eyes and spit splattered sentences.

There wasn't a dry eye in the place. Phoebe still wasn't out of control, but holding it together pretty well, considering.

We listened as they recited the last poem. I was afraid to look at Phoebe the wrong way, for fear of shattering our relationship as we finalized theirs.

I watched as Phoebe retreated from me to console Cliff's mother when she finished the eulogy. I admired her in the moment and although she was just ten feet away from where I was standing, when she spotted me again out the corner of her eye, she turned and ran full force into my arms, the ceremony putting it all in perspective.

In a welcomed, yet entirely unexpected embrace, we stood for what felt like an eternity. Despite how emotionally distraught the past two hours had been, I never wanted this moment to end. Phoebe made even the worst of times feel ceaselessly amazing.

I was jealous of Cliff. I was jealous of Max. They each had a part of Phoebe. Something I never thought redeemable, yet as I stood there with her in my arms, a montage of everything I thought Phoebe would be flashed in my mind. I squeezed her a little closer, because she far exceeded my expectations on all accounts. I wasn't jealous anymore. I let go of my hostility and aggressiveness. Looking at her was what it felt to love.

I thought for a moment that I had a change of heart and that I may just end up staying rather than leaving shortly thereafter, but I knew it was unrealistic. I couldn't stay there with Max and Phoebe, for I was never technically invited to begin with. I'd tell them tonight that I was eternally grateful for the few days we shared, but that it was time to move on. I wondered how Phoebe would take it when she slid her hand in mine as we made our return to the car.

Phoebe was mine all along. I had some part of her that nearly possessed her, made her think hardest, and challenged her to be everything I could never be. As cruel, selfish and ignorant as I blamed myself for being, all Phoebe ever gave me back was hope, restoration and the strongest sense of love that could possibly ever be felt.

Yet there I was, choosing to leave it all behind ...again.

***

It was a Monday, the day of the week with the worst reputation. I love Mondays, personally. If you spent your time hating Mondays, there would be so many precious days of our lives gone to hate, all because you weren't able to fall into the groove of a fresh start. That's what Mondays do, they give us a little renewal at the beginning of each week. When I was walking, I'd lose track of the days, like I did in middle school when I was on summer vacation. I just knew I needed to be disciplined if the journey was going to work in my favor.

My time with Phoebe and my walk to her had taught me a lot about the days in our lives. Mostly, it taught me to be prepared for the unexpected. Today, I was prepared for a sad day as I said goodbye to Phoebe and Max.

I packed my things solemnly. The news of my leaving only allowed Phoebe to cling to me more. She didn't take it as well as intended, which surprised me. I wholeheartedly expected the daughter I've excluded my entire life to despise me, and even rebel against me, and above all else hate me, but it was quite the contrary.

"When will I see you again?" She asked while tossing me a pair of my beaten up shoes in an effort to help me pack.

"You're welcome to come visit any time."

"And where exactly will you be? Back in New York?"

"I suppose I don't really have a home there any-more. I'll send you a postcard when I get wherever I decide on going...?"

Even I couldn't convince myself, as hard as I longed to.

I considered calling Warner, but decided not to rush into that option either. Although he offered to have me stay with him an absurd amount of times, I had been doing this on my own and surviving. I just might not need him as much as I missed his sweet, sensible personality and his warm touch. He was my cherry on top.

It made me giddy just thinking about it. On second thought, maybe I should call him...

"Sage, it has been wonderful to see you again," Max appeared in the room, dressed for work, "I'm already running behind schedule for today, but I must see you off."

His formalities sickened me, mostly because that was not the way I remembered him. I took his tone gently, and avoided the slight condescension in the air.

I wish you the best, as if you already haven't ruined our daughter's life and now you've come back to complicate it even more...thanks a ton!

Maybe I was just paranoid because I felt like a guest in a house I expected to feel more at home in.

Regardless, "Thank you, Max, for your hospitality. I appreciate you taking me in on a whim like that."

"I really am proud of you, Sage, and even grateful for you taking my sixteen-year-old, disillusioned advice, if it led you to us even just for a while," he continued, extremely genuine.

We hugged a meaningful hug. Last time we embraced to part ways, it felt like goodbye forever, but this time a sense of *I'll see you soon* lingered.

Still it made me emotional. I didn't want him to let me go, knowing the second I stepped foot out the door I would regret leaving.

"You did it, Sage," he said, putting a hand on my shoulder in approval. Again, it was far more formal than he had to be with me, but I supposed that's who he was. "Don't forget about us."

I nodded simply because even though it was an odd dynamic, I knew I was always welcome.

A tear trickled down my face. At first I let myself accept that I tried, but in all actuality I had done it; I had succeeded.

Max slid aside so I had a straight shot at Phoebe.

I spent a few more hours with her before she walked me to the bus station. Her car was still out of commission, and Max needed his to head to work. I laughed at the irony of walking with her now and how juvenile, and even out of practice, it felt.

It was not even noon and I felt like I had already given the day all my emotions. I had been seeming to do that a lot lately, just giving them away like they were extra change...

"Thank you for coming here, Mom," Phoebe said to break the silence.

"I'm so happy with how things turned out, honey," I said, whipping out a term of endearment, totally and completely unlike me. "You've changed my life, Phoebe, more than anyone in this world ever has, and I need you to know there hasn't been I day I haven't thought about you, and a day I never will forget to."

A single tear fell from her eye, which triggered mine to do the same. She handed me the snapshot I took of her that day at the diner—the day we met—a lifetime of four days ago.

"Thank you," I said, knowing I didn't need the photo to always cherish that moment, but it was good to have, of course.

"It can be the first piece of decor in your new place," Phoebe said more excited than expected.

"New place, yes. I love that." I held the photo up lovingly to the light and bit my lip. It was hard being the one who had to be brave when you were so damn scared. I hoped she couldn't read my very obvious demeanor.

"Well, I guess the bus will be here in..." her index finger trickled down the bus list, "...three minutes. Made it just in time."

I turned to face her and smiled, running a finger through her hair. "I'm so proud of you," I said, "Be good!"

At that it was her time to smile, hugging me one last time and said, "Good to see you."

She walked off just as the bus arrived, wasting no time with dramatics as I secretly hoped to watch her disappear from the rearview. Rather, I hopped on with a few business executives, a couple of hipsters and another few of which I couldn't categorize. I felt out of place there, knowing if I went back to New York, I'd feel even more out of place. Plus, the explanations I'd owe there were something I'd rather not begin to think about.

I got off at the airport. Everything I owned was in my one small bag, which was what my life had become.

I didn't need the extra baggage though, anyways.

An overweight man, who flowed over into my tiny aisle seat, snored in my ear as his half-drunk glass of ginger ale tempted to spill on his lap. Conditions had been better in the past, hoping that moment didn't foreshadow my time to come. I was on a plane headed west, where no one can stop me; not that they ever dared to before.

PHOEBE

I laid under the stars beside the river, which topped
the list of things that still reminded me of Cliff. I
couldn't help but think as I laid there in our spot by the
water, in the most content and relaxed state that I'd been
in a long while, that we'd all end up where we needed to
be when we needed to be there.

In the meantime, I'd just revel in small, happy
moments to get me by, before I too say goodnight and
goodbye for good.

PART III

NOW

January 1, 2017

SAGE

I hang the first picture on the wall: the one of Phoebe. She kept the collection of snapshots, but I kept the one of her. I was forever wishing we took more photos those few days together, but I didn't plan on that being our last goodbye. I sent her a postcard with the landscape of the mountains on it, as promised.

The view here is unlike anything I've seen before. As I strain the pasta and sauté the spinach for the night's dinner-for-one, I am reminded of the fateful night I decided to walk in the first place, mirroring the actions and scene of right now, just in my New York apartment.

As similar as it appeared, it truly was different in every way.

I am fulfilled, and that changes everything. With a new year, comes new hopes.

The mountains of Montana are foreign to me, but now I call them home. The air outside my window is fresh, and the landscape is to die to for. Coming out here I know no one; not a single soul. There is so much solidarity, but also palpable satisfaction. The move here was a rash decision, but no mistake. I keep in touch with people like Melrose, as I promised I'd write her when I reached the end. I'm thankful to have friends all over now.

It's crazy how you can go through life, not knowing ninety-nine percent of the humans that coexist along-side you, but get by just fine.

Some may say I'm insane for moving out to a remote cottage and living alone, especially from where I've been and what I've seen, but I believe that humans are designed to desire a change in pace. There are two ways to gain a new perspective of the world, and that's walking through an area you thought you knew and secondly, moving to new land.

Adjustment is not impossible. It's been one week, and day by day things get better, as things in life often do. Do I miss the hell out of Phoebe? Yes. The thing with Phoebe is that we met at a fragile time in both our lives. If I didn't rekindle a passionate romance with Max, my original intent, I'm blessed to have Phoebe in my circle now.

What I've learned from this experience is that even though certain people are meant to be in your life, sometimes the timing will never cooperate and rarely ever align, but that doesn't mean you don't try. It took me nearly fifteen years to wise up and realize that there is no time better than right now to do something, if it means anything to you.

I applied for a new job as a receptionist at a hospital. The long hours would keep me occupied so I wouldn't feel so alone.

I wouldn't flaunt that I walked across the east coast, but I would tell my newfound friends about my daughter, speaking only of her lovingly, picturing her face the day of the funeral, needing me in her eyes. Trying times reveal true colors, and that's how I'd describe Phoebe, with all her vibrant colors.

I talked to Max time and again, just as I did Phoebe. They promised to come out and visit as soon as the summer came and I was fully settled. Even Warner promised to make his way out here, but couldn't, until his latest home improvement was complete. Lord only knew when that would be, so for the time being, I decided to be happy just fulfilling whatever it is in life that makes *me* happiest, sometimes that changing every day. I wanted all these people to love me and for my relationships to be solid, and I could feel myself getting so close to a journey complete, however, I believe the journey to self-betterment is one that will never be completed wholly.

"Excuse me," I said, walking to the desk on the sixth floor, "I'm looking for Dr. Emerson."

"You'll need to go up one floor to cardiology," a grumpy elderly woman voiced, not even making eye contact with me as I was eager to submit my final paperwork to the hospital staff. Dr. Emerson, the head doctor of the department, wanted to meet with me personally.

As I turned to the door, I saw a packed elevator full of nervous eyed people preparing to visit fragile patients. If that wasn't enough to deter me from the elevator, my own mind was, because everywhere I go now, I take the stairs. You never know when you're going to need to step away from your life and step into a journey of a lifetime.

You can never be too prepared.

ABOUT THE AUTHOR

Taylor Hartshorn is a 24-year-old Pennsylvania native who currently resides in Atlanta, Georgia with her miniature Dachshund, Finn. *Different Walks* is her debut novel.